TEN ENCHANTED STORIES

CELTIC
LOVE

CAITLÍN
MATTHEWS

HarperSanFrancisco
A Division of HarperCollins*Publishers*

Caitlín Matthews's Web site at
www.hallowquest.org.uk gives details of
books, courses, and events worldwide.

FIRST EDITION

Library of Congress Cataloging-in-Publication Data
Matthews, Caitlín
    Celtic love : ten enchanted stories / by Caitlín Matthews.
      p.   cm.
    ISBN 0–06–251609–4 (cloth)
    ISBN 0–06–251610–8 (paper)
  1. Celtic literature—Adaptations.   2. Tales—Great Britain—Adaptations.
3. Love stories—Celtic authors—Adaptations.   4. Mythology, Celtic Fiction.
5. Celts Fiction. I. Title.
PR6063.A8625C45   1999
823'.914—dc21   99–40709
                                                   CIP

00 01 02 03 04 ❖HADD 10 9 8 7 6 5 4 3 2 1

FOR JOHN

There is one man on whom I'd gladly gaze,

To whom I'd give all the bright world,

—All of it! all of it!—

Though you think it a poor bargain.

—Anon. Irish verse
   spoken by Gráinne of Díarmait

CONTENTS

THE ONE STORY WORTH THE TELLING

May stillness be upon your thoughts and

silence upon your tongue!

For I tell you a tale that was told at the

beginning

. . . the one story worth the telling. . . .

—A traditional storyteller's opening

THE SOUL ALCHEMY that causes one person to love another remains a mystery to us. Love cannot be evoked by love philters, it cannot be commanded by persuasion, it cannot be summoned by violence. But once we are under the burning glass of love, there is no escape from its spell of passion. The desire of the lover for the beloved is fanned by restraint, by absence, by whisper and glance, by stolen kiss, by secret embrace, by song, poem, and story.

"The one story worth the telling" is the one we most wish to hear. For each of us has our own passionate resonance that quivers sympathetically when particular love stories are told: at the echo of trials remorselessly endured, of loves lost and yearningly sought, we are retuned to love's own string.

In every listening heart there is complicit support for lovers who love against parental consent or against the conventions of their station in life, for those who dare to love against all the odds. Listeners who were young once remember the bittersweet pain of first love; those who are still immersed in their own youthful strugglings know the sharp imperative of desire; those lost in the featureless middle course of a dull marriage rekindle to remembered passion.

Our ears are sensitive to the strains of love themes that echo our own experience, even though the nature of our own amorous adventures may have less intensity than the stories told here.

This collection draws on the rich treasury of Celtic love stories that have enthralled listeners and readers alike for centuries. Some stories, like those of Deirdriu and Naoisi (see "The Blood in the Snow") and Drustan and Isolt ("When Leaves Be Green"), are well known to us. Others are like jewels, lost in the intricacies of Celtic tradition, that I have polished and reset.

Here are faithful lovers, women who entice or endure, couples who contend or who are contented, eternal triangles that revolve around the marriage of May to December and the younger man, lovers lost and found, emotions that are harmonious or touched by the fiery sear of jealousy. Erotic and secretive or blatantly celebrated, love stories here come from the heart of the passionate Celtic tradition.

Many of these stories weave in and out of the Otherworld—a common feature of Celtic lore, where enchantment and unbespelling are often necessary parts of the lover's quest for the beloved. The ancient gods and faery races occasionally meet and mate, adding complex elements of magic and mystery to already difficult relationships.

I hope I have kept faith with the irony, starkness, passion, and longing interwoven through these stories in the original. For these early Celtic love stories are not romantic in the modern sense of the word. They are neither tame nor domestic but of a primal nature, often changing the course of events, causing wars in a Homeric way or creating internecine strife. In some, their legacy reaches down generations to afflict the unborn descendants (see "The Stretching of Time").

Each of these stories carries its own blessing with it, whether it be the wisdom and understanding with which experience gifts us or the enduring vision of the beloved of our heart. Whether we have loved and lost, or whether the image of the beloved is burned upon our memory, whether we enjoy the fruits of love in full measure or seek to rekindle the spark of a relationship gone stale, we all long to be loved in return.

In these tales where heroism, patience, endurance, longing, and faithfulness are spent in the service of love, we are able to borrow qualities to reinvest our own relationships with a constancy and delight that live forever.

The one story worth the telling is the one that strikes most nearly to the heart. For each person, that story will be different, for each heart is like a harp with its own distinct tuning. When the melody of love vibrates the strings, that one story is the distinctive music we shall make.

Caitlín Matthews
5 June 1999
Oxford

AUTHOR'S NOTE

The pronunciation of major character names is given in brackets after their first appearance in each story. Stress is upon the capitalized syllable, for example, Gwalchmai (GWALKH'my), Fearbhlaidh (FAR'ly), Cu Chulainn (KOO HULL'in). Frequently used terms that have no direct English translation are given here:

fidhchell (FISH'el): a board game; see p. 122 for description

geis (GYESH), pl. *geasa* (GYA'sa): a negative or positive obligation of honor, binding upon an individual as an expression of one's fate or role in society; the higher one's social standing, the more *geasa* one had to observe

grianan (GREE'nan): a south-facing room used only by women

ogham (OH'am): a form of writing used for public inscription on pillar stones or for covert messages on bark-stripped slips of wood; each *ogham* letter derives from the name of a tree

CHAPTER ONE

WHEN LEAVES BE GREEN

While leaves were green, I gave

Veneration to my sweetheart's leafy bower.

Sweet it was awhile, my love,

To live under the birch grove,

Sweeter still to clasp fondly

Hidden together in our woodland hide . . .

To keep love's secret cordon, covertly:

Truly, I have no need to tell you more.

—From "Y Serch Lledrad,"
by Dafydd ap Gwilym,
trans. Caitlín Matthews

The story of Tristan and Isolt has one of the longest lineages of any in this book. In its earliest version, it concerns Drustan (DRIST'an), the Pictish nephew of Cornish king Mar'ch (MARK) and his love for Mar'ch's Gaelic wife, Isolt. It is a story that passed from British into Continental tradition with great rapidity and spread throughout Europe, even as far as Iceland and Serbia. Wagner made it into one of his great operas.

In "When Leaves Be Green," my reworking of an early Welsh text, the tale stops short of the fated denouement of the medieval stories, as we follow the early adventures of the lovers' unfolding affair. Their secret love begins before Isolt's wedding to Mar'ch and has to remain a secret after she is married.

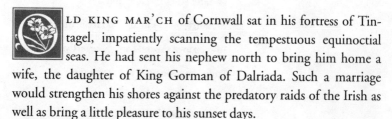

LD KING MAR'CH of Cornwall sat in his fortress of Tintagel, impatiently scanning the tempestuous equinoctial seas. He had sent his nephew north to bring him home a wife, the daughter of King Gorman of Dalriada. Such a marriage would strengthen his shores against the predatory raids of the Irish as well as bring a little pleasure to his sunset days.

Mar'ch prided himself on having sent the perfect ambassador for this delicate task: his sister's son, Drustan, who had lived under his uncle's fosterage since he was seven. Though Drustan had none of his mother's fair goldenness, being pale and dark haired like his Pictish father, Talorc, he had the gift of languages.

From moody and often stubborn youth, Drustan had grown to be an accomplished, single-minded warrior and a fine harper, becoming the companion of Mar'ch's empty hours: one whom he could match at board games, ride with to hawk, and discuss the finer points of a horse's breeding with, and who could tell as good a story as any bard.

Mar'ch had placed in Drustan's hands his own sword: "Let the daughter of Gorman be married to me by this sword: until she comes to my bed, let it lie beside her to remind her of her duty."

And Drustan had received the sword solemnly then, with the agility of one long skilled in swordplay, tossed it into the air, and, catching the heavy, smith-crafted iron as if it had been of wood, made a deep obeisance with it to his uncle. "Go bring me my wife, nephew. And shorten the journey for her by your skills until she sits safely at my side."

Mar'ch knew little about his wife: Gorman had merely sent a gyrfalcon with a long strand of Isolt's hair in its beak to kindle his curiosity. The hairs of that gift were as long as the wires of Drustan's harp and as brightly golden. Mar'ch knew true gold when he saw it, and the urgent appetites of his passionate youth revisited and surged through him at the thought of the owner of that hair.

"Come home soon, Drustan!" he breathed impatiently to the savage sea.

In the shelter of Gorman's hilltop enclosure in western Scotland, Drustan sat playing chess with Isolt under the vigilant eye of her mother, Queen Languoreth (LANG'or-eth). The priest who accompanied her inveighed against their unrestrained hilarity, arguing that it was Lent and therefore a time for more moderate behavior. Languoreth pushed aside her dogs with an easy knee and argued for her daughter's pleasure. "She'll be soon enough in an old man's bed. Let the young people enjoy themselves," she repeated, indulgently. Languoreth herself had been younger even than Isolt when Gorman had taken her.

Drustan did not hear; his eyes were fixed covertly upon Isolt, his uncle's intended wife. Ah, she was golden fair! The golden harp wires of her hair had not lied. Her heart-shaped face, soft brown eyes, and gentle mouth spoke of a modest maiden, but this was belied by her husky voice and the incisive curve of her jaw. She was of an age with him, certainly, but she was older in cunning than he by many lifetimes. Perhaps in the loose-limbed easiness of her mother, he might glimpse the woman Isolt would one day be. At this moment, he could do nothing but stare at her like any simpleton.

"You have won again, Drustan!" Isolt cried, laughing. Flirtatiously, she pushed a ring across the ivory board. "Take it for your service to me and to settle the wager between us."

Drustan shook himself out of his reverie. Truly, he played chess so instinctively, he had not even noticed that he had beaten his host's daughter. "For the discourtesy of beating you, lady, I will recompense you with a story."

The golden head turned. It was a dangerous moment, for the soft brown eyes made Drustan relate a story he did not know he knew: "There once was a warrior who knew no love. No ladies courted him; he laid no tokens in their laps. He was passionate for combat and hunting. One day, he was in the forest when he shot a white doe. The doe turned her head and said, 'You have wounded that which you should not have wounded. I lay this *geis* upon you: you shall know the ardors and hardships of love to the measure of my wounding. And as you shall be a sorrowful warrior, so shall you have a dolorous lady.'"

"How curious!" remarked Isolt. "A man who loves no woman! Did he love men instead?"

Drustan blushed scarlet, since this idle accusation had been covertly leveled against himself and his uncle within his hearing, so much were they in each other's company. That there was no truth in it made such talk hard to bear, especially from the lips of this lovely creature. But he merely said, "Love is faithful to its own. You shall see."

He told how the warrior fell straightaway in love with an image of a woman in his heart and wandered till he came to the shore of a sea and took ship. The moon led the ship to the shore where the woman lay. But his ship was wrecked and he swam ashore, to be washed up at the very place where she was. In that castle the lady, who was a queen, was securely guarded by her husband. He would allow no man to look on her, save only her priest through the grille, so jealous was he.

Noting Isolt's stillness, the strange moody introspection of Drustan, Languoreth placed a fearful hand to her mouth, recognizing the double truth of Drustan's story: she was a Pictish woman and had the second sight.

Drustan continued. "She lived alone and apart, with only her women, in an enclosure bordered by the sea. Walking upon the path of her enclosure, she found the man and brought him to her chamber, where they fell in love, for she was the living flesh of his vision. He fastened round her waist a belt that no one but he could untie. . . ."

Isolt drew out a ribbon from her dress and passed it about her own waist, laughing up at Drustan. "I wonder what would have happened if she had been pregnant? She might have died before it could be unfastened by her lover."

Her pragmatic questions had wrecked the telling. "Oh, no! She could not have been pregnant. She could have no children."

"How do you know?" Isolt frowned with pique. He had spoken in such an emphatic voice.

Drustan felt the slow coil of his ancestral knowing and knew that he had spoken the eternal truth of his lineage.

"The lovers had no children. It was their fate."

Isolt looked at Drustan, Drustan at Isolt. There were no others in that place: only they two.

The priest, impatient at the way the story had been suddenly broken off, asked, "And what became of them?"

Languoreth hustled him away with, "Love found a way. And the knot was broken."

Her prophetic words resonated long in the silent room.

The alliance between Cornwall and Dalriada was ratified with an exchange of gifts, and Isolt was married in the presence of her people to Mar'ch's sword. Because of high seas, it had been decided that she would ride south to Cornwall with Drustan to meet her husband.

Each night they made camp, Drustan would spread his blanket next to Isolt's couch to keep her from any danger. Mar'ch's sword would be thrust into the turf between them, that all might see the proprieties were honored. But in the watches of the night, when the snores of the attendants and the long breathing of the horses proclaimed the amnesty of sleep, Isolt would lie sleepless. The first few nights, she merely gazed at Drustan in the firelight; then she extended a hand to touch his shoulder or back. Once, very daring, she touched his cheek and he awoke with a start that roused several of the watch.

Now she grew crafty and stroked his leg with one white curved foot. "Drustan!" she sighed. This time, he woke motionless. There was no mistaking her intention, and he turned over with some anger. "Oh, Drustan! Don't be so unkind!"

He hissed moodily, "Kindness is for kindred. You do not belong to me, as well you know!"

"But you are kin to me now! I'm your aunt and your elder now— you had best obey me!" she giggled.

"I'll be no Joseph to your Potiphar's wife!" he almost howled at her and strode off to dash his head against the bark of an ash tree in frustrated ire.

And so it went, by day and night, with little touches, glances, and meaningful sighs.

Two days following, Isolt took a deep ford at a stiff canter, shrieking with laughter as the water splashed up her legs and soaked her skirts. Drustan rode into the water beside her to guide her mare through the treacherous waters, and, as he led her ashore, she said reproach-fully, "The waters have been bolder than you, Drustan. They have penetrated where you have not dared come yet!"

That night, Drustan bade the attendants draw apart, saying that Queen Isolt was going to pray by the light of the stars and that he him-self would stand watch over her. The shame she had put upon him was intolerable, but the yearning she roused in him overwhelmed all other concerns.

Drustan tossed Mar'ch's sword into the blackthorn bushes that bor-dered their camp and strode to where she sat looking up at the moon. God, she was fair! Golden fair. There was no stain upon her. Anger, shame, guilt, and longing—he shed them all with his clothes, coming to her wrapped only in his mantle as she combed out her waist-long hair on the banks of the moonlit river. She glanced up at his footfall, taking in his look of determination, and rose to meet his challenge.

Drustan enveloped her within his mantle, and she twisted up to meet his fierce mouth, eager as he to be devoured by the conflagration that consumed them both. Held tight against him by his terrible strength, under the shelter of his mantle, she knew herself to be truly loved.

"Ah, God! What joy is this?" she flung to the distant stars as he spent himself within her.

The lapping of the plangent river and the haunting shriek of owls in the spring woods were the music of their second coupling. Drustan threw down furs to keep her from the seeking wind, but neither needed them, since their very blood was warmth enough. And if he had been savage before, with all the urgency of his ancestral lineage, now Drustan was all tenderness, encouraging her pleasure and pro-longing his own as the moon set.

Tears stood in Isolt's eyes as the light faded. He kissed them away. "What?"

"Only that it's too dark to remember your face!"

"Why should you have to remember me? I shall be with you daily."

And that made her weep the harder. "You are my love! Only you! They will wed me to a gray-haired grandfather. And I must bear it because of my people. . . . I can bear it—but only if you are not daily by me. And so I need to remember every line of your face." And she leaned over, hungrily conning each feature of his face by the dim starlight.

As they neared Mar'ch's lands, they planned. Love made them cunning and resourceful. It was Isolt's young servant who provoked them to think beyond the next bedding. Golwg Hafddydd (GO'lig HAV'theeth) had a practical nature. Now she fretted for her mistress. "It's no use trying to hide it from me: I know all about the prayerful vigils every night!"

The lovers looked abashed.

"What you have to think of is when my lady is laid in the king's bed. What then?"

Isolt's blankness exasperated Golwg into explicit explanation. "He's going to be expecting a virgin—that was what he sent for!" Golwg appealed to Drustan: "You know your uncle, you know the custom! He's going to want proof he's had a virgin on his wedding sheets."

Drustan blushed, causing Golwg to suppress a smile: really, neither of them had the first clue. Golwg sighed. "Well, I've thought about this. It only matters the first time. If it helps you both, I will go to Mar'ch's bed on the wedding night. I'm still a virgin. In the dark, we will feel alike. My hair is not as golden as yours, mistress, but it's long and fair enough. So, if he's drunk and bit too eager—well, it's no worry. But you will have to beg that the chamber be darkened, mistress!"

Isolt's eyes opened very wide. "You would be willing to do this for me, Golwg?"

"My life is as your own, lady."

Drustan stopped his horse and kissed Golwg's hand. "By your blessed gift, may you never fail in promise or purpose!"

And together they rode on, until the miles and days brought them unavoidably to Tintagel.

~ ※ ~

The wedding feast was as elaborate as Mar'ch's riches could decree. The king received his new queen with courtesy and a sharp quickening of desire that in recent years had been less eager but was now piquantly provoked. If only the feast could be soon over! What were fancy dishes compared to this, his own rare dish? Placing one bearlike hand over his wife's diminutive fingers, he kissed her on the nose and cheek—the only parts of her his lips could reach, so ornate was her headdress.

Isolt shifted in her carven chair and looked for Drustan. Their eyes met miserably over the throng. To Drustan, she looked doll-like beside Mar'ch's massive body, her beauty quenched by the reality of marriage. To her eyes, Drustan looked far gone in drink, his features bitter, blurred, melting.

It was time for Isolt to speak up, or it would be too late. "My lord king, I have a request."

Mar'ch lowered one hairy ear to her mouth to catch her precious words over the music. "Speak, my dear!"

"Please, may the chamber be darkened when we go to bed? I am a maiden and . . ." Her lip quivered so violently that Mar'ch broke in with, "Of course! Of course! Don't fear me. I shall be gentle and kind."

As Golwg prepared Isolt in the antechamber, Isolt embraced her servant tightly. "Never was woman so generous!" she whispered in her own tongue. And she in turn prepared Golwg, stripping her down to her shift and anointing her with the powerful perfume that she herself always used, before seeking Drustan.

In the darkness, Golwg slipped in beside Mar'ch. They said it wasn't too bad, she consoled herself. That she had kept her virtue this far was due only to her sharp wits; many a man had wanted her for her body, but none had taken her fancy. Mar'ch began to heave himself over her with determined skill and considerable haste. As he fumbled with her shift, she resolved, "After this, I will seek a man of my own choosing. . . ."

Before dawn, Drustan led Isolt to the door of Mar'ch's chamber. With the extortion of desperate kisses, and with promises of another assignation, he finally left her there, to slip into Golwg's place.

The servant was in the antechamber at the open shutter. "It is done," she said, chin held high. "He suspects nothing." Drustan looked away, sick at the knowledge that his golden fair, who had twined with him all night, now lay beside the unquickening lead of his uncle's bulk.

Wind salted the castle walls with spray. Wildness of winter drove maid to kitchen, groom to stable, and king to bower. Drustan twisted the pegs of his harp, trying each string with a crescent nail. Each time he touched the string, Golwg noticed how the others quivered, resonating sympathetically with the harp. Isolt sat with hands twisted into embroidery, looking steadfastly into the empty pit within her heart. Mar'ch moved the chess pieces with idle hands, eyes full of territorial hunger.

The summer had come and gone. The days were short and the nights long. Nights that were a haphazard pattern of bliss and torment to the lovers, depending on whether Mar'ch wanted his wife beside him.

As if the confinement wasn't bad enough, Drustan launched into some wandering Pictish melody, throwing up a *pibroch* of notes like winged hands asking for help. Golwg noted the rapid beating of the pulse at her mistress's neck and the unconscious flicking of her fingers on her skirts, as though to flick off an irritating insect.

The signs were clear for all but a fool like Mar'ch to see. Isolt without Drustan was a woman without her soul. They had enjoyed only a few snatched hours that week. Golwg felt, not for the first time, the dull, slow hours of women's waiting, endlessly dictated by men. She could wish her mistress the distraction of a child, except she knew that Isolt would bear none. Her mother, Languoreth, had looked beyond the horizon of time and found only the same barren story.

Isolt had put off Mar'ch for several nights now, pleading the need to make a vigil in the chapel, to beseech the saints to aid her to conceive. Mar'ch had clasped her to his broad belly and nuzzled her ear, whispering, "Better that we spend the time in bed, my honey. Since time began, that's how women get children." And Isolt had detached herself with a sweet "I will fast and pray to prepare myself." And had gone straight to Drustan in an outbuilding.

As for Drustan, he now felt the prophesied trap close about him. It was as Isolt said: to be together and yet parted was beyond torment. He ripped out chords from the wires of the harp with harsh fingers, playing a sad ballad with the insistent rhythm of a horse's hoofbeats. Now it was an Armorican air that synchronized all heartbeats into the motions of a dance.

Only Golwg herself was exempt from dancing to that music. Her own life had fallen into no easier lines: Mar'ch treated her like one of his own concubines, using her whenever he wished. If only the king would die, then Isolt would have her desire and Golwg herself would be free of the king's importunities. She muttered a charm against the korrigans, the faeries who make people dance till they drop, and made the spiral sign of the Three with her fingers: let the priest preach; she didn't care which Three, and, if truth be told, neither did he. There must be a better life than this one, she told herself, but she only hoped that it would be this side of paradise.

As the harsh music washed over them, Mar'ch pulled the queen to her feet. "Too many melancholy songs, my lady! Let's to bed. You've prayed and sighed enough, now let's to work!"

With a despairing look, Isolt trailed after her husband.

Drustan raised a ruined face to Golwg. "How shall I bear it? When she goes with him I want to murder him—my own uncle!" He groaned aloud. "What shall I do?"

Golwg dropped the spindle of flax with a brisk spiral motion, moistening the thread and letting it grow between her fingers. "Better that you go!" she observed. "If you stay, murder will be done."

"Without saying good-bye? It will kill me!"

"Go to your father's kin. I will be your go-between. Somewhere there must be a place where Mar'ch cannot find you."

In the inner chamber, Queen Isolt lolled on King Mar'ch's bed, her head moving like a doll's, her body as unresponsive as a corpse. King Mar'ch, meanwhile, rode her like the grim Lord of the Underworld himself, in search of souls. She had schooled her body not to think of Drustan while Mar'ch was at his kingly work.

He would raise no heir from her womb. For all his efforts, her womb might as well have been sown with salt. She thought hard upon the spirits of salt, their hard, crystalline whiteness that bit the tongue.

She became salt. Lot's wife, looking backward, not to Gomorrah but to—Drustan.

No! Not that thought! Thought betrayed her body into response, and Mar'ch grunted in recognition, like a gardener at last drawing out the deepest root of a rosebush.

Queen Isolt's face was a wasteland of tears.

Mar'ch withdrew into the adjoining chamber. Seeing Drustan absent, he beckoned to Golwg, who sighed heavily. "Again?"

"Aye. Your mistress does me no good. No! Don't take off your dress! Just slip it up, like so. Ah! Better!"

Golwg rotated her hips to accommodate him. It was like giving suck, having Mar'ch. She clung to the back of the chest and waited till he had done.

The king strode away toward the mews, where lived the hooded and jessed provisioners who brought small birds to his table. He could just fancy a spit of larks.

In the chamber above, queen and servant cleansed each other with the same cloth and threw away the water with the same curse.

Golwg said to her mistress, "Slavery comes in many forms. You kept me from the worst of it when we were in Dalriada. Here in Cornwall we share it together!"

❧❧

Somewhere in the depths of the Celydon forest of Scotland, Drustan wandered. His horse and weapons had been lost upon the way. As the sun sheared through the heavy darkness of the pine branches, he stopped.

Who am I? His head was planed of thought, empty of memory. Since leaving Isolt, he had wandered northward in increasing agitation and despair. Taking the knife from his belt, he carved a play upon his name on the bark of a struggling rowan tree:

Drust

Trust

Trist

Sadness or madness was it? Pictish ancestors gibbered and sighed in the roots of his bowels. He felt their coiling, clustered obsessions like a knot of adders within him.

His sorrows had made him mad. His duty to Mar'ch, his ancestral honor, his love of Isolt. Unable to bear the burden of trustlessness any longer, he had reverted to a timeless childlike reverie wherein nothing but Isolt figured.

Ah, the neck of her! White as the swan—No! Swans were as crows to her! He kissed his hand, as if kissing again that neck. He grew rigid thinking of her. Was the relief to be a poem or hand-love? Shamefully, the images already began to squander themselves in his hand. He cast his seed into the swift stream. "Pass to the inlets of my own love, Isolt," he prayed. The intensity of her image floated in the deep waters, foaming upon the mossy stones.

In his madness, he carved on the neighboring tree, rendering the queen's name into his own tongue:

Isolt

Easily

Essyllt

. . . Ah! If only!

Mar'ch had raged all day and most of the night, falling at last into a stupor from which Isolt both feared and hoped he might never rise. On finding Drustan departed, he had first sent messengers in every direction. Then, suspicion roused, he had put the blame upon Isolt. Surely she must have insulted or slighted him for him to leave them without a word? Despite her protestations and the pleadings of Golwg, Mar'ch disbelieved her.

He seemed to suffer a kind of fit, as if stricken by lightning. His great bulk toppled over, and he soiled himself. But this was not the seizure of death.

In the early morning, he rose, cleansed himself, and put on fresh garments. Mar'ch was contrite. "Forgive me, wife. There is a vein of melancholy in our line. My sister died of it. Drustan's mother, she was.

Goleuddydd (Gol-EYE-theeth)—aye, Fair Day she was called indeed! But her day was a short one. Her sojourn among her husband's folk was not good for her. The Pictish northern winters are long and without sparkle of the sun. She died most dreadfully, running mad into the forest and giving birth to Drustan in the wretched sty of a swineherd amid all the pigs. . . . Ah, if only my dearest nephew were back among us!"

And Isolt stroked his grizzled hair with a full heart. On that matter they were at least in one accord!

"There has been little to do here, my dear. Perhaps Drustan has gone to find deeds of arms?" she suggested.

"Aye, likely you are right!" And for the first time in their marriage, Isolt felt a faint pity for the hope that played upon his stricken face.

To take the king's mind off his troubles, Isolt demanded to be taken to market. The fair before Christmas was always lively, and she longed to be out of the confinement of Tintagel. It was her idea, to distract Mar'ch from his depression, that they go attired as plain country people. "Golwg and your chamberlain can ride with us," she urged. "We will be able to move among your people without anyone knowing who we are."

Her ruse rallied the king. They rode out the next morning, dressed as a prosperous merchant and his wife. Isolt's beauty turned many heads, and she soon veiled herself against recognition. But they had not taken a full turn round the stalls when Mar'ch pulled at her arm. "There are players—come, let's see!" Seating themselves upon up-turned kegs, the king and queen watched the players perform the Christmas mystery. Their drollery and capering made Mar'ch laugh. But then came on a comedian with a long pair of sheep shears, snipping and snapping away.

"Now, goodfolk, I'll tell you my work: barber at the court, that's me! You need doctoring or dosing? You have a fine beard to trim? Then

I'm your man. But, I tell you, some jobs you'd never want to have. I goes to the court the other day, and they says, 'Trim the king's hair!'

"What an honor! thinks I, maybe I can put 'by royal appointment' over my door?—but—just you wait and see. . . ."

Isolt looked uneasily up at Mar'ch, but he was laughing loudly with the others.

Another player came forward with an ornate tall crown upon his head to represent Mar'ch. The barber went to work on the beard and then pulled off the crown to reveal—horse's ears! He clapped horrified hands over his mouth.

The crowd howled with mirth as the barber tried to cram the huge ears back under the crown. The barber cast looks into the crowd and called out, "When does a door serve no purpose?"

The crowd roared back, "When it's ajar!"

Mar'ch began to shift, puzzled, but Isolt realized the player's drift.

"Well, no good to lock up the barn after the horse has bolted, they say," the barber cried cheerily, trying to cut round the player-king's hair with his sheepshearing shears. While he was busy snipping, two other players entered behind them—a boy attired as a queen, with a huge pair of false breasts, and a dark-haired man with a harp.

The harper started to play to the player-queen, making outrageous love to her.

Mar'ch stood up abruptly, ignoring complaints from those behind whose view he blocked.

The song of the harper pretending to be Drustan had a silly tune, but it took all of Mar'ch's understanding to hear what he sang:

King Mar'ch has horse's ears, they say.
So while he's trimmed, let lovers play.
Under the greenwood, against the wall,
Over the hills and—get away all!

The player-queen and the harper fell shrieking to mock copulation on the platform while the barber tried to creep off to a general roar of neighing from the rest of the company.

Mar'ch dragged Isolt back to her horse, and they rode back home unspeaking. In his ridiculous merchant's cape, Mar'ch fixed his wife with weary sorrow. "Is it true? Do I have horse's ears—or a cuckold's horns, more like?"

Isolt looked out of the window over the sea.

"Is that why my nephew has taken himself off?"

"He has gone to spare your honor," said Isolt, facing him at last.

"You seem to have had little regard for it till now," Mar'ch spat bitterly.

The silence between them screamed with accusation and vengeance.

Mar'ch threw off his cape and said, "I will send to Arthur. Drustan is a mighty warrior, and it may be that he has gone to Caerleon. Arthur will give me revenge or restitution; it is my right."

While Golwg combed out Isolt's hair that night, they made their plan. "I told Drustan to go north to his kinfolk," she whispered. "Maybe we should go thither ourselves?"

"I will send a message to Talorc myself and beg him to receive us," breathed Isolt. "Make ready, Golwg; we are going to find Drustan."

In Celydon Forest, on the borders of Pictland, Drustan lay among the pigs. In the midst of his madness, he dreamed the true dream again. Ever the green leaves. Never the brown.

He dreamed of the green and flaming tree that grew and was never consumed; it grew out of a single root that was a man and woman, the Parents of Life. Whoever looked upon it looked upon the roots of life itself and was changed. Almost he averted the eyes of his soul, so as not to be wound in the tree's branching life. It was dragonish, coiling, multiform—partaking of plant, serpent, faery, and human fashioning. It was the original of the roof-tree that supported the roof of the hall of his father, Talorc, and that was carved in likeness of the ancestral line.

In the dream branches hung a woman by her hair, her mouth one scream of recrimination. What ancestor cried out to him or what child-to-be? It was not Isolt, his divining liver told him with foreboding. Did *she* not lie across the deep root whence sprang the burning leaves? Oh, spirit of the tanged lightning! It was she—his lovely Isolt—wound loathsomely with a crowned toad that was in turn growing out of a fluted fungus.

In the true dreaming, the ancestral Father of Life at the root of the green and flaming tree awarded him the accolade of the green leaf once more. And Drustan clutched it, no gratitude more humble than that of a captive given the dubious mercy of one more day's portion of life.

He awoke to memory, to the loathsomeness of a pigsty. Confusion and recollection clutched at him together. God! This was how he had come to be born! The shame of his mother's madness had long been purged by the kindness of Mar'ch, but here he was in the mire with swine, with no more sign of who he was than if he had indeed been born this very day. Not even a knife or a garment. He had on a cloak of fennel stalks woven together. With great disgust, he threw off the primitive covering and vaulted out of the sty. Nakedness was better than this!

He found a stream and bathed himself in its icy waters, pulling handfuls of frost-crusted soapwort from the bank to purge his skin of the smell of the swine.

He presented himself shivering with cold to the swineherd, desperate for human company, for food, for news of what passed. The man gave him a shirt to cover his nakedness and fed him a dish of boiled roots, pleased to see that his guest's madness had flown off. Drustan urged him go to Talorc with a message that the Son of the Fair Day would have words with him. In his shame, Drustan could not bear to reveal his true identity before even a swineherd: Talorc would know who was meant.

"But who will tend the swine?" asked the man, reasonably enough.

Drustan sighed with lovesick heaviness. "Let me tend them—if you think me trustworthy. The pigs know me and trust me. I will see that they don't wander."

"Make sure you don't. These are the gift of King Mar'ch to Talorc, from his own herd."

Drustan said, modestly enough, "I have had charge of Mar'ch's property before this."

The swineherd looked narrowly at his guest. "And you were not discharged for unfaithful service?"

"I have ever treated Mar'ch's possessions as carefully as my own," replied Drustan solemnly.

<hr>

Messengers from Mar'ch came to Talorc, Drustan's father, that his son was lost. Strangely, only that day Talorc had received word of a stranger who had been found wandering alone in the great Celydon forest: a stranger who lodged with a swineherd who let him lie down among the pigs in the sty and eat of their food.

But Talorc had received another message, from Isolt. The Pictish king astutely assessed all the information at hand and slyly invited Queen Isolt to come herself and hunt the deer in his forest, to see if the quarry was to her liking.

The swineherd returned to the forest after a few days, with great excitement. "Talorc bids the Queen of Cornwall to come hunting in these woods. I must move my swine to the northwest quarter of the forest, that they might not be harmed. The Lord of the Picts sends this to you. For the Son of Goleuddydd." Drustan tore open the leather bag to find a set of clothes suitable for his station and a sword with the crest of Talorc upon it: it was the lightning-struck tree, emblem of their line.

Here was a sign of his father's favor, a renewal of kinship and of the honor that he had lost these last few months. News of Isolt was balm to his soul, but surely, where Isolt rode, Mar'ch would not be far behind. He would have to prepare.

Drustan ranged about the woods, creating hides of fallen limbs and platforms in the high branches, the better to move about and spy upon who came there. He made ready in another way, cutting a hazel branch and preparing it to engrave his message to Isolt. Squaring the peeled branch to expose four clean sides, he carved Pictish *oghams* upon its whiteness—ah, if it were only her own sweet sides, he breathed, what secret script would he not write upon them?

The message would be meaningless to anyone but Isolt, for had he not instructed her in his own language over several dreary days? It read,

Woodbine round the hazel twines:
In the wood they both survive.
But when they are torn apart,
Cob and woodbine lose their heart.
As with them, and so with us:
Without you my green soul pines;
You without me never thrive.

Lying along the branch of an alder that grew over the best fording place within the forest, Drustan waited. Here horses would come down to drink. And indeed, later that day, a string of mounted travelers came that way, including a heavyset warrior and Golwg, with Isolt trailing behind. As Isolt slackened the reins to let her strawberry roan mare lower her pretty neck toward the crystalline waters, Drustan let fall the hazel branch. Her groom noticed the stick but merely kicked it onto the bank.

"Give it me!" begged the queen.

The youth handed it to her, incuriously.

She read slowly, wrinkling her brows to remember the letters' sound. Drustan watched her gloved hand tremble and clutch the hazel wand close to her breast, and he uttered a low wood pigeon's call overhead. Looking up, she saw him and gestured with her hand to a nearby clearing.

Dismissing the groom with the excuse that she wished to relieve herself, Isolt left her mare and slid away unnoticed, her dark green gown merging with the forest's own dark foliage.

He drew her silently into the hide of fallen birch branches that he had covered with fern.

"My mouth is confused: how shall I both kiss and ask you how you have been?"

"Typical of hazel to think of words at a time like this! 'Kiss first, tell after, said the honeysuckle,'" teased Isolt, drawing him down upon her. "It is hazel's duty to be straight and to the point!"

"Fair instructress! You teach me to be bold with you." And they ended their exile in that moment.

"Lady Honeysuckle, you are true to your name," said Drustan, afterward. "Has Lord Hazel leave to speak? . . . Sweet love, how has it been?"

"As it has ever been! Golwg and myself share the burden of Mar'ch. But I have sworn he shall have us no more."

The pain of it! He kissed her eyelids to cleanse them of the shame. "She is a good servant to you! But how will this end? We are as ships torn apart by contrary tides: as your tide ebbs, so does mine, and we are separated further by the fury of Mar'ch."

"There is hope, my love. I came to this forest accompanied by Golwg and by one of the noblest of Arthur's own host—the mighty Cai Hir (KIE HERE). He will be our spokesman. Will you speak to him?"

"Gladly! What deep plans have you laid, you cunning little vixen?"

"Wait and see!" Isolt gave a low call for her groom, who returned with Cai leading a black horse, on which sat Golwg.

Cai stopped and shook his head unbelievingly at sight of the leaf-covered lovers. "Fine deeds in the forest, Drustan!" he grinned.

With dignified appeal Isolt knelt to their champion. "Brave Cai, you alone can reconcile Drustan and Mar'ch. If you help us, I will give you whichever of my women you choose to be your own paramour."

Cai looked down his long nose. "I seek no paramour, lady. Only one glimpse of a summer's day do I desire . . ." and his eyes seemed to scorch Golwg with desire.

Isolt saw how it was between them. She joined their hands together with a blessing. "If you can help us, I will give you Golwg."

Golwg felt her heart would burst. Cai's long, fair eyelashes, his long limbs, his extraordinary deeds of arms to be hers? Then to Isolt she said, "Mistress, I have served you since I was born. Let me have this one gift: the freedom to be myself. I would come to Cai as a free woman, not as a slave."

Cai laughed, "Well said! Since love is free as the wind and blows us where it will. Of all stories I like best the ones that tell of love!"

Isolt drew out a ribbon from her cloak and wound it round Golwg. "Give me a knife!" The slave stood patiently as Isolt sawed through the ribbon. "As this tie is cut, so you are no longer bound to my service. As Cai and Drustan are my witness, I declare you, Golwg Hafddydd, to be a free woman."

Cai took Golwg in his arms. "Will you have me, free woman?"

"With all my heart!" She kissed him but turned to Isolt sadly. "I wish I might free you that easily from Mar'ch, but we must place our trust in Arthur's judgment now."

And the two women wept together, to Cai's evident discomfiture. "Never fear; I will persuade Arthur to treat fairly with you." And he drew Drustan aside, and the two men fell to planning.

Winter's grip kept the lovers safe from discovery. Outlawed from home and family, kindred and tribe, they loved each long night and had no evil dreams.

But as the first snowdrops bloomed, Celydon Forest was filled with sounds of men in great numbers. Isolt clung to Drustan fearfully.

Mar'ch's voice bellowed through the forest: "We have the forest surrounded! Come out and fight, coward and traitor!"

"Leave go of my arm, Isolt. I must fight him, and maybe this can be ended."

Taking his father's sword, Drustan came into the clearing where Mar'ch stood with twenty-four chosen warriors of his household about him. At the sight of the tall, black-haired Pict who seemed to magically melt out of the trees, the men began to murmur superstitiously. Many of them had fought a passage of arms with Drustan and knew the force of his blow. It was popularly rumored that whoever drew blood from Drustan would die, and whoever Drustan struck would most certainly die.

"It's not our fight, lads," said the leader of Mar'ch's war band, for what was this but a fight over a woman? It was shameful to come against one man with such a number. The warriors drew back, leaving a path between Mar'ch and Drustan.

"You have stolen a sword of mine, nephew! I give you from now till sunset to return it, or the justice of Arthur will fall upon you," Mar'ch called. It was long since he had been out campaigning, and the bitter winds cut him to the bone and made a winter of his voice.

Drustan chose to misunderstand him. "The sword that I hold in my hand is my own, given me by my father. I give up this sword to no man, uncle or not." And he stepped toward Mar'ch, flourishing the blade with its engraving of the lightning-struck tree. In Pictish incantation he sang the rallying cry of his tribe, "Father of the lightning-leafed blade, grant me liberty of soul!"

Mar'ch stepped backward, muttering, "I will not kill myself for the sake of killing him! For the love I bore you, nephew, I pray that Arthur's judgment brings me redress for the faithlessness of your kinship to me. Be at the court of Talorc by this week's ending." And he turned his horse.

༺ ༻

At the court of Talorc, Arthur sat in the high seat. As emperor of Britain, his authority was respected by most people within the realm. For did his lineage not spring from the primary family of the island, sealed by the blessing of the red and white dragons of the holy ancestral tree? Akin to Talorc, Drustan, and Mar'ch by countless links of blood, Arthur had the duty of bringing peace to the family. But since he had no family connection with Isolt, he was the best arbiter and impartial judge of the case.

Cai stood to champion Isolt, supplied with the able information of Golwg to plead her case. When Isolt had been heard and her preference for Drustan established, Arthur turned to the two plaintiffs.

"Mar'ch and Drustan, closest in blood as men can be—for is not a nephew better than a son?"

Talorc the Pict affirmed this with a nod, since his whole tribe accepted only the son of a royal sister as their ruler. Here under the carven roof-tree of the Old Ones, where the green and burning tree was figured, could the ancestral judgments best be given. In no other place could a woman give evidence in her own defense with more impartiality.

Arthur looked squarely at both men: Drustan, mutinous and defiant; Mar'ch, dangerous and dishonored. "Which of you is willing to give up Isolt?"

"Never!" cried both men.

At his elbow, Talorc sardonically reminded him, "Drustan is one of the stubbornest men in Britain, Arthur."

"So I see! Uncle and nephew are both adamant!" Arthur cupped his bearded chin in one hand, consideringly. His eyes fell upon the great carved, totemic roof-pillar where the green and burning tree sent up its ancestral leaves from generation to generation, and he received their inspiration thankfully. "My judgment then: that one of you shall have her when the leaves are on the trees, and the other when the trees are leafless . . ."

There was an outcry of astonishment, but Arthur was not finished: ". . . and her husband is to be the first to choose which."

Mar'ch gave Arthur a long, thankful look and said without hesitation, his voice quavering with gladness, "Then I choose the long nights of winter when there are no leaves." And he strode toward Isolt with predatory purposefulness.

Drustan gave a terrible howl.

Arthur raised his hand, staying Mar'ch. "Let us hear from Isolt. What do you think of this judgment, lady?"

Isolt knelt at Arthur's side and kissed both his hands with seeming compliance. Then, raising to the company a face of radiant joy, she sang out to all, "Blessed be that judgment and he who gave it!"

She found and held Drustan's unbelieving eyes with encouragement, saying with a little smile, "For while the holly, ivy, and yew still grow, they are never without leaves—which means I shall be Drustan's as long as he lives!"

"It is the judgment of Solomon all over again!" breathed Cai to Golwg, who stood beside him, the tears spilling down her glad face.

Mar'ch reeled back, slack jawed in defeat.

Talorc wrung his son's hand and kissed Isolt: here was a daughter-in-law of such cunning that she could have sprung from his own line!

Mar'ch's hollow voice cut through the lovers' rejoicing. "Emperor of Britain, you mete out uneven justice! What of the alliance that I won by means of this woman? I need troops to defend my shores against the Irish."

Arthur considered. "I judge that Drustan shall use the dowry of Isolt to maintain a host in Cornwall against raiders and that he himself shall captain it. Will that restore honor and protection to your shores, cousin Mar'ch?"

And with that Mar'ch had to be content.

For two fortnights of feasting under the carven roof-tree of Talorc's hall, Drustan the Pict and Isolt the Dalriadan sat together, while, at their sides, Cai Hir and Golwg Hafddydd raised the pledge to lovers everywhere.

And, on the northerly coast of Cornwall, King Mar'ch sat once more alone, loveless in his hall, regarding the bitter, turbulent sea.

CHAPTER TWO

A HARP OF STONE

I heard thy music,

O melody of melody,

And I closed my ears

For fear I should falter.

I tasted thy mouth,

O sweetness of sweetness,

And I hardened my heart

For fear of my slaying.

I blinded my eyes

And I closed my ears

I hardened my heart

And I smothered my desire.

—From Padraic Pearse,
  "Renunciation"

"The Harp of Stone" is a heartrending ninth-century Irish tale whose theme will be familiar to all who have yearned over the story of Abelard and Heloise. Liadain (LEA'dan) and Cuirithir (KOO'reer) are two poets whose deep love is thwarted by circumstance and religion. Liadain is a career woman whose art fills her whole life. Marriage is not part of her life-plan. When love calls on her, professional pride and fear of her art being subsumed in child-bearing stand in the way. Love's disruptive effect, however, is nothing when compared to the terrible consequences of ignoring love. Many of the poems in this story are my translations of the lovers' own originals.

THE EYES OF the ivory crucifix carved by a master maker from Ravenna gazed down unsparingly at the prostrate nun. It saw a beautiful, even willful, woman submitting herself to severe Celtic austerities.

The floor of the chapel was chill, even for February. The nun's habit was of worn, coarse cloth that once had been weatherproof but now was thin enough to be worn as a summer garment. Under a dun-colored veil, her hair spilled dull and ash strewn, for it was Lent. An icy blast blew unheeded through the unglazed, unshuttered chapel window, straking the prostrate woman with a spear of light.

All this was visible to the eyes of the crucifix.

But what the *woman* saw, her eyes clenched tight, seared by the brightness of her inner vision, was something quite other.

A man with the gray eyes of an otter, lambent with desire, whose hands and poetic tongue caressed her secret places with carnal pleasure. Under him moved a woman, the twin of the nun, save that she was half-clothed in a cloak woven in a royal mix of colors; her hair was glossy from washes of nut dye, spilling like water to her waist; upon her wrists bracelets of cunningly wrought bands of red gold set with Baltic amber. She moved beneath the man, receiving his sunlit caresses with equal passion. Her hand sought to grip his member and guide it into her, but he played with her, delaying the moment, as a warrior plays and feints with his opponent before thrusting home his sword.

The gritty impact of a sandal entering the chapel brought her vision to an abrupt conclusion. The sea-lilted accents of her confessor slashed through the gray-eyed dream lover's murmuring. "If you have finished your prayers, sister, I will hear your confession."

Liadain rose from the floor and knelt with Abbot Cummine (CUM'een). Despite her prostration in prayer, she had served only to call up visions of her carnal past; despite her vision, she had submitted only to the ravishment of the wind.

From youth onward, Liadain knew that poetry was her key to the door of the world. Raised by her uncle, the master poet Flann ua Fáelann, she took every opportunity to learn from him.

By the time she was nine, Liadain knew most of the major verse forms and their complex rules of scansion. Flann accepted that his niece was one of the most gifted pupils to have come through his hands and ensured that the best teachers in the land give her skill a well-polished luster. When questioned by a doubting fellow student about her possible usefulness as a female poet in a man's world, Liadain answered:

> *Verse has chiseled veins in me*
> *Deeper than all other thirst.*
> *Poetkind who weave no skeins*
> *Know themselves a race accurst!*

At nineteen, Liadain was the product of everything the Irish poetic system could make of her. "Although what she'll do with such a dowry of words, the Lord alone shall tell us!" exclaimed her aunt, Dercomanath, to Flann. "Women of her age have two children already."

"Her children will be remembered longer," remarked Flann.

"Poems don't keep you in old age and enfeeblement!" Dercomanath gibed her aging husband.

"She will have pupils of her own one day: they will be children enough" was all he said.

On that day, he placed into his niece's hands the golden branch of her office, scion of the holy otherworldly tree of verse, which was ever fruitful, leafy, and blossoming all at once. Its chiming bells told everyone that she was now an *ollamh,* a master poet, and stood in the highest ranks of skill. "Go now upon your poetic circuit of the land, and return covered with fame."

Liadain blushed with pleasure and pride. "Uncle, I will do all I can to reflect the honor upon your teaching." And she meant every word of it, for she loved him dearly for cherishing her gift.

At last she was a full poet, by everyone's criteria, for she had completed her twelve years' study, astounding her examiners with the breadth of her knowledge and the resourceful depths of her skill. She had emerged from the houses of darkness, where she had lain day after day for a week, searching the darkness for the metaphors, rhymes, and rhythms of her set subjects, to recite poems of sparkling skill, composed in the stillness without quill or parchment, etched only upon her remembrance.

In whichever household Liadain lodged—and she stayed only at those who could, with honor, entertain her—she was assured of a welcome. The novelty of a female *ollamh* brought a good many from the surrounding settlements. Her name passed before her into five provinces of Ireland.

It was so that Cuirithir, chief poet within the household of Guaire (GUE'ry) Fiangalach, heard of Liadain's approach. A certain male pique rose in him, and he desired to see what this young woman could do. Disguising himself as a mercenary soldier, he came to the settlement of Cathal Brega, where she was lodging, to judge how true was the reputation put upon her. Taking his place at the lower benches reserved for grooms, itinerant entertainers, and cowmen, and drawing his sleeves over his telltale white hands and long harper's nails, he combed down a strand of his long dark hair to twist into the characteristic lock of the lowborn over his forehead and waited patiently for Liadain to begin.

He found himself wondering at her youth but checked himself, for many young poets manifested this confidence and skill. It was only because she was a woman that he judged her differently from the rest of the poetic class. For this injustice, he made an honest attempt to listen without looking at her but found that his eyes sought her out with an urgency that confounded him.

She was tall. The golden fillet of poets bound her long, flame-bright hair in that hall, as she took upon her lap a silver-mounted harp of bog oak, whose sides were carved with starlike eyes and set with iridescent crescents of shell. He found himself envying the harp and swore that he would lie in that lap before the month was over.

Liadain's theme was the gift of music, and, like a true descendant of her people, she sang truly of the gift that she had inherited from Corco Duibhne, birthplace of music.

> West's where music first was sung,
> Munster's peace where songs begun.
> Each soul seeks its nature's twin,
> In the cradle of its kin.
>
> Framer of all mystic deeds,
> Quickener of cold's hidden seeds.

Stirrer of sorrows in women's hearts,
A voice not heard in faery parts.

Memory of abiding grievance,
Wakener of valor's lost achievance.
Melody shortening winter's day,
Hastener of delightful May.

Lifeless shape that yet revives,
Carven side that swarms with eyes:
Freed by fingers from its nest,
Sings harp music of the West.

Cuirithir withdrew without betraying himself to his host or to Liadain but left word with the steward that Liadain and her party were welcome at the household of Guaire; if she would extend her circuit that far, an ale feast would be held in her honor.

Cuirithir needed the long, chill walk home. But it did not displace that voice "not heard in faery parts" that sounded still with confident mastery through his being. Would he win her? Since he had seen and heard her, he no longer thought of her in terms of a poet's amorous conquest but as soul of his own soul.

Liadain was warmly welcomed by Cuirithir's patron, Guaire. "This ale feast is in your honor, Liadain. I have invited all the notable poets of Connacht to honor you."

A male poet of lesser talent would have quailed before the august company assembled there that night, but not Liadain, Cuirithir noticed, as he sat apart with the men of lesser account.

After all the fuss, and as the evening became less formal, Liadain sat quietly, wrapped in her long mantle, far from the fire. Only her red-hued long hair spilled fire-bright in the dimness, and a ring of rock crystal sparkled upon her thin hand. She watched the company, taking no part in the boasting, the competition of poet with poet, the riddles and elliptical kennings of the speech that flashed like beacons across the dark spaces of the hall as poet tried to best poet.

Liadain watched silently, looking for another island of quietness such as she possessed in all that noisy throng. It took her some time to note it. A man of about thirty summers, dark hair framing his narrow head, alert as an otter watching teeming fish, his bright gray eyes darting about the company but his shoulders held taut as a harp string. She waited curiously for the harp to come into his hands. He took it eagerly, and she could see how impatient of his turn he had really been, disquieted that uproar and drunkenness would intervene before he had shown his worth.

The grizzled harper who sat beside her stirred himself and set down his ale cup in expectation. "It's young Cuirithir mac Dobarchon, the Otter's son."

As he thrummed his nail over the strings, Cuirithir scanned the sea of faces and deliberately caught Liadain's attention as she leaned forward out of the shadows to hear him. His fingers struck a chord from the bronze strings to her in homage, like the greeting of a blackbird to the new day.

He began with a short melody to see if the strings were in tune. Liadain found herself listening more intently than she had before. The firelight shone upon his left arm and flamed sparkling upon the arm ring that circled his supple forearm. She found herself envying the curve of the harp, cradled upon his left shoulder, and suddenly wished herself pillowed there.

Cuirithir spoke the first line of his poem, touching the harp with three hooked nails to draw attention to the next line. As line succeeded line, rhyme and assonance swelled to accommodate foot and scansion, so the intricate fingering of those nails grew and melted upon the strings, now assaulting the ears with sword shavings of finest silver from the growing moon, now laid on with lilts of the smoothest hand-woven linen folded under hot stones and cool to the limbs as a garment fresh from the loom.

Forever afterward, Liadain could not remember the poem, only how her body yearned to be within the weaving of that voice, held secure and strong, to be clothed with the majesty of love after years of frugal virginity. It seemed that Cuirithir knew her with an intimacy only vouchsafed to her own poetic teacher, where metaphor and personal symbol are exposed in all their nakedness.

Transformed by the promise of his musical caress, she rose at the next opportunity when the drink came round again. The magic would be withdrawn, lost to her forever, if she stayed. All too soon, the poets would be beyond coherence with the richness of the ale. She would withdraw to the women's quarters to savor this moment.

Outside, as she drank in the cold dark night, letting the mantle fall from her shoulders and the brisk sea winds wrap her in their raw embrace, she felt, rather than heard, someone behind her.

"You are Liadain."

Without waiting for her eyes to adjust to the light, she said, "You are Cuirithir."

He laughed. "We are good at poetic recognition, then!"

She replied, "Our teachers would be proud of us; we did it without the need of the seership of touch." She spoke of the manner in which poets might recognize unknown colleagues for the first time by grasping each other's walking staff and intuiting from the wood the antecedents of the other. It was one of the three old prophetic skills of poetic vision.

"St. Patrick outlawed the other two illuminations, but I bless him that he left us that one." And before Liadain could respond, Cuirithir's hand made a seer's trial of touch all of its own, cupping her breast and laying his mouth over hers, breathing, "Not a stone I am touching, but a flood of songs unshed."

Liadaín met his kiss with a smile at the pun he made upon her name: for *Lia* meant both "stone" and "deluge," and *dan* was the name that poets give to the gift of song.

As she gained her breath again, she whispered, "And is the earth sown with your kisses?" And it was Cuirithir's turn to smile at the compliment of her kenning on his own name, which meant "plant the earth."

"I am accounted a good husbandman: I plow the earth to raise up many songs."

Then her arms were about him and his body pressed into hers in a fit so perfect that even the fierce Connacht winds themselves might never part them.

At dawn, Liadain stretched her aching limbs and rose from the byre where they had made their tryst before the household slaves could arrive with their milking pails and find them still entwined. As she combed her long hair free of hay, she looked upon her lover. In repose, he was pale and vulnerable, whereas last night he had been assured, incandescent with passion.

As she fastened her gown, Cuirithir stirred and stretched out a hand round her ankle, kissing her foot. "Lady of my heart . . . We should not be parted, you and I."

"Nevertheless, I have my circuit to finish," she replied.

"But think!" he sat up, shaking the hay from his shoulders. "If we were together—two great poets—just think what a prodigy our son would be!"

Every nerve in Liadain's body twisted with a sickening jolt. Who was this man to speak so unguardedly of these matters? To whom had she given her body, that he so disregarded the courtesies to talk of children? And then a sharper fear gripped her: "What if I am truly with child because of this night's work? What will become of my fame? Will it wither, only to flourish in some scion of this man's blood? Will the name of poet be denied me and the common title of mother be inscribed instead in the branching tree script over my tomb?" The thought was horrifying.

She made no response to his banter, regretful now of her passionate disclosures of the night. Cuirithir saw how it was with her and discreetly turned to clothe himself. He had had enough wellborn virgins in his bed to know how things must be with her, so gently raised: the passion of the night doused by the chill dawn, the compliant twining of midnight starkly exposed by noonday convention. By all the angels! She had been like a faery woman the night before, hot and sportive, eager as a freshly fledged filly on a firm, straight track. Now, her downcast eyes were even ashamed to meet those of the beasts stalled in the byre, let alone his own!

That afternoon, he found her company readying their packhorses for departure. Saluting her with style, Cuirithir cupped her foot once more in his hand as she mounted her roan mare. Her long-tailed eyes gave away nothing, but her toes curled over his hand.

"Shall we make a double circuit, you and I, Liadain? Shall we be together forever?"

She smoothed the horse rod against her own thigh, in consideration, badly wanting to say yes but fearful of the consequences. "I must finish my own circuit first; I owe it to my uncle. Call for me at my house in Cill Conchinn, and I'll come with you."

"May the sun shine on that hour!" Cuirithir cried out as she turned toward the south. "I shall come, never fear!"

Each hoofbeat hammered fear and dread into her. What had she done? No man had ever wakened even a glimmer of the desire she knew other women to feel. She was acquainted with the stories of passion: she had examples aplenty in her repertoire. Lovelorn women who wept alone; fierce, independent women who coerced their lovers to deeds of madness; wives whose husbands abandoned them.

That she knew now something of the secret metaphor of man with woman was one thing, but that she knew so little of its meaning was another. Knowledge and ignorance battled in her.

What was Cuirithir's meaning—a double circuit to honor poetry, or a marriage between them? She had not questioned him closely enough to find out. Her mind swerved from his meaning, confronted as she was by the implication of her unguarded actions.

The need to clarify and understand the consequences of her actions mingled with anxiety that she might be with child. That she might lose her hard-won livelihood through association with him was uppermost in her head. Each fear fought within her as she rode through Connemara down to the coasts of home.

On her return, Flann was gratified by the honor heaped upon his niece. Together with her foster parents, Liadain made the pilgrimage to the church of St. Ita to give thanks for a successful circuit. She offered a tithe of her earnings to the foundation, which had the reputation of rearing abandoned children and educating promising young clerics.

Abbot Cummine was staying in the guesthouse. Now founder of his own monastery in Offaly, he had the reputation of having a singular insight as a confessor, being a man of virtue and wisdom. In her confusion, Liadain schooled herself to sit through the liturgy.

The preaching of Cummine was persuasive. He had a poet's understanding of how the heart leaps ahead and learns to love at hearing the text of love. He had spoken of the Divine Lover of all people at the offering that day, and Liadain had been moved, for her own heart had been touched with that same transforming fire. The song of Christ and Cuirithir, Cuirithir and Christ: they blended together within her. What Cuirithir had wakened in her was akin to her service to poetry, to God. On impulse, she begged that Cummine become her soul-friend and give her the physic of holy advice.

Unsparingly, she poured into his ears the story of her ecstatic but shameful night of passion. Unsparingly, he gave her her penance: "Take a vow of chastity. Give to no man the knowledge of your body. Fast twice as hard as laypeople generally do. Pray to the King of the Elements for his mercy."

Liadain had come so far on the wave of passion that she found herself on shores unknown. Cummine's penance was a map by which to return to the house of her soul. She promised to visit the abbot again, returning home to Cill Conchinn. And as Cummine waved her upon the road, he swore that he would win her for Christ, for he had rarely known such a resolute, passionate soul as hers.

During this time, Cuirithir had left Connacht to seek Liadain. As he approached Cill Conchinn, he saw a strange-looking fool converging with him at the fort where Liadain lived. His clothes were on backward and inside out.

"Well met, friend!" called Cuirithir. "What's your name?"

"Mac Do Cherda (MAK DOE KHER'da) they call me."

"I've heard of you," Cuirithir marveled. Mac Do Cherda was a famous poet. He had, it was said, slept with a druid's wife, and the druid had sent him straw-mad in retribution. In his foolishness, Mac Do Cherda would roam the wilderness and shun the company of men. In his sane moments, he was one of the sagest poets in the world, able to deliver true and kingly judgments on matters that few could resolve.

And this was why he was called Mac Do Cherda, the Son of Two Arts, since he had the skill to be foolish or wise.

Cuirithir hesitated outside the fort, not knowing how he might be received. He said to the fool, "Friend, will you do me a favor? Go into the house, and, using the secret, dark speech of poets, inquire if my lady Liadain is within. Do it so that no one else knows who waits for her here. Tell her that Cuirithir mac Dobarchon awaits her at the well."

Mac Do Cherda grinned and entered the main house, hovering at the foot of Liadain's *grianan*, where she sat with four of her women. He bumped into one of the pillar stones that held up the wooden floor of the *grianan*, kissing it and saying loudly,

> *Oh, great house on pillars stood,*
> *Bright your fruit within the wood.*
> *Has any gray stone here a date?*
> *—At the sunset she must wait.*

The women above giggled, and Liadain cried down the stair, "Why do you speak to the pillar stones?"

Curling one arm about the stone, the fool called up to her,

> *Darkness is upon my eyes,*
> *And I fail to note the signs!*
> *Every woman that I see,*
> *I call her the Gray Lady.*

And then Liadain rose, knowing that a poetic kenning game was afoot, for few knew that her name might also be construed as "Gray Lady." "Who seeks the Gray Lady?" she called down the stair. Mac Do Cherda replied,

Yonder there the beast's son sighs,
In the pool all night he lies.
Waiting by the well to greet,
On his pale, gray, pointed feet.

And then Liadain knew that Cuirithir had come for her at last, and she flew down the stairs to the well outside the fort, where he stood in his purple cloak of feathers.

"I have come, as I promised," he said, making to encompass her in his arms.

Liadain drew back, drinking in his precious presence. "You are too late." She wrung her hands. "On my poet's honor, I have taken a vow of chastity."

Cuirithir was like a man taking a death blow. "Liadain, it was *marriage* I promised you, not the dishonor of an unblessed bed. Why could you not have waited till I came?"

His reproach was terrible. But how to tell him of her girlish fears? It was not three weeks after her return from St. Ita's that she had had her flow of blood again. Had her penance been for nothing?

"Abbot Cummine bound me to this penance, and I shall maintain it to cancel the sin of our coming together."

His voice became a lover's again. "Dearest woman, ours was no sin—only an anticipation of what is lawful and loveful." And his hand crept up her sleeve, renewing the uncontrollable passion in her body. She suffered the ecstasy for a few heartbeats and then withdrew again. "Cuirithir, I beg you come with me to see Cummine. He can be your soul-friend too! I swear to you that his penance is one that only honor can discharge."

And though he cursed himself for a fool, Cuirithir could do no more than accompany her to keep her bargain with God.

Mac Do Cherda, who had been watching them from the bank,

looked at them both, intrigued. "I shall come with you to the house of this great saint and taste his wisdom for myself." Later, on the road, he looked curiously at Liadain again,

Woman of the sturdy stride,
Your fame's twin's not been descried.
No nun's veil can ever fence
Such a fine intelligence.

"Or such a foolish one," Liadain's secret soul silently replied, as they went forward, three fools together.

At Cill Cummin, the abbot welcomed them to his foundation. He saw immediately how it was with them and gave Cuirithir no opportunity to claim Liadain or expostulate with him. He spread wide his arms in compassionate blessing and proclaimed, "The power of my soul-friendship be upon you! While you are here together, I will strive to win your souls to God, for many of my little crumbs—the penitents who seek soul's counsel—have I offered up, and they are become the bread of angels in their turn. Tell me, while you are here, which would you rather: would you see each other without speaking or speak together without seeing?"

As one being, the lovers said, "Speaking!" and looked upon each other hungrily as they said it, grinding each pigment of skin's, eyes', hair's color upon the palette of memory to last forever.

"Then this is how it will be," said Cummine. "When Liadain is in her cell, Cuirithir shall walk abroad. And when Cuirithir is in his cell, Liadain shall walk abroad. And you shall speak together once a week through the wattled wall of your cell."

It was only with Cuirithir beside her that Liadain began to realize how hard this would be. They were led away to separate cells where penitents fasted and prayed.

Then Cummine turned to Mac Do Cherda, taking in his bedraggled appearance. "It is wet in the wood."

"I am always wet."

"But you have come into a dry place."

"Everything we have is wet," responded the fool.

"We have a fire by which you may dry yourself."

"It is not right that wet and dry be under one roof," said the fool, looking at the lovers significantly.

"Ah! You would say, a hound and a full cauldron should not be left together?" probed Cummine.

"Only that some wet things never dry out!"

Cummine blessed the fool. "What is your name in God, my son?"

Mac Do Cherda set his thin face on one side, as if hearkening to remembrance. "They call me Mac Do Cherda."

Cummine blessed the fool. "Will you be my foster-brother in Christ?"

"I will, if Christ so pleases."

That Liadain had overturned her former vow to marry her fellow poet, Cuirithir, and had precipitately taken the veil was soon the chief gossip of Munster. That Cuirithir had then become a monk in order to accompany her in some manner of strange fellowship was even more hotly discussed. For a man to turn from the profession of poet to that of monk was unusual, but for Cuirithir, who was a master poet and at the height of his reputation, it was considered a sorry shame.

Unknowing of the gossip, Cuirithir sat in his cell of penance, reviewing the eight chief sins as set out in the book by St. John Cassian and how he had fallen into their grasp at different times in his life. It was extraordinary how each of these involved Liadain in some way. Out of long habit, he spent an idle moment composing a poem to her, incidentally weaving Cassian's physical occasions of sin into his confessional review:

My two eyes are jealous that others look upon you,
My two ears smart at hearing your beauty slandered,
My tongue speaks ceaselessly of your virtues,
My heart delights in all that you do,
My belly is hungry with need of you,
My hands are raised to protect you from harm,
My feet wander ever to where you stand,
My manly part is as a compass to my true north—Liadain.

He wondered that Cassian's eightfold bill of sins did not include the sense of smell. He dwelled upon the enjoyment of pleasant odors— of flowers, of freshly made cheese, of roasting meat—the scent of Liadain's flesh. . . . Even through the wattled walls of her cell, he could smell her. His daily walk took him past where she lay, but only weekly could they converse. Cummine's method of soul-friendship had at least brought them to better knowledge of the other. "If only we two could have studied together in the houses of darkness, we would have known each other better!" was their joint complaint.

Cuirithir had taken the habit of a penitent in order to keep her company, submitting himself to Cummine's direction only so that he might show his constancy to Liadain. No great sense of sin had been upon him, though that burden was now heavier the longer he remained in the monastery.

How ironic that his ardent journey from Connacht to Liadain should end in this place! He cursed himself for a fool but knew himself incapable of being anywhere other than where she was. Cummine had trapped him well and truly.

As part of her penance, Liadain was cautioned to meditate upon Eve. The realization that there would be no winter, no hell, no death, no fear, no sorrow were it not for the first woman hung heavy upon her. Her mind could not encompass the notion.

Again and again she was told that Eve had stolen heaven from all who were born of her. Eve been steward of Eden's household, and had she not touched that sacred store in her larder—the fruit of the Tree—there would be no evil in the world. She was a gateway to evil; hence her image was to be placed at the doorway of churches, chapels, and monasteries of women so that all women might be reminded of their foremother.

"Like Eve, you have given away the jewel that should illuminate the garden of your soul, when you lay down with Cuirithir," said Cummine, severely, to Liadain's weeping argument: "But it was sweet and tender to lie with him!"

"Aye! Forbidden knowledge tastes sweet when it is stolen, but it soon sours the soul."

Seeing his penitent so cast down, Cummine would remind her that, for all her sins, Eve was also the ancestress of Christ and that, as the teachings were harsh and unforgiving of Eve, so they were tender and loving of Mary.

That was why, thought Liadain, to approach the altar of the crucified savior, all people had to pass under the open gape of Eve's womb. Born into sinfulness, only through shame and blame might they come to glory. Eve's womb had opened to bring mortality and death into the world: Mary's opened to bring immortality and salvation again.

She both believed and disbelieved it. The Irish, poetic part of her nature knew and yearned after that which was native and familiar to her—the ancestral wisdom that flowed at the water's edge, where poets sought inspiration.

She gazed down on the waters of the lough that bordered the monastery while upon her daily walk at the vesperal hour and knew that yearning now to be part of her own ancestral tradition. To be joined to Cuirithir would make her part of it, but that relationship would omit Christ. If she were joined only to Christ, it would include Cuirithir, poetry, everything.

These thoughts festered in her heart. She felt as exiled from herself as Eve had been from Eden.

Cummine was well aware of Liadain's obsessional prayer. He dimly knew how poem and prayer stretched out together upon the bed of Liadain's soul, how each—God forgive the metaphor!—strove to enter bliss before the other. He did not hold with the long hours of meditation and prayer that the Roman church prescribed.

Long meditation tended to lead such penitents as Liadain and Cuirithir into the ancient druidic and poetic darkness where inspiration was kindled. Keeping them occupied was of far greater efficiency.

He knew also how instructive and impressive it was to his flock for two such nobly born poets to enter into manual labor. But he was aware too of how shocking and potentially feud making it was to keep them at their labors for longer than necessary. It was not wise to humiliate penitents of noble fame by such menial works.

He looked down the long corridors of penance for some spectacular example of piety that would render their sexual heat for each other less torrid. He had reduced Liadain's food to a level where, if he thrust a pin into her hand, the blood would not spurt proudly out but only slowly seep. Cuirithir's lust was of a stronger order, fueled by the vigor of manhood, untouched by slight penances. He had forbidden Cuirithir to make any verse in an attempt to reduce him to a truly penitent state, but with little avail.

Both had the staying power of those long trained in poetry. Cummine's mind wandered to and fro. The stories of the desert monks whose virtue was not thrown by proximity to young virgins or loose women came to his mind . . . the temptations of St. Anthony. A scheme so daring and so startling came to him then, as if an angel had thrust its lance into his blank vision and cleared its obscurity with a flaming ray of light. Even in his own rigorous penitential he had failed to mention this thorny test: a *consortium,* whereby man lay with woman, but with an innocent soul lying between them.

Of course! Why not put them to bed together and see if their resolve could be tested. It was a test not found in any penitential, but it had the biblical warrant of old King David and Abishag, the young Shulemite woman, whom David had taken into his bed in order to warm his chill bones; yet that virtuous king had had no carnal knowledge of Abishag.

On the day on which the lovers were permitted to speak together, Cummine watched and listened, covertly. Liadain scratched at the wattled wall of woven hazel and called softly within to Cuirithir, who made immediate response in a dull voice:

Sweet to me the voice I hear,
Though I cannot make good cheer.
This alone is what I say,
Sweet the voice that greets this day.

And Liadain responded with shame,

Though this voice sounds through the wall,
You are right to blame its fall.
What your own voice does to me:
Shades of joy won't let me be.

Cummine's foot stirred a stone, and Liadain turned angrily at being disturbed during this precious time. So terrible was her ravaged, reproachful face that Cummine spoke of his plan before he had truly thought it out fully. "Listen! I have a penance for you. I bid you sleep by each other tonight, face-to-face, but let a little boy sleep between you to keep you from carnality."

Through the wall, Cuirithir's irony was colored with some amusement:

One night's passing, you confide,
I shall lie by Liadain's side;
It would not be a wasted year,
If it were a layman lying here!

Swift as thought, Liadain threw back the answering stanza,

If one night by Cuirithir's side,
You command that I abide:
Though one year we gave to it,
We'd not lack for ready wit.

Cummine did not like their tone, but pride in his penitential contest blinded him to everything else. That night, the lovers were laid together, with a little acolyte between them in the darkness. When his stertorous breathing showed that the boy was asleep, Cuirithir ventured a word to his erstwhile love: "Words are all we have had for the best part of this year, Liadain. Would you turn these into deeds of love?"

"In this bed?" she inquired, looking askance at the little boy between them.

Cuirithir stirred as carefully as he could and lit a rush light from the flint and tinder he had concealed in his garments.

For the first time in a year, they gazed upon each other. He was appalled to see the wastage of her beauty, wrought by severe fasts. She was chastened by the deep etching of disappointment scored upon his face.

"I have borne you company for a year, Liadain. Tell me, will you at least return to poetry, even though you will not be my wife? Or you can cast off your veil and come with me."

But as Cuirithir reached to embrace her, the acolyte stirred, feeling their movement, and made to cry out. Cuirithir covered the boy's mouth. "I will kill you if you say a word! Get outside, lie still till morning, and then return, and no harm will come to you."

The boy got from between them, shaking, and lay wakeful in the lee of the cell all night.

The next morning, the child would say nothing of the night's events; neither was he able to report their speech to Cummine, who wrathfully sent for Cuirithir. Tight-lipped, he said, "It is clear that the penance was too hard for you! I command you to make your pilgrimage to the east, where you shall be housed at another monastery, and may God's guidance bring you to the heart of heaven!"

"And Liadain?" Cuirithir asked.

"She shall remain here, under my protection. She shall not be exposed to you again after last night. You will be well companioned on your road," indicating where Mac Do Cherda stood. The fool had become the favorite of all in the monastery, but he was eager to be once more upon the road. Seeing how Cuirithir's discontent hung thick upon him, like bog water on a hound's back, Mac Do Cherda said, "Let the otter's feet take him away to the pools of Cill Letrech; the fish are fatter there."

As they traveled eastward, Cuirithir contemplated the void into which his life had cast him. Knowing that Mac Do Cherda would speak only the truth, he asked the wise fool, "What is sin?"

The fool replied, "You wouldn't ask that if you knew a pure soul."

"What use is going to church?"

"Nothing, if not done with goodwill."

"What about taking the monastic tonsure?"

"Long hair is no worse, if there's no disgrace beneath it," smiled the fool.

Cuirithir sighed heavily. "The selfishness of women empties the storecupboard."

"And the selfishness of men ravishes cornfields."

Cuirithir pressed on with his catechism, more humbly. "What about when one is angry with another?"

"It is bad for the one who fosters it and displeases the King of the Sun."

"What of a woman who has been promised to one man and then beds with another?"

"Whoever has no shame receives no reward." Mac Do Cherda could not be brought to speak ill of Liadain, whom he respected. So Cuirithir asked instead about himself, "Then what of the man who is given to adultery?"

"However pleasant for his body, the evil stains the soul."

"And hell?"

"If you were to see it before death, you would not do another evil till doomsday."

"What about heaven?"

"The lowest rank in heaven is better than kingship of the whole earth."

Cuirithir was silent for the rest of the journey, digesting these answers. He then resolved to make his own penance for the sake of Liadain's lost love. For what use was a discipline given to him by another when he could barely master himself? Abandoned by her, angry, and in pain, Cuirithir took the vows of a monk at the monastery of Cill Letrech and—more terribly—relinquished poetry as his self-imposed penance.

Back at Cummine's abbey, Liadain would make no response to the abbot's questioning. Since she would say nothing of her actions the night of the *consortium,* Cummine was hard upon her, sparing her no detail of the extremity of Cuirithir's action: his forsaking of poetry would surely strike her hard? But she was merely spurred to respond, angrily, with eyes hard as stones:

> *The Otter's son has left his pool,*
> *Submitted to the chanting school;*
> *They'll not hear his eloquence,*
> *For he'll make but little sense!*

Cummine found himself moved to respond in verse,

> *Liadain, wife of Cuirithir,*
> *I like not the words I hear!*
> *He left here with spirit glad,*
> *Never say that he was mad!*

And Liadain, broken at hearing herself called his wife, spat one final defiant stanza in Cummine's face, even though there was no truth in her allusion:

Bright Friday, when we bedded last,
Honey took the place of fast.
On the fleece of my white skin,
Cuirithir laid and entered in.

Appalled at his penitent's lapse, Cummine's face fell. "Woman, what have you done?" And that question thereafter became Liadain's self-reproach: a reproach that had nothing to do with displeasing God or abbot and everything to do with the true veneration of her heart. In the solitude of her cell, she made her poem:

Without joy
My disastrous action:
I have broken him whom I loved.

It was madness,
Not to bring him pleasure:
Yet Heaven's King is my reprisal.

No hindrance
For him to run his desired track:
From pain's wrack toward paradise.

Such small offense
Embittered Cuirithir's heart:
With him great was my gentleness.

Liadain am I,
My love was with Cuirithir:
Never was truer word uttered.

A short while
I was companion to Cuirithir:
Our tenderness gave him joy.

Wood's song
Enchanted me with Cuirithir:
And the sea's dark tide.

My constant wish:
No harm shall come to Cuirithir,
Whether early or late.

No hiding!
He was my heart's treasure,
Though all the world I loved.

Flame's scorch
Has roasted my heart:
True, without him it beats no more!

Then Liadain left Cill Cummin and followed her lover to Cill Letrech to beseech his forgiveness, but when Cuirithir heard that she was coming, he took ship in order to avoid her. The abbot of Cill Letrech would not tell her his destination, only that Cuirithir had chosen "the white martyrdom" of self-imposed exile rather than sin again.

Mac Do Cherda alone had pity upon her, leading her to the stone upon which Cuirithir had daily prayed. Setting her knees into the hollow that he had worn in that stone, she let her sorrow shape itself into his requiem:

Cuirithir, ex-poet, won the prize,
Yet no profit meets my eyes.
My lord of the two gray feet,
Never more we two shall meet.

This stone, south the oratory wall,
Where my ex-poet used to call,
Here I'll take my pilgrim way,
After evening prayer each day.

And as she pressed bony hands into tear-drained eyes, the vision of Cuirithir as he might have been came powerfully to her, only to be replaced by the waste, the loss. If only she might have been privileged to bear him children!

No wife for him under the sun,
No dear children round him run.
No warm thigh next his will lay,
No verse, no music light his day.

And there Liadain could be found, every evening, facing into the east—the direction into which Cuirithir had gone. The monks of Cill Letrech mistook her moving lips for prayer. They saw her steadfast, flintlike face set toward the place of the Lord's crucifixion and mistook her faithful penance on that unyielding stone as a final renunciation of her carnal love. And when she died thereon, they buried her under it, proud that their own monastery should be the resting place for one who had made her soul. But had they had windows to look into that secret place, they would have averted horrified eyes, for her soul was as a shrine to Cuirithir and not to Christ!

Many years after, there came from the east a tall, gray-eyed monk who had spent his life in the service of others in far Alba. He knelt beside the stone that covered his soul's love on knees whose calluses were as thick as the saddle sores on a pack animal.

His dim eyes peered closely at the stone.

Only Mac Do Cherda could have scratched the inscription upon the stone, for none but he had the poetic knowledge: a harp with eyes upon its side, and along the strings had written her name in branching tree script.

"Liadain, poet of Corco Duibhne."

And the heart within him broke, as Cuirithir set his fingers on the stony strings whose music would sound no more in this world.

CHAPTER THREE

EDUCATING THE SEA-GOD'S SON

I am a man upon the land,

I am a selkie in the sea,

And when I'm far and far from land,

My home it is in Sule Skerry.

—Scottish song,
"Sule Skerry"

In this tongue-in-cheek tale, Mongan, the half-immortal son of Manannan mac Lír (MAN'an-awn MAK LEER), god of the Otherworld, is given a complete education in how to be human. Mongan's wife, Dubh-Lacha (DOO LAK'a), has a far shrewder grasp of mortal affairs than her husband. It is only when he foolishly loses her to his rival, Brandubh (BRAN'duv), that Mongan really begins to grow up.

The beginning of this story is known to modern readers through the "Ballad of Sule Skerry," when Manannan becomes a seal who goes night visiting.

IT HAPPENS, ONCE in many aeons, that the gods bring a child into being. The coming of such a child is usually prophetically heralded, but there is always the matter of how and on whom it will be conceived. This was the manner in which I, Manannan mac Lír, god of the blessed islands beyond the seas, became the father of the Mongan.

Of all the women in the world of men, I found only one who was worthy to be the mother of my child: the virtuous Caintigerna (KEN'tig'ERN'a), wife of Fair Fiachna (FEAK'na). And that was the trouble: she was faithful to her husband and would never lie with me, not for even one night.

I caused her husband to leave Ulster to help his friend, Aidan of Scotland, fight against the Saxons. And while the coast was clear I visited Caintigerna one winter's night as she sat lonely at her hearthside. "Sleep with me!" I begged her.

"Not for gold nor jewels will I disgrace my man," she proudly replied.

"Would you sleep with me to save your man from death?" I asked her. "For, even as we speak, he is about to fight the deadliest of the Saxon foes and will certainly die in that combat unless you sleep with me. If you consent to spend but one night with me, you will conceive a son of great renown; and, in return, I will go to Scotland and kill your husband's opponent with my own hands before he can strike his deadly blow against Fiachna."

What else could the beautiful, proud woman do? Not that she found me unappealing! All that long, wintry night, we explored the lovesome variations of pleasure that only one who lives forever in the Plain of Delight can fully know. In that one night's work we made a child: a boy who would be half mortal, half immortal. As the pale, pure morning dawned the next day, I told Caintigerna with whom she had lain. As her pale gray eyes widened in awe that she had slept with a god, I promised her that our son would be known as Mongan mac Fiachna in her world, though he would ever have my protection in his life. Which is just as well, as he grew up to be a trouble to more than me.

On the night that Caintigerna gave birth to Mongan, there were two other significant births: souls whose lives would touch my son's. On that night, the wife of Fair Fiachna's servant also had a son, Mac an Daimh (MAK'n DAVE): he was the one I had chosen to accompany Mongan when he became a man. Also, there was another birth: Dubh-Lacha, daughter of Dark Fiachna. She would be Mongan's wife in the fullness of time.

Now Dubh-Lacha's father, Dark Fiachna, was joint ruler of Ulster with Mongan's father, Fair Fiachna. There was little love lost between the two kings, whose enmity went back to some paltry feud so far beneath my notice that I don't remember the cause, but it was an enmity that I did well to pay attention to. On the third night after Mongan's birth, I came secretly by night and took my son away from Caintigerna.

Her gray eyes were clouded as I took the infant in my arms, but I assured her, "I will bring up Mongan in the Land of Promise and endow him with skills that will surpass those of other men. I promise that he will return to Ireland when he is ready to take valor as a man."

"It is so long a time!" mourned Caintigerna, kissing her baby and giving him into my hands. But, within the week, both she and Fair Fiachna were dead at the hands of his rival, Dark Fiachna, who fell upon their settlement and burned it to the ground. And though the people of Ulster begged and prayed to me that Mongan might be returned to them, that they might make him the rallying point for retaliation against Dark Fiachna, I hardened my heart until my son was old enough to deal with the situation himself.

Mongan grew into a tall golden-haired youth, with a dreamy smile and engaging appearance: amiable and slow to harm, he had a sharp mind if he would but use it, but only experience would hone that faculty into an edged weapon. I taught him all that an inhabitant of the Otherworld might need, nor did I neglect his schooling in the earthly affairs of his own world. Looking deeply into the pools of seeing by which we immortals view the earthly world, he scanned the tides and affairs of Ireland, ever returning to one particular household—that of Dark Fiachna. He learned the motivations and actions of his enemy well, but, when he thought I wasn't looking, his attention would stray to Dubh-Lacha, spying upon her with an attentive rapture that gave the game away.

Dubh-Lacha, whose smooth dark hair was like plumage of the black duck, whose skin was pale as the blossom of the arbutus tree, whose mouth was the color of the ripening wild strawberry: ah, his gaze would fix upon her like a man gripped by a vision.

And she? The power of Mongan's longing bored into the secret places of her heart, even to the depths of her dreaming, where, upon the dream paths of the night, she would encounter his likeness and long for him—unknowing of his name. To her, he was a dream stranger, a night-visiting lover. And I, who am the king of dream lovers, felt pride that the dream likeness of my son had roused the love of such a beautiful girl.

Seeing him so, I knew that it was time to send him to his own domain. As soon as he landed upon Ulster's shores, the warriors of his clan met and acclaimed him as their leader. And Fiachna the Dark, fearful of the popular acclaim of his rival's son, made a peace with Mongan, offering him one-half of Ulster and his own daughter to seal the pact.

I believe that Dubh-Lacha thought herself in my own blessed realm the day that she was married to Mongan, so great was her joyful surprise in learning that her intended husband was none other than her own dream lover. I left them to their honeymoon but returned a few weeks later. Dressed as a drab-robed cleric, with the distinctive broad-browed tonsure of the church, I was presented to them as Mongan and Dubh-Lacha sat at *fidhchell*. Their game did not advance very quickly because, as either considered the next move, the other would stretch out a hand and caress arm or breast or lean forward and catch the lower lip of the other in a questing kiss.

It is hard to divide lovers from their loving, but my heart was burning with injustice against Dark Fiachna, who had slain my son's mother. Caintigerna at least should have vengeance, even though Mongan disregarded his putative father, Fair Fiachna. "This dalliance is unbecoming in a king, Mongan: your father and mother lie unavenged while Dark Fiachna lives yet!"

The lovers looked up as my words broke the spell of their caresses. Mongan saw at once who I was, but Dubh-Lacha pressed her lips together reprovingly. "Who are you to reprove the king?" Mongan stayed her with, "It is the truth, Dubh-Lacha. Your father killed mine, and there will be no true peace until I slay him."

Dubh-Lacha smoldered with sulks in my direction. "What kind of cleric councils death? It is a strange brand of Christian faith that you preach!"

Mongan bit his lip, unhappily realizing that his actions would alienate his wife. "This is my new confessor, Orbsen. And he speaks as my conscience, Dubh-Lacha."

"Then if you follow his course of advice, let me pronounce your penance: you shall fast from my bed until you make restitution to me for the loss of my father!" cried Dubh-Lacha, her face like stone, and swept out without another word.

An astute and faithful woman, Dubh-Lacha! I could almost find it in my heart to pity my son, but a father must train his offspring to stand upon their own two feet and bear their ills bravely.

Before the week was out, Mongan had killed Dark Fiachna and completed the rites of mourning over the graves of his parents, according to the old custom. Turning his face to me under the shelter of his cloak, the dark thunder spots of rain making their own mourning runnels down his cheeks, he reproached me. "Dubh-Lacha will scarcely speak to me now: she has taken herself from my bed. How can I win her love again when I have slain her father?"

I spoke the truth to him and he knew it. "If you had left your father and mother unavenged, your popularity would have quickly waned. Now you have done a man's deeds and secured your position as sole ruler of Ulster. Now you should strengthen your kingdom by making alliances with the kings of the other provinces of Ireland. All this you do for the good of Dubh-Lacha, and she will see it and acknowledge you again as her love. She has asked for restitution. . . ."

He looked at me yearningly, like a little child who looks to his father to take away the pain of a bruised knee after a fall, but, though I could indeed make his affairs come straight should I wish, yet I knew that his mortal nature must be strengthened by necessity: that is how humans reach to the pit of their resourcefulness and find solutions. So I merely said to him, "I am sure you will find something that settles the matter."

And that was how my son began his quest to win back the love of his wife. Visiting the provinces of Ireland one by one, Mongan came to the lands of Brandubh of Leinster, where he was royally entertained. Now Brandubh was a wily king and Mongan but newly come to manhood, and so the trouble began.

His command of all that I might teach him of the blessed islands of the Otherworld was remarkable; but every mortal has his flaws, and Mongan needed to learn the virtue of good common sense. He was young but still short of a complete education. Only an immersion in the tides of mortal affairs would mature him now, for men are born to trouble, as their scriptures attest.

Mongan wakened early one morning and strayed past a meadow where fifty white, red-eared cows grazed, each with her calf. It was a sight to lift the heart of any ruler, but, for Mongan, this sight brought to remembrance the fields of my own dear realms, where cattle of this color are to be found in their droves. Mooning over the wall at the cows, Mongan sighed a deep sigh: "Surely such a herd would gladden the heart of Dubh-Lacha and be sufficient recompense for the hurt that I have brought upon her?"

Brandubh overheard this remark and, seeing how Mongan brooded over the cows, said, "Such beautiful cows are surely a fit match for the beauty of your wife?" Mongan opened his eyes wide with surprise as Brandubh made this offer: "I will give them to you if you will make a pact of special friendship with me: whatever you ask of me I shall grant you, and whatever I ask of you, you shall give me."

Ah, my son! Your rash acceptance of that offer was the worst day's work of your life! But now you were a man in your own realm, and I could not intervene any longer. Such is the pain of the gods: to see the mistakes that humans make and be unable to change what will come.

I watched the fond youth ride home beside the herd that his followers drove triumphantly before them to Ulster. I saw how Dubh-Lacha peeped out from the shutter, how he coaxed her out to take possession of the exquisite herd, how he made her smile upon him again. And Dubh-Lacha drew him down onto their bed and opened her thighs gladly to receive him whom she had missed so sorely and rained a mixture of tears and laughter upon the one who had killed her father.

But that very week came Brandubh with his hosts to demand the fulfillment of Mongan's promise. "It is a large company you have there, King of Leinster, if you truly come in friendship!" cried Mongan.

Brandubh slapped my son upon the back. "It is but to demand the reciprocation of our promise, King of Ulster."

"I thought friends made requests, not demands," said Dubh-Lacha, speaking freely before them both, and wiser than Mongan of the danger in which they stood.

"This is my request, then," replied Brandubh, revealing his shark-bright teeth. "You promised to refuse me nothing, Mongan . . . so I request . . . Dubh-Lacha."

Silence fell upon Mongan then, and the shock of mortality blanched his cheeks. His speech stumbled like a drunkard. "I never before heard of someone giving away his wife!"

Dubh-Lacha said speedily, admonishing his manhood to action, "Though you have never heard of such a thing, give me you must." She implored him with her eyes. "Mongan, honor is more lasting than life! Do as you are bidden!"

Then a deep anger stirred Mongan from his silence. "Take her then, especially since she is so willing to go with you." He believed he had lost her love forever, but I heard the words of Dubh-Lacha to Brandubh: "King of Leinster, I'm sure you know that one-half of Ulster would rise against you for my sake had I not fallen in love with you. I shall come with you only if you grant me one thing. . . ."

Brandubh smiled with self-congratulation but answered guilefully, "I grant you whatever you wish, reserving only my eternal soul till it come to the house of judgment."

Dubh-Lacha looked sharply at him, fluttering her lashes, "It is but a small thing to ask, and you, being a man of sensitivity, will understand me. I cannot go from man to man like a whore. Grant me a year during which I shall be given time to prepare, and that, during that year, we shall not sleep under the same roof, and that you shall not sit beside me but sit opposite me. This will give us ample time to be courting, while I shall school my great desire for you and forget the husband that I once had."

Now Mongan took his wife's wise words at their base value and immediately fell into a decline at her loss. But clever Dubh-Lacha had given them both time and a means of rescue, which I at least understood, though not my poor son, by his doleful expression.

However, it was not otherworldly powers that brought my son to his senses but good old-fashioned scorn. His servant, Mac an Daimh, seeing his master's unmanly languishing, gave him the rough edge of his tongue. "It was an ill day's work, your going into the Land of Promise, Mongan! All that time in the house of Manannan, master of magic, and all you can do is sigh and eat while you wife has been stolen away into Leinster. I hope you realize that my own wife, Gormlaith (GORM'ly), accompanies her. Not only are you without a wife this night, but your servant also! Where are your wits, man?"

Mongan's rare anger flared. "No one thinks worse of me than I myself! Go! Fetch me two sods of earth: one from Ireland and one from Scotland."

"What for?" asked the puzzled servant.

"Because, when we set off for Leinster—as Brandubh will be expecting us to—I will have each of those sods of earth in my shoes, and, when his druids seek news of me—as they surely will—they will be able to truthfully report that I have one foot in Ireland and the other in Scotland, and Brandubh will think himself safe from assault!"

And that was how Mongan came to the plains of Leinster. Looking down on the great settlement, Mac an Daimh cursed. "Power of God! Will you look at the place—swarming with his men. How will we get into the fort?"

At that moment, the priest called Tibraide (TEE'bra) came by with his clerk. They were busy praying and did not see Mongan draw a thread from his cloak, throw it down, and create a river with a bridge over it on the path ahead.

Tibraide looked down, astounded. "Why, this is the place my father was born, and I never remember a river being here before, nor this bridge, either!" But, as there was no way of passing, he and his clerk began to cross over the bridge. They were halfway over when it collapsed beneath them. As they fell, Mongan snatched the gospel book from the priest's hand and let the two men fall into the river.

"Shall we not drown them?" asked Mac an Daimh.

"Let them swim downstream until we have done our work at the fort," said Mongan, taking the shape of Tibraide upon himself and turning Mac an Daimh into the likeness of his clerk. And away they both went into the fort of Brandubh, who greeted them effusively. "It is long since I saw you, Tibraide. Read the good news of the gospel to us before you go to visit the queen and hear her confession."

And so Mongan made best use of the education I had given him and read dramatically from the gospels the incident where Christ drives out the moneychangers from the temple. At every pause, Mac an Daimh uttered pious "amens" with much crossing of his breast.

Then Mongan made his way to the queen's apartments. Dubh-Lacha immediately recognized her husband under his clerical disguise. "Leave me, all of you, except my attendant!" she commanded in her clear voice. "I must make confession to this good priest, and my sins are not for your ears."

All the women left the *grianan,* save Dubh-Lacha and Gormlaith, Mac an Daimh's wife. The four of them breathed one huge breath, and soon there were only two couples making good their absence: Dubh-Lacha and Mongan upon the queen's bed, and Mac an Daimh and Gormlaith upon the maid's bed, behind the screens.

"Long have you been in finding me, Mongan!" Dubh-Lacha said between Mongan's devouring kisses.

"Soon you will be out of here!" he replied, easing himself into her.

"Not too quickly, I trust!" said Gormlaith through the screen as Mac an Daimh drew her down upon him, saying, "You can trust two pious men as we to be diligent in our office!"

But this was no time for dalliance, for, outside the *grianan* door, an old hag had concealed herself, and now she began to sing out when she heard the unmistakable sounds of lovemaking, not of holy confession, coming from within.

Mongan breathed out a magical breath upon her, misting her vision. "Do not rob me of heaven, O holy cleric," the old one wept. "I must have heard some devils making merry. Let me repent fully, and no harm will I tell!"

Mongan held a knife before him, saying in the voice of Tibraide, "Lean closer, grandmother, and I will hear your confession gladly," and thrust the blade into her body.

"I like not the killing of women," he said to Dubh-Lacha.

"Do not be ashamed of your deed, husband. This old hag would have blabbed to Brandubh, sure enough."

Just then there was a knocking at the door of the queen's apartments. It was none other than the real Tibraide, who had been plucked from the river by his monastic students. The queen's women waiting at the door frowned at one another and said, giggling at their own wit, "We never saw a year for such a plentiful supply of Tibraides! There is one outside and one within the *grianan*."

And the guard was fetched to investigate this matter. He hammered on the door of the queen's house. "Who is that within?"

"It is Tibraide here within," replied Mongan, "and the one who is without is none other than Mongan come to steal away his wife. Those with him are his warriors disguised as monks. Deal with them, as you love the honor of Brandubh!"

And the guard called his fellows, who fell upon the real Tibraide's attendants, killing them.

"Too long have we tarried, Mongan!" cried Dubh-Lacha. "Go quickly through the shutter in some other shape, for there are too many men for you and Mac an Daimh to overcome at this time."

Mongan realized the truth of the matter—my clever, idle son! "I will return for you, never fear!" And, planting one kiss upon her brow, one upon her mouth, and one lingering kiss upon her pale breast, he and Mac an Daimh leaped from the house and made good their escape.

Brandubh came to investigate the matter, grimly interviewing his queen himself. "Tell me truly, Dubh-Lacha: who is the cleric outside whom my warriors hold by the scruff of his neck? Is it Tibraide or Mongan?"

Dubh-Lacha let her shift fall down over her shoulder to blatantly reveal the love bites upon her breast. "It is the cleric Tibraide whom they hold. You had best let him go, lest you have to pay him an even higher honor price than you already owe him for the death of his men!"

Brandubh snarled an order but restrained his arm from striking his queen. "And it was Mongan who was with you?"

"It was," she said, plainly.

"I did not grant you leave to entertain your husband when I gave you my promise."

"No," said Dubh-Lacha, a smile playing about her mouth, "but you did grant me anything I wished and reserved only your eternal soul till it come to the house of judgment. . . ."

Brandubh frowned, not understanding her meaning.

"A husband's soul is his honor and is guarded by the virtue of a wife; but you reserved your soul *co tigh breithe* (TEE BRE'ha)—till the house of judgment—in your promise, but *ti braide* (TEE'bra)—the house of judgment—has already been and gone from this place. Tibraide—or one bearing his name and shape—has been with me. And so I have had my revenge upon you, taking that which was most precious to you, Brandubh!"

And Brandubh's face became as black as the raven at her words, for by his own promise he had been tricked, since the Irish for Tibraide is said precisely the same as "the house of judgment."

"You will not leave this *grianan* until the year's end, when you will lie with me, Dubh-Lacha, and then I will have my soul's honor again!" he swore, resolved to humiliate this cunning woman.

Meanwhile back in Ulster, my hopeless son, Mongan, lay on his bed, despondent. The noblemen of Ulster came to him and begged to be allowed to follow him into war against the treacherous friendship of

Brandubh and to help Mongan liberate his wife, but he replied, "Dubh-Lacha has been stolen through my own fault. I swear that no man's son shall die because of my lack of wit. If I cannot win her back by craft, then she is truly lost and I alone shall suffer it."

When word came that Brandubh was preparing to marry Dubh-Lacha, Mongan took Mac an Daimh back down to Leinster.

Mac an Daimh was nervous and ill prepared. "Master, what plan do you have to rescue our wives? We have only the clothes we stand up in and the weapons in our hand. What good are these against the hosts of Leinster? Or will we go into other shapes again?"

But Mongan would not reveal his plan. The reason for this was clear enough to me, the truth being that my son had no idea how he was going to accomplish the rescue.

Now the two men were passing by a broken-down old mill and saw the hag of the mill, Cuimne (KIV'na), a tall, ugly old woman with her ferocious dog and the bony old packmare that she used for carrying the flour sacks. Tall as a weaver's beam was Cuimne, with long shaggy locks and tombstone teeth. As Mongan passed by, she called out coarsely as if she had been a winsome young whore ogling a couple of cruising young blades: "Look no further, my lovelies, but set your eyes on this," and flicked her skirts up.

Mac an Daimh shuddered but called back gamely, "A man might well drown himself in your come-to-bed eyes, grandmother."

To his master, he added, "But saints preserve me from her gone-to-bed legs, for your nuts would be truly cracked if she got her thighs round you!"

Mongan brightened suddenly, as a plan presented itself. He bowed, very courtly, to Cuimne, "Grandmother, how would you like to enjoy the delights of a queen and lie with the king of Leinster?"

The old hag cackled raucously and eyed him with a knowing look. "I know you, Mongan, whom they call the son of Fiachna. If you truly had Manannan's gifts you could make such a proposal worth my while."

Mongan twinkled back at her, "In what shape would you like to be, good Cuimne?"

With a broad grin, Cuimne said swiftly, "I would be like Ibhell, the king of Munster's daughter. She is called 'shining-cheeked.' Give me her shape, Mongan!"

Then Mongan struck her with the tip of his staff, and the old hag Cuimne became like young and beautiful Ibhell. And he changed himself into the likeness of Aedh, the king of Connacht's son. Mac an Daimh became their noble companion, while Cuimne's old snaggle-toothed dog became their fairest white greyhound, and her broken-down mare, their fleet-footed palfrey.

Together they made their way to Brandubh's fort, where they were greeted with surprise, not having been invited. To Brandubh, Mongan said, "We are traveling secretly, for I have stolen the king of Munster's daughter." But Brandubh was already eyeing Ibhell's magnificent charms and sat her next to himself at the feast.

So besotted was Brandubh with the transformed hag that he sent her a secret message to meet him. Cuimne showed it to Mongan, who smiled like a cat with the cream. "The bait is dangling nicely! Cuimne, send back that Brandubh must back up his love with gifts. Ask him to send you his drinking horn."

Now Brandubh's drinking horn came from the hills of faery and was a great wonder, but so badly was his desire roused that he sent the horn to lovely Ibhell. Again, he sent to her to beg her to lie with him, and Mongan told the hag to beg for a healing belt that Brandubh had: it would heal the wearer of any wound. Though all of his household bade him keep this treasure and not waste it upon some big-breasted girl from Munster, send it he did.

Brandubh was consumed with longing to possess lovely Ibhell, to lie between her beautiful white breasts, to twine her long silken hair in his hands. As the next day was to be the day when he bedded Dubh-Lacha, he let her out of the *grianan* to be at the feast that night. He covertly compared the two women as they sat at the table. Dubh-Lacha he had once thought beautiful, with her smooth helmet of dark hair and her pretty strawberry mouth, set now in a dark line at the thought of being in Brandubh's bed.

But she did not compare well with the charms of Ibhell.

He turned to Mongan and said, "Fair Aedh of Connacht, you see this woman beside me? She is Dubh-Lacha—a virtuous woman whom I took off the hands of Mongan." He gave a wry grin and leaned forward conspiratorially. "Actually, between you and me, I bound the foolish youth to a 'friendship that cannot be refused.' He took it to be a nobleman's agreement, poor fool he! Now, here's what I'm proposing—a pleasant exchange. What if you took this woman as your own and I took your woman, Ibhell, eh? After all, you are in some trouble for stealing this woman from her father, are you not?"

Mongan, as Aedh, allowed his anger full rein. "This is not what I expected when I sought guest-friendship at your hearth! If I had come with herds of horses or jewels, you could have asked for them without affront. However, since it is dishonorable to refuse what has been asked of me," he screwed up his eyes as if to steel himself to the dreadful prospect, "I give you Ibhell for your own woman." And he put Ibhell/Cuimne's hand into Brandubh's.

But when Brandubh handed Dubh-Lacha to Mongan, it was seen that Prince Aedh was very quick to kiss the long-imprisoned lady and she to receive his kisses. Seeing Brandubh's surprise, Mongan had the wit to respond, "Lest it be said that I received the lady unwillingly and that some dishonor had been done—it seemed only right," and, to demonstrate his evident willingness, he kissed Dubh-Lacha once more before the whole company, thrusting his tongue clearly into her mouth.

The feast began to wear to its end, with Brandubh impatient to be abed with Ibhell and both attendants and nobles within an inch of falling off their benches onto the rush-strewn floor with drunkenness.

Mongan flashed a warning look at Mac an Daimh, who had located Gormlaith, now firmly plastered to his side. Mac an Daimh said loudly to the heedless attendants, "It is a great dishonor that my lord's cup goes unfilled!" But no one listened, and he nodded back at Mongan. The four of them went swiftly to the poorly guarded stables, took the best two steeds in the place, and rode off toward home, Dubh-Lacha behind Mongan and Gormlaith clutching Mac an Daimh. They were not pursued.

But only I, Manannan mac Lír, had the cream of the jest when, in the morning early, Brandubh woke with a mouth so dry that he called for ale. The butlers were already wondering whose was the snaggle-toothed hound and the clapped-out packmare that lay sleeping before the king's door. But they gaped with amazement at the sight that greeted their eyes in the chamber, for there, in the great royal bed, lay their lord's wife . . . only she was no longer in the shape of Ibhell of Munster.

The sight of Cuimne of the Mill at the crack of dawn was not a pretty one: at least Brandubh did not find it so. Instead of the firm-fleshed beauty of the night before, here was the slack-breasted hollowness of the hag with her unbound tresses like a horse's mane and her great gap-toothed grin, wide as the door to hell. "Is it with you that I lay last night?" Brandubh stuttered apoplectically.

"Yes, my lovesome king, it was!" Cuimne nodded, her empty teats dangling before his eyes as she straddled him another time. "Shall we do it again?"

And from that day onward, Brandubh was a chastened man, never able to live down the shame of having taken the hag of the mill for his wife. Never again would he try to deceive my cunning trickster of a son!

And so Mongan's earthly education was almost complete.

Such was the love between Mongan and Dubh-Lacha after their troubled separation that nothing could divide them again, save the short parting of death, which is the price of mortality and the last bitter lesson that any human learns. But it was into my own realm that I received them when that time came so that their blessed souls might longer enjoy the felicity that had illumined their earthly lives.

CHAPTER FOUR

THE GOLDEN SHOEMAKER

They took the violet and the meadowsweet

To form her pretty face, and for her feet

They built a mound of daisies on a wing,

And for her voice they made a linnet sing

In the wide poppy blowing for her mouth.

And Llew came singing from the azure south

And bore away his wife of birds and flowers.

—Francis Ledwidge,
  "The Wife of Llew"

In the Welsh myth, Blodeuwedd, the wife of Llew, was created out of flowers, becoming the first in a long line of women called "the Flower Bride": one of the central appearances of the Goddess of Britain, who has been embodied or represented by many royal women, among whom we may count Arthur's Queen Gwenhwyfar, Henry VIII's Queen Jane, and Princess Diana.

In "The Golden Shoemaker," the theme of the Flower Bride is explored in another way. This lost British story relates that Caswallawn (kass-WAHL'own) lost Fflur (FLER) and that Julius Caesar tried to take her away but that Caswallawn found her again. In my reconstruction, myth encounters history. Caswallawn, or Cassivellaunus, was chieftain in what is now Essex at the time of Julius Caesar's invasion of Britain. Fflur is the representative of the land's sovereignty. For those who think I must have invented it, the role of footholder is attested in Welsh law and custom. The story is narrated in turn by Caswallawn and Fflur.

CASWALLAWN

It begins with a head and ends with a foot.

The head of my great and courageous uncle, Bran, was brought back from the carnage of the wars with Ireland by his own household warriors. With his last breath, Bran had bade them cut off his head and bring it to the White Mount and there bury it. For Bran had sworn that even in death his virtuous head would defend the land against all comers, and he had dedicated his spirit to that task.

This sacred interment was done secretly, reverently, and with some speed, for the island of Britain now lay in imminent danger of invasion from the Romans. Not content to conquer our brothers in Gaul, they looked across the water to Albion.

As the last bucket of soil covered the hallowed place of the Sacred Head, I, Caswallawn, was consecrated as battle chief of all the kings of Britain, chosen to lead the White Island of Albion against the Romans.

After my inauguration, I withdrew from the rejoicings of my drunken followers to my apartments, with only Wally for company. Wally had been my mentor in so many things, almost an uncle, one in whom I could confide the thoughts of my heart and whose advice was always earthy and astute. He was neither wellborn nor good to look at, one more used to tracking game through difficult terrain than to sitting by my side in full assembly, but, in the midst of fawning and flattery, it was good to have his honest, lopsided, gap-toothed features to remind me of my tribal duties.

We sat sipping the thin red ale thought best for kings, regretfully mourning our favorite brown beer. "I could send to Beligdunum for Cerwynna, you know," I said to Wally. "She could brew something with more belly in it than this gnat's piss."

As he nodded gravely, there was a beating on the log outside. Wally rose to see who wanted me, returning with, "Bor, it's that oak-mad druid again. He's got some maid with him."

Brimapon was a well-fed, smooth-fleshed ox of a druid, now one of my chief counselors. Without waiting to be announced, he strode into the pool of light from the fire, while the blue-veiled woman beside him hugged the shadows.

"Lord, now that you are installed as our battle leader, it is proper to your dignity that you have a footholder to maintain your realm," the druid said.

"What nonsense is this?" I remember crying out with scorn, little knowing what a gift he brought me.

"The wise ones of this land believe that the virtue of Albion resides in maidens who have been chosen by the gods to serve them as their oracles."

"And am I become some kind of god that you offer me one?" In the shadows, the woman shifted: the barest rattle of her rush-plaited crown reminded me of the solemn interment of my kinsman, the mighty Bran, and made me plaster my ironic tongue to the roof of my caustic mouth.

The druid licked his lips, uneasy and discountenanced by my rudeness. "Not so, lord. It is an ancient custom. The maiden who represents the virtue of Albion is the proper attendant of our battle leader in the assembly of tribes. In the royal footholder resides the spirit of this island. Hers is the virtue of peace. When war threatens, only then may the maiden leave from holding your feet."

Annoyed by his rebuking reminder, I began combing my mustache. I knew the slippery ways of druids. If they wanted to place a spy in my bed, better it were a maiden, I supposed, since by their arts they would know my very thought before it reached my tongue or my hand.

"It seems an ill-chosen time to give me an attendant who is vowed to peace," I said testily, "but let me see her." I blush now to think how I sounded in her ears, petulant as a slave owner about to inspect new goods.

The druid raised his brows in admonishment. "My lord, you mistake me. This maiden must remain, as I say"—he coughed a little cough—"a maiden. Only if she is untouched will her sacred power protect Albion."

I dashed my mustache comb to the ground in disgust. "You mean that I must have a woman in my chamber, handling my body, and yet I must not lay hand on her? Man, are you clean witless?"

"Lord, you may have pleasure of whichever women you please within the boundaries of your realm—any, save this one woman. In her lives the untarnished honor of Albion, and your feet will rest in her lap whenever you sit in assembly to remind you and others by what virtue you are our leader."

He beckoned the rush-crowned shadow forward into the firelight. It wasn't until she removed her veil and crown that I saw how small she was, little more than a girl in height, though with a woman's body and dignity. She had honey-colored hair and an impassive face, schooled in the silences of seers. Her downcast hazel eyes shot up to mine and down again, but I could see that something more interesting lay behind the passivity.

Brimapon was saying, "She has been schooled in the duties of her role, lord. She has been trained never to lie and to be able to detect a lie." But I was not attending, only staring, for, under the dark blue garments, at neck and wrist, the flesh of her body was covered by tattoos of every flower imaginable. "Your name?"

"Fflur, lord king."

Ah! Flower!

FFLUR

A footholder's duties are not onerous, less so than those of a vowed seer tied to a temple, at any rate. Caswallawn was less testy than the overseer of the shrine, more moderate in his expectations than the druid who served there, and considerate of my needs. He insisted on coming to me straight from his bath, in clean garments, to show me that he honored his obligations to me, in whom the land was present, a living heart and soul. He put me to no servile task and never laid a finger upon me save in play or conversation, when he would stroke my arm—

but as he might stroke a cat or a child. But there was a woman's wisdom within me that battled with the sacred wisdom schooled into me by the sisters of the shrine.

Every careless stroke of his hand inflamed new and irreligious thoughts within me. Until I stood in Caswallawn's presence, I had never yearned after any man or boy. I did not know myself a woman until this moment. I had been told over and over by my sacred sisters that I was a vessel for the tall, majestic spirit of our island, She who stands victorious with mighty forests in one hand and great cities of people in her other. It is not an easy thing to contemplate when you are a girl, but any personal pride in such a role was threatened or beaten out of me, with due respect, of course, by those who had the raising of me.

But now I began to bargain with myself. If I was truly dedicated to the land, then, if the Island of the Mighty might be a woman, would she not covet the caresses of such a king as he? Would she not take what was on offer, casting one mighty hillside leg over him, and draw into her the goodness that was the core of his manly strength? Such was my reasoning, and what woman would argue with me?

Caswallawn was a big man in his prime, muscled and scarred with warrior proof, cleanly limbed, with broad, long-fingered hands. His ash-colored hair fell about his shoulders; his slate blue eyes were keen; like the hairs upon his body, his long mustaches gleamed with glints of gold, framing a mouth that was made for kissing. Whether he sat in hall, in council, or in private, when he spoke to me, when he issued orders, when he sang the after-dinner boasts of his kindred, I longed to still those lips with mine. But I remembered my duty.

The first few days attending him were full of awkwardness. "How are you to hold my feet when I go riding or hunting?"

"Lord, you need only have me in attendance when you are in council or in repose. If you have to go about your daily affairs, I will remain in my chamber or attend the shrine of Camulos on your behalf."

For the God of Battle was the tutelary deity of his people, the Catuvellauni.

"And when I travel to outlying regions to confer with my allies?"

"Then I will travel in your company, at your convenience."

"Can you really ride—at speed and for many hours? I cannot stay for stragglers."

"I will do the best that I can, on horseback and in wagon."

He paused, looking uncertain. "What of—when I am with my women?"

"Then I will retire to give you privacy, lord."

He looked relieved.

The fact was, I was not looking forward to sharing the quarters of his womenfolk. Kings like Caswallawn have many women. At the Shrine of the Nine, the strict exclusive presence of women together had been a burdensome thing, unlike the shrine where I had grown up, where many people came and went. I knew that here at Beligdunum I would have the unpleasant task of ignoring, or trying to ignore, the innuendo of the king's women, their pointed and unsubtle boastfulness at knowing something substantially more interesting about their king than I ever would. As a dedicated seer, I would find no belonging among Caswallawn's concubines.

"Tell me about yourself!" he said.

"I was given to the shrine of Nethent when I was a child because I had the gift of the two seeings." (Nethent was on Caswallawn's disputed border with the neighboring Trinovantian tribe.) "Then I was taken to the Shrine of the Nine at Thorney Island, in the mouth of the Tame, to be made ready as footholder."

"And were these done then?" He turned back my wrist to show the tattoos on my inner arm.

"They were done over the last few months, yes." Nine months of daily agony as the flowers bloomed over my body, each dot of blue ash pricked in with sloe thorns. The Keeper of the Patterns had reminded me, at my every wriggle or suppressed squeal, that if I thought the tattooing was painful, I was indeed fortunate to remain a virgin and never suffer the pangs of childbirth.

But Caswallawn still grasped my wrist in his strong hand, and his breath was upon my shoulder. "It must have been dreadfully painful!" Then, realizing that his voice and breathing had grown deep and desirous, he carefully let me go and retreated into bluster. "By Beli, let it never be said that the footholder of Albion was any less a warrior than her king!"

And he made good his words by gifting me with a pair of spears, with hackles of the river-wading herons about their necks. It was the first time that I had received a gift, or felt honored, the first time that I had a friend and knew the delight of meaningless banter. He took pains to make me laugh. Laughter had not been part of my training.

But after that, Caswallawn was more careful. Though his hand would often stretch out to touch me as he talked, he would draw it back in time before . . . No, it was already too late then! He knew and I knew that it could only be a matter of time before we betrayed our true feelings for each other. But I was his appointed footholder, and I schooled myself to be only that.

To those who peer into the timeless depths of the times before and learn my story, know that it was no dishonor for me to hold the feet of Caswallawn. To him I was inviolate, like a sister or a mother, to be held in highest honor. For myself, I daily marveled at my good fortune in being in his company and pondered on the circumstances that had brought it about.

When Bran, grandson of the great Beli, had been chosen high king and defender and had gone off to fight against the Irish, Caswallawn had been appointed in his place to lead a sevenfold council to steer Britain, but this confederacy of elders soon fell to fighting. Caswallawn, also a direct descendant of Beli, had restrained some, killed others, before succeeding to the position of battle leader himself on the death of Bran. If he had not done so, then I would never have been brought to him.

But in all actions, so the Seer into Waters says, we must ever consider the ripple that spreads over the pool. One of those counselors whom Caswallawn killed was Immaneutix, of the neighboring tribe of the Trinovantes. Now, in Albion's extremity, Immaneutix's son, Afarwy (a-VAR'wy), ran to the Romans, plump with their conquests in Gaul, and bade them come and support his claim to the chieftainship of his tribe. Nowadays, no one calls him Afarwy; he is remembered only as Mandubrad—the black traitor—for it was he who sold the island of Britain to Caesar.

CASWALLAWN

I was relieved to hear that the footholder did not have to literally hold my feet at every turn: it was expected in full assembly and in formal encounters with allied chieftains and the like. Those who entered the hall would behold me as the spiritually appointed protector of Albion, with my feet supported by Albion's very earth in the person of Fflur. She had her own cushioned stool at my feet, and after the formalities were concluded, she would move it beside my own chair.

For the first few weeks, I was suspicious and had her private moments watched. But it was soon clear that she never passed any intelligence of my council meetings to anyone. As I had feared, the proximity of a woman was not easy for me, especially one so gravely beautiful. It was impossible to think of her as just a sacred cipher to my role as battle leader. As a woman, she demanded to be loved and honored, to be touched, to be kissed. . . . I dared not think of that.

Yet, despite these natural urgings, soon I began to rely upon her ability to discern truth more and more in the following months as the Roman situation worsened.

Three years ago, the Romans had tried to enter Britain, but our British chariots had driven them seaward. Now Afarwy's betrayal threatened the well-being of everyone in the Island of the Mighty. I gave orders for Trinovantian hostages to be executed, since as guarantees of Afarwy's good behavior they were no longer useful. It was time that the Trinovantes accepted my authority in this time of peril.

But I needed the advice of one who had firsthand knowledge of the Romans and their ways. I commanded the presence of Commin, one of the Atrebates of Gaul, who had known the Romans at first hand.

I asked him forthrightly, "What manner of man is this Caesar, and what does he seek with us?"

Commin spoke plainly. "Caesar is a sharp and ambitious commander, eager for honors, a daring strategist who is loved by his men."

"Then he is young?"

"He is well past his youth, but neither is he fully established. He has enemies at home. By his deeds in war and conquest he hopes to win power in Rome."

So, then, not a king or chieftain but a battle leader seeking the position of one higher. I asked again, "What does he seek with us here?"

"To the Roman way of thinking, the Narrow Sea that borders our land is the very edge of the known world. To all in Rome, Albion, the Island of the Mighty, is the realm of legend, since none but daring shipmasters venture to our shores. He seeks—"

"—to be remembered by his ancestors as a hero who went to the Otherworld," I continued and bit my lip, now that I knew this Caesar for the most dangerous of men—one who does not fear death, one who would lead his men across seas of terror to strike at the very heart of fear, and then return from out of the otherworldly regions so that stay-at-homes might lard honors thick upon him for his daring.

I then conferred with our scouts and spies to gain intelligence of Caesar's movements. He was busy readying his ships to carry horses and men to our shores. And, ever at his side, he had Afarwy, the

Manubrad, filling his ears with tales of my wrongdoing. But I had to credit Caesar as a doughty warrior: "So far from Rome, and yet the man still sails to Britain, leaving enemies at his back!"

"He holds Gaulish hostages for their tribes' good behavior," Brimapon pointed out. "Lord, you have heard the words of Commin and know the devastation that Caesar has brought to Gaul. Now he comes to our shores to print his cursed foot. I have sent word to the sacred groves that Rome's luck be tested by whatever force the gods allow. We have spoken to the winds, to the seas and the high places. What action can you now take?"

"I will do my part, as will we all. One thing is clear: the confederacy of the tribes is essential. The many feuds between tribes caused the downfall of Gaul." And I began to regret having been so harsh with the Trinovantian hostages, yet not as sorry as I would be.

When they had gone, I asked, "What do you see, my Flower?" for I had learned how good she was at gauging the true intention of those who came to me in council. The merest tremor of her reaction as she held my feet gave me many insights in a wordless way.

She raised her hazel-flecked eyes from the pattern of the floor rushes and said ruefully, "Soon, I will be holding your feet no longer, my lord."

"I need no seer to tell me that! Will you come with me to battle?"

She shook her head sadly. "It is not my place. I shall return to the Shrine of the Nine on the Thorney Island until this work is done."

Like a seer myself, I looked into that dead, empty time we spoke of. Already the pang in my belly: I had not expected to miss her so very much. "But you will uphold my cause before the gods?"

She smiled her downturned smile with such acceptance that I nearly kissed her then and there—to bring real joy to the one who I felt loved me more nearly than any of my women.

"When this war is over, we will go together through the land that the people may see you and honor you, as I do" was all that I could say.

But the words fell from my lips too glibly, like a warrior's empty promise to treat his girl after a battle from which he may never return.

FFLUR

Leaving Caswallawn was one of the most difficult things I had ever done. But I had other duties to perform. I did not stay long at the Shrine of the Thorney Island. Each one of the Nine Sisters was needed to aid the commanders of our forces. Not for me, the incitement to battle, the calling down of curses, the blessing of spears. I was called south to the encampment of Madoc and his men to look with my seer's sight into the dispositions of the Roman troops and speak as the voice of the gods to its commanders.

Gazing into the black liquid of the cauldron, the words arose from immense distances. "I see a silver host upon a board of gold. They stream forth and do not return. A levy of picked men I see marching from these shores." The difficulty with oracles is that the gods' time is not like ours. I cannot pick the words that come, nor can I interpret their meaning: they must fall as rain upon the earth and seed what meaning they may.

The commanders asked questions of me. And I was busy tracking the answers as they floated to the top of the cauldron like the fatty stars on a mutton broth when the attack happened. Uproar filled the camp as our men rushed to defend it.

Sick and dizzy from my sudden journey from the cauldron's depths, I gathered my soul to myself and grasped one of the heron-hackled spears Caswallawn had given me. Around me, Romans in corselets of leather were stabbing with their short swords, their breath rank with rotten fish, their skin brown as nuts. They seemed to fight as one man, obedient to the blaring call of brazen trumpets, possessed by the spirit of their eagle totem, which towered above my head.

As I struggled to regain my grip on the present moment, a Roman captured me, knocking the spear from my hand and twisting his scarf about my wrists.

Soon I lay bundled in a wagon with other hostages, some dying, others bleeding or crying out, unable to bring comfort to any of them as we drove toward the coast, to Caesar's camp.

"Sir, we bring you the wife of Cassivellaunus."

Some traitor must have known my association with Caswallawn—but not one who had been long in Albion, I thought, as the clerk ushered me into Caesar's tent.

Caesar looked briefly upon me: eyes curious and head still, like a man arrested by some sudden freak of nature as he walks along his daily road. He was almost bald, with a thin combing of hair smoothed upward over his pate to hedge his vanity. His olive skin was like fine leather, and when he came close to me, he had not the fishy, garlicky breath of his soldiers. His face held the most frightening intelligence I had ever seen.

His eyes pierced through mist and deception alike. In those eyes I saw my death, or was it the death of Albion herself? In those eyes, I knew exactly the difference between Roman and Briton. There would be no hiding places from such eyes.

"Are you Cassivellaunus's wife?" The interpreter translated his words.

Caesar's long eyes lit upon me, seeing the understanding in mine. I shook my head and looked through the floor.

"Is that the modesty of virtue or the shame of a wife?"

I did not answer him, wanting to deny him any intelligence that would help his cause. But my heart was singing, "Yes! yes! yes!"

"Let her be detained near the horse lines, but not too near—I mind me that some of these Britons can divine from and bring chaos to the movements of animals."

Later, after dark, I was brought back by the clerk and an escort of two soldiers. The clerk dismissed them at the door of Caesar's tent and brought me within.

Caesar sat by himself, one sandaled leg extended, while on his knee, by the light of two hanging lamps, he wrote with a stylus upon diptych of wax. Looking up, he folded the tablet together and laid by his stylus.

He saw my interest in the thing. "You know what this is?"

"I use them for scrying bird flight at the major feasts."

"What does she say?"

The clerk translated. I knew then I had spoken too freely.

He asked me a few questions about our religious customs, which I answered truthfully but circumspectly.

"You are a seer, then, as well as a wife?"

"I am . . ." the words would not, could not be spoken. I should not say, "I am Britain." I should remain silent and unknowing, lest I give him myself as a weapon against my land and people. Instead I picked up his armored corselet from its rack and placed it in front of my breast; I held up a vision spear in my hand as if in defense.

Caesar followed this with keen interest. "You are the armor bearer of your king?" I neither confirmed nor denied the clerk's translation. Caesar considered me, appraisingly.

"What is her name?"

"Fflur—it means flower," the clerk replied.

I saw Caesar's eyes open wider in full knowledge of what I was. He dismissed the clerk without taking his eyes off me.

I felt devoured by his eyes.

When we were alone, he slid the chains further up my arm until they were clamped tight to the broadest part of my forearms. He drew back my sleeves to look upon my sacred tattoos. Like a healer, he drew aside the fold of my cloak to see the flesh under my tunic. He traced the flowers over my breast with great gentleness, kissing them and drawing back my garments to kiss them all the way down my body.

Custom commanded me to run, to strike, to call out, but I did not stay him. Contempt for myself rose up briefly before I was overwhelmed by his kisses.

He kept asking me, "Does Cassivellaunus do this or this?" His very voice ate into my marrow, consuming my discipline, corroding the metal of my virgin shield. Hand's touch, voice's touch, and mouth's caress were my triple enemies. Part of me shrieked, "I do not belong to this man, but to Caswallawn," and another voice told me, "No, you do not even belong to him!" A distant part of myself watched this thin middle-aged man fawning upon my body.

Then Caesar stopped and spoke to himself with low triumph, leaving me slack legged and ashamed to have responded to the conqueror. Then he did a curious thing: covering his head with the corner of his soldier's scarf, he muttered some invocation, took a little dish of oil and wine, and made a libation of it down my thighs, as though I were some shrine. Though he must have wanted to finish what had plainly excited him, he called out brusquely to the guard outside, and I was taken away. Which was as well, as, in one moment more, I would have been on my back, no better than any camp follower.

That night was the worst of all. Although Caesar had ordered me a softer blanket and given me a Roman gown to cover my body, I fell into self-hatred. It needed no seership to tell me what he intended: cunning as any druid, he had called upon the power of the Goddess of the Land, wooing her with embraces and libations, thinking to woo her through me. I scratched my face with deep gouges of shame, letting the blood trickle upon the dear earth in propitiation for my shameful response.

Trained from youth up to spurn such advances as blasphemy to the Goddess herself, I had no place to hide within my soul. If there had been a blade nearby I would have taken it and used it against myself rather than run away that night.

But near me lay a fellow hostage, a Gaul. I saw that he knew who I was by the sacred marks upon my body. Although we did not speak each other's tongue with fluency, we could comprehend each other in the dark language of the druids, which common folk do not understand.

In whispered, half-snatched conversations, I learned that Dumnorix was a druid who had been performing his religious duties when he was taken. He believed Caesar had brought him to Britain only to assassinate him in obscurity.

"Footholder of Britain, beware of Caesar! He is a lascivious man. Even his troops brag openly about his exploits in bed when they march. He is descended from the line of Aeneas, son of the whoring goddess Venus."

I grew more silent in the straw but said, "He seems to think that I am worthy of honor—at least since he heard my name."

Dumnorix snorted. "Aye, he would! For, know you, that Flora is one of their secret names for Rome—he remembers through you the spirit of his mighty city. Though those who have seen it say she is a great spreader of her legs."

His words sank reproachfully into my soul. What Caswallawn would have thought of me, I dared not even entertain.

CASWALLAWN

Caesar had landed, with Afarwy to negotiate and interpret for him with the British. The Mandubrad's price was the kingship of the Trinovantes, and Caesar, like a big brother at his back to defend his sibling from a bully, would enforce his claim.

Brimapon and his kind had stirred up the elements to defend the island. We had reports that the easterly gale, magically summoned, had wreaked havoc upon Caesar's fleet riding at harbor, but that had not blunted his advance.

Now, as the protector of Britain, I must go forth. It is the fear of every commander that combat will be joined as harvest ripens: people must eat, and stomachs often loom larger than the common good. It was rising harvest now, the wheat no longer green but standing tall and golden in the sunlight. But cursing the time of year would do no good now.

I sent war chariots and skirmishing parties to harry Caesar and slow his progress. Every step of the way he would be harassed and his men tempted out of their neat columns to pursue what would seem obvious targets.

Our initial impact was impressive, but the fight soon went out of our men when they saw the battle order of the Romans, who fought as if possessed of one head. Our champions charged again and again with their chariots, but I was forced to sound the general retreat when I saw how few Romans were moved by our assault. We made a well-ordered retreat, and I gave instructions that the skirmishing parties should continue their valuable work.

The Romans could not be defeated by outright confrontation but by guile, endurance, and cunning.

Word was brought to me of the death of Dumnorix. He had tried to escape Caesar's coastal camp, and in his death throes he had cried out clearly that he was a free man of a free nation and that the Flower of Britain still bloomed.

I could not believe what the spies were telling me. In the middle of all the battle intelligence, the bare mention of Fflur's name was enough to distract me from the extremity we were in!

"Why was the royal footholder anywhere near the coast? She should have been in a place of safety by now," I roared at those who should know.

Ironically, only Brimapon was as grave as I at this news. "If she falls into the hands of an enemy, the whole of Albion could suffer defeat!"

"Not while there is a sword in my hand!" I exclaimed.

"Greater kings than thee have fallen, Caswallawn, mighty son of Beli!" Brimapon fell into the archaic speech of his kind. "She was trained to know that, under such circumstances, she must not let herself fall to the lusts of a conqueror. She will kill herself rather first!"

I could not restrain the shudder that passed through me. The thought of my Flower in Caesar's foul hands! The memory of her still patience, her grave beauty burned upon me, as if in blessed reassurance of my fears. Did she, even now, speak to me as I stood in the field of battle, fearful for her safety? With sincere heart, I spoke to the gods to keep her safe and breathed my blessing upon the soul of Dumnorix who had sent her message to me.

Retiring from the campaign discussions as soon as I could, I called old Wally. "Bor, I need a service only you can do for me now!" Only the language of my boyhood came to my lips at this extremity. "Find Fflur! You're the best tracker in the land. Find her for me! I would go for her myself, but with Britain so beset . . ."

His old eyes shone at the challenge. "I'll be off directly then, bor. Meet ye at Beligdunum, shall I?"

I was not the only one to receive ill news that day, for the druids had struck out at Caesar himself, so Brimapon relished telling me that evening. "And for the loss of the Footholder of Britain, we have sent out the Unappeasable Spear spell, the curse of the Goddess Adsagsona, to claim the life of the one whom he most cares for in this world—his daughter."

It was said that Caesar loved his daughter more than any other of his family—Julia. I averted my mind from the horror of the thing that Brimapon had done, even while my heart gave its assent if it avenged the indignities he might bring to my Fflur.

As harvest beckoned, we were in full retreat. It was clear that no reinforcements from the Trinovantes would now appear. Afarwy's poisonous persuasion had robbed me of any local support. With lessening forces, we fought a retreating line toward Beligdunum.

I issued severe orders that brought protest on all sides: all standing crops to be burned, all habitations leveled. Nothing should be left standing to offer shelter or nurture to Rome. There had never been as good a harvest as this one, men complained, but burn the crops they did, knowing as well as I that the farther Caesar penetrated into our land the hungrier his troops would become. His supply lines were now well overextended.

That we would have nothing to feed our people the following winter did not stop us. The tribes to our north had promised to keep aside grain for us.

I sent messages to the four chieftains of the Canti to destroy Caesar's coastal base camp and to rescue Fflur if she was held there: her lovely, painted skin was unmistakable. She was to be given all honor. Such an attack would also be sufficient to draw Caesar back and give time for my forces to regroup. But I was not to be that lucky.

It was Lammas, a time for what should have been the celebration of the harvest. The vast, tree-girt enclosure of my earth-ditched fortress of Beligdunum stood gleaming triumphantly over the shining arm of the river Lea. But it towered over a devastated land, the once-gold wheat blackened by fire.

What followed I can tell briefly—for what commander can speak boastingly of his own defeat? The Trinovantes aided Caesar, showing him the secret ways, revealing local wells, and supplying them with food, until his legions ringed Beligdunum. We Catuvellauni fought a short siege, but the Roman's strategy soon overwhelmed our earthen ramparts and the fort fell. All our livestock and many prisoners were taken by the Romans, while I fled with my household to a more secret and defensible place.

Shortly after the fall of Beligdunum, Wally returned to me. He had tracked the Romans skillfully and passed himself off as a friendly Briton, even selling their quartermasters game that he had caught in order to penetrate their camps. "She's still alive, bor. Held in his coastal camp. He's not harmed her, that any can tell."

But there are worse scars than those made by torturers' knives.

Knowing that Fflur yet lived gave me the strength to treat with the Romans, repugnant though it was. My people had suffered enough. I was forced to treat with Caesar through the mediation of Caius Trebonius and a Trinovantian druid in the pay of Afarwy. Seeing the druid's contemptuously confident air, I was sickened. He brought the Roman's terms for withdrawal: "Three hundred hostages, a fixed annual tribute, and a promise that you do no harm to Afarwy, whom Caesar establishes and supports as king of the Trinovantes."

If I had known to what uses these hostages would be put, I would have delivered myself into Roman hands before I let one of them cross the Narrow Sea to Rome, for they were sold into slavery and the money raised from their sale put toward paying the troops on Caesar's campaign. The people of my tribe—to whom I owed duty above all other and who had elected me their king—dispersed, killed, or enslaved. No! There is no greater disgrace than one who sells his own flesh.

Fflur

Brought before Caesar again, I shuddered to think of my former behavior. I determined now to do nothing to shame myself. But before his tent were gathered ambassadors and spies—men I had seen before in the runs of Caswallawn, including Afarwy the Mandubrad. There was a druid with his attendant, who bore the green bough of truce. They looked on me with horrified eyes.

Caesar spoke slowly and clearly, his words being translated for my countrymen.

"I have divined that this woman is of some importance to your worship and defense. She has been treated with respect, but I must ask now that you withdraw your troops, since Caswallawn has agreed to our terms."

There was hurried conferral between the envoys, and the spokesman of the Canti made his boastful response. "Do what you will! Our battle leader will come against you and defeat you yet."

Caesar then made a curt gesture to his aide, who stepped forward and stripped my garment from me. All eyes stared upon the sacred tattoos of the footholder of Britain, which none but the Nine Sisters had ever looked upon before.

Caesar nodded and two soldiers came forward. They seized me, forcing my legs apart. Caesar allowed himself a stretching of the lips, which might have been a smile, and then walked toward me with his commander's baton. Briefly, but symbolically, he laid it between my legs. I shuddered as the cold metal kissed me.

"You see, gentlemen. Your land lies open to me."

The Britons stared, appalled, while the druid cast dreadful eyes upon me. Afarwy put one hand over his mouth to stop his laughter.

Caesar nodded again, saying to Afarwy and his party, "Take your painted girl and go!"

When his generals demurred at my dismissal, he said to them, "She is their vestal. I will not shame her further. Let *them* deal with it, and her blood be upon their hands."

One general was persistent. "But an executioner could deflower her and finish her."

Irritated by their dogged lack of understanding, he swore. "By Venus, if we keep her, we will lose the land. I have drawn the virtue from her here today." And he kissed the tip of the commander's baton in a manner so suggestive that some of his hard-faced generals looked away, while the legionnaires standing by stifled sniggers.

CASWALLAWN

With the shame of dishonor thick upon me, only Wally could salve my soul. In his easy way, he listened to my despairing anger. "The traitorous Trinovantes sicken me. I need the help of the gods. Which will assist me now?"

Wally smiled his slow smile and then said, "They say the prophetess of the Old Ones, the goddesses before the gods, has a word to say."

"What is the normal offering? An animal, iron?"

The old fellow hissed warningly through his remaining teeth at the very prospect and spat copiously to propitiate the spirits. "Grain, milk, eggs—that's all they'll ever take. Never offer them iron, bor, lest it be sent against you!"

So it was that I spoke to the priestess of the temple of the Old Ones, the Veras, propitiating them with the correct offerings, abandoning Camulos of the Battles, as he had abandoned me. The woman was calm but stern of demeanor. "Seek purification. Become as low as the lowliest for a season. Take the initiation of the Shoemaker, he of the Great Hand. Turn your fortunes. Move to the east, and found a new city in the name of those who help you best."

Accordingly, I went to the Temple of the Long Hand, humbly offering myself to the mysteries of the god Lug. I may not speak openly of these rites, which initiate men into the society of those who call themselves the Shoemakers. The Shoemakers go unseen, marking by their very footfall the passing of the god—but I say too much! I can only relate that the priest clipped my hair, shaved off my mustache, put my clothes upon the wooden statue of Lug to stand in my place as king till I returned. Then he gave me the clothes and tools of a journeyman shoemaker and took all the gold upon my arms as payment for the privilege.

Kings do not sully their hands with any trade that involves pig keeping or the tanning of leather, but now I was without status, without even my own name, which had been taken from me while I served my apprenticeship to Lug.

As I stood waiting naked before the shrine, shorn and in dishonor, I felt acutely the poverty of a king who can command whatever he wishes yet who may never live a life that he can call his very own. I had wanted to be worthy of my country and had lost my tribal home. I had wanted to be a warrior of renown, and now I was only a defeated soldier, forced into the greasy compromise of tribute and forced sureties.

I did not bargain with the god, as once I might have done, but prayed from my heart: "Let her only be safe and the land will be safe! I relinquish all right to her." And I was not able to tell whether I meant land or woman. "Even though these eyes nevermore behold her, I am willing to go into exile for her sake—only that she be safe. Spread your broad hand over her, and let her darkness be made light by your long spear!"

The priest brought out a hooded cloak, the kind commonly worn by travelers or by druids when they are at their rites. He spoke spells of guarding over it and placed it about my shoulders. "It will be to you a cloak of concealment, that you might go invisibly among the Romans themselves and learn all that you may."

Now, in that simple woolen cloak, name, rank, and honor set aside, I moved invisibly through the land to find the Flower of Britain and bring her safely home. Wally at my side, I made my way through the ravaged lands with their stinking harvest of death stooked high instead of barley and wheat sheaves. We went by coracle, by hidden track, between Roman lines, but mostly on foot, always following the unmistakable route that had marked our retreat. And it was with a strange, high hope that I walked or ran all the way to the coast.

All the way to the coast, with the long summer spear of Lug beckoning us to the southeastern seaboard where Caesar had his camp. If any stopped us, we were traveling shoemakers—which might be believed as long as no one noticed my callusless hands. Wally himself was my surety; his good-natured expression and meandering gait made him appear harmless, though I knew his hands could crush throats and his knife make short work slipped between one rib and another. He made me stoop to hide my height and smeared my face with unsightly stains.

The Roman camp was well guarded. From the cliff tops we could see ships already embarking, laden with horses and slaves. Wally's long sight could pick out the chains, while my sharp ears caught their wailing.

"Could Fflur be on one of those?"

"Best find out" was all he would say, though he knew me well enough to realize that we might have to swim to Rome if she was.

We had brought wild fowl and oysters to barter our way into camp. As we waited to be checked in by the guard, I was reminded of the manhood testing of my youth—to perform an act of utter, foolish daring and live to tell the tale. It was all I wanted then and now. If any recognized me now, I was a dead man.

The guards searched every Briton, except for those who were obviously under the branch of truce. We had no weapons about us but had hidden them up on the cliff top—not unless you counted the knotted string in Wally's pocket, deadly around throats, and the tiny sharp awl and hammer in my cobbler's roll.

We searched the camp with our eyes, meeting back later at the cookhouse. We squatted together to share a platter of meat stew and some bannocks of bread. Dipping the bread into the gravy, Wally said quietly, "She's not gone to sea. Caesar handed her over to a druid last night."

I nearly made outcry of joy, but Wally dragged me closer, turning my telltale face away from a curious glance, and spoke as if threatening me. "Be bloody quiet, you fool! She's been took by the druid who was with Afarwy. Likelihood is, she'll be in Trinovantian runs by tomorrow or the day after."

I groaned aloud. All this way for nothing! Out of the hands of one enemy into the hands of another! Now I cursed myself for my high-handed execution of Afarwy's kinsmen.

FFLUR

Afarwy's delight at gaining the footholder of Britain had been distinctly dampened by learning that now I was fit for nothing. His glee at having stolen me from Caswallawn and Caesar had been quickly dispersed by his druid, Gormodial. "She has been dishonored by Caesar. The virtue of Albion does not lie in her lap."

Afarwy had bitten his sulky lip with pique. "I'd like to be there when you deal with her," he began to wheedle, but Gormodial silenced the Mandubrad with an outraged look. I thanked the gods then that I had fallen into Trinovantian hands and not into those of Brimapon, for he would have handed me over to the Nine, on whose island I would have become fish food quicker than a poet can ask for his fee. The vengeance of women is total: they would have been merciless.

I was returned to my home temple, to the precincts of Nethent, like a sack of badly tanned pelts. None but the nonfree handled me, I was so vile. The once-kindly guardian of the shrine looked upon me with the utmost disgust. I was not permitted to inhabit my former room but was removed to an outhouse. I was allowed nothing by which I might end my own life, but then I knew my fate already, for I had witnessed such a death when I was very young.

She had been a seeress who had stolen out to meet her lover. She had been executed at night, her eyes and hands bound. The ovate had put the cord about her neck and throttled her, while another struck her with his knife, and together they threw her dying body into the quicksands.

After I had been handed over to Gormodial and Afarwy, I had done my best to escape, and when that was made hopeless, I'd started to make my farewell to life. The wagon in which I had been thrown was heaped up with meadow flowers, at Caesar's command—his way of honoring the Lady of the Land. So, as we trundled over hill and ford, I'd thrown out a flower at every place we passed—a trail of blossoms to bless the land and bring fertility to the scars that Rome had wrought.

Caesar's gesture of conquest in front of the Trinovantes was no more than a gesture. I was virgin still, and none could rob me of the duty that my skin itself proclaimed. I would be the Flower Maiden to the bitter end.

That night, Afarwy's druid, Gormodial, came with his followers to interview me. I was tethered to a stake by a noose so that I might not pollute their sacred presence. The ovates were the only ones to touch me; they who had been the old priests were now the oak-kind's sacrificers, so my old grandmother had once told me.

Gormodial related the evil story to his cronies, and there was much pious shuddering and shaking of heads. In the light of flaring torches, his long gray hair twisting in the wind, the convener of my judges spoke for them all:

"It is the decision of this court that you be denied sight of the sun, lest you pollute its light and ruin the harvest. We dedicate you to the gods above, around, and below, that you be accorded the threefold death: you will be given to the gods above by stabbing, to the gods of this place by strangling, to the gods below by drowning, that you be forever bound in their service and be denied rebirth through the air, the earth, or the water."

I tried not to think how it would be to have earth in my mouth and nose if I didn't die immediately from the cord or knife. Perhaps instant death at the hands of my sisters would have been preferable after all? Gathering my courage to me, I called upon the Spirit of the Land herself to come to my aid. Along the salt marsh winds came a certainty and a lifting of the clouds of fear. Although I might no longer be footholder, yet would I go with the integrity of the land around my shoulders. As I breathed in the welcome air and pressed my foot deeply into damp earth, understanding came to me.

I had seen what it was to be among the Romans and suffer their arrogance. They regard all other people as worse than themselves, and women as lower than all. It was clear that Caesar had not understood British honor. Standing here at the end of my life, I tried to remind myself of Albion, of the honor of its people, of Caswallawn, who had thrown himself into her defense. For their freedom I would die and become their advocate, I vowed in that instant.

I spoke silently to the Goddess of the Land: "Mother, protect Caswallawn, and he will protect You till his dying day."

The ovates dragged me off to the lonely place on the moors where I was to meet my end.

CASWALLAWN

I came to the place just in time, unrecognized, just as the bloody sacrificers were sharpening their knife and laying out their cord. Wally breathed into my ear, "You're on your own now, bor!"

All the way from the coast, we had followed the path of flowers, right into the Trinovantian lands. Wally's sharp eyes were our guide.

Now, into the circle of torches I came with the unclean tools of the cobbler's trade—the tanned hide, the greased thread of swine's sinew, the sharp awl for piercing leather.

"I claim the victim in Lug's name!" I cried, leaping out of the darkness.

There was uproar. Fflur lifted her face in startled hope, and we spoke with our eyes in that moment.

"How dare you abuse this holy place with your profanity! This victim has been dedicated to the gods of the three worlds," cried the convener of the judges.

"And I claim her in the name of Lug's long spear, which shines beyond all those realms." I hoped I had remembered the formula properly!

One of the ovates, a dark, thin fellow with a gash for a mouth in the darkness of that place spoke up boldly to Gormodial. "What the cobbler says is true. It is the old law of this land. An offering may be given in place of the sacrifice."

They muttered together, like a buzz of hornets.

The convener spoke up. "It is the old law, but there is an accompanying duty—that the one who claims the victim must himself be sacrificer and bear the consequences. If he be a man of low honor-price, then his life will not be long."

Speedily as I knew how, I severed the rope from Fflur's throat and set her beside me. I drew out the weasel that Wally had captured for me from the bag on my shoulder and slipped my cobbler's sinew over its neck, hanging it from the post. Then I stabbed it with my awl and, throwing it to the ground and covering it with the hide, crushed it beneath my foot till it died in the way they had planned for my dear.

"As this beast dies, so die all enemies of this dear land," chanted Fflur, her eyes toward the dark-robed band of weasels gathered for the kill, her lovely, honey-colored hair flying free in the wind.

The dark-haired ovate standing by cracked open a grin of admiration and recognition of who I was, but I knew I could trust his silence.

Then I took Fflur's hand and we ran.

FFLUR

We rode swiftly into Catuvellauni territory, the winds and rains cleansing us both of doubt and dishonor. Like children, hands clasped, we entered the temple of Lug together.

Here Caswallawn returned the clothes and implements of the Shoemakers to the altar of Lug with great humility. Standing naked before the shrine, he turned to me, saying, "A king should know his place. We are not going to escape druidic justice."

"I think we might!"

"How?"

I hesitated, fearful to voice what my heart screamed to my head: "I can no longer be your footholder, no longer subject to druidic laws, if I am made a woman by the king."

He wrinkled his brow in puzzlement. "But you *are* a woman!"

"Not until you make me one, my lord."

His expression was comical. Then he pressed me to him, naked as he was. "By Lug, I'd do it here, if it will make you safe!"

The priest, amused and not a little alarmed at this turn of events, discreetly led us to a side chamber with a couch in it.

Ah, to be no more chained to the cold service of the oak kind! To be at last free to be what I had always been, a conduit of the land's love to the one who served her best!

The taint of Caesar was upon me no more, but as a wildflower blowing in the free winds I was myself, a woman in that sunny place where I slept with one of the Golden Shoemakers of freedom.

Together we established a new settlement and called it Verulam, out of thanks to the broad hand who had protected us and to the Old Ones before the gods we know. And there Fflur wove about Caswallawn's shoulders a new cloak, a cloak of peace

In due time, Caesar sent to us for his protection money. But when the annual tribute was due, the Trinovantian envoy in the pay of Rome whispered a private message to the ears of Caswallawn alone: "For the safe return of the Flower Woman, I demand gold."

And Caswallawn said, "I will send Caesar my best horse, Meinlas."

But it was no living horse that he sent, only the image of Meinlas struck upon coins of gold. How we laughed! And in succeeding years, no further tribute was sent or collected as Caesar forged a high place for himself in Rome.

And when Brimapon complained of how his Trinovantian colleagues had been duped by a common shoemaker, Fflur said to him, "You chose me as footholder from all the girls of Albion. But since these wars have been joined, it is Caswallawn, battle leader, who has spared *my* feet from the steps of dishonor. As his wife, I will help him maintain the integrity of the Island of the Mighty, for he has seen to it that the flowers of the land shall bloom without the conquering foot of Rome."

And Caswallawn told the druid, who realized at last what man had dared come into the unhallowed sacrificial circle, "I have a payment for you, druid! As one of the Golden Shoemakers, I have humbled myself to save the royal footholder from dishonor and death. This is my honor-price, to shield her honor." I tossed him a leather bag of gold pieces. And I, Caswallawn, knelt and kissed Fflur's foot in homage to a love more mighty than I had ever known.

As it began with a head, so it ends with a foot.

CHAPTER FIVE

THE CASKET OF MEMORY

Fair woman, will you go with me far

To the land of wonders, under the star?

Hair grows yellow as primrose flower

All skin is like a white snow shower.

Woman, if among our fine race you would live,

A crown of gold to grace your head I'll give;

Fresh pork, ale, milk, and mead you'll take,

—And me as well, Fair Woman, for your sake.

—Anon. Irish,
  from "Midir's Invitation to Etain,"
  trans. Caitlín Matthews

In most Western romantic literature, the compass of one lifetime alone is the usual arena for a love story, but in "The Casket of Memory" we learn about the legendary transmigration of Etain's (AY'thaw'in) soul into different shapes and lifetimes and the faithful search of her husband, Midir (MIJ'ir), down the aeons to find her.

It is worth noting that in Ireland the faery races, or *sidhe* (SHEE), are tall, shining folk, taller than humans; they are, in fact, the gods of the times before ours. In Britain, faery folk come in different shapes and sizes and are often held to be the same as the undying ancestors.

N A TIME far from this time, yet as close to our own time as the touching of a dream, there lived a great king among the *sidhe* folk of the faery, called Midir. He was tall with long black hair and gray eyes, wise and ageless like all his kind, for the passing of the years did not diminish their vigor.

The faery people of Ireland had inhabited the land since before the first humans came to its shores. In those far days, the faery realms were avoided by people, and the faery folk still lived within the invisible borders of their magical protective cloak, the *feth-fiadha* (FAY FIA), able to come and go at will. Their skill was to enjoy all the wonders and joys that were in the world.

Now it happened once that Midir was visiting his foster son, Aengus mac Og (AN'gus MAK OGE), at the crystal white hostel of Brugh na Boyne. As they sat together watching a hurley match, Midir was struck in the side by the speeding puck, which flew up at a masterly stroke from one of the champion players.

Aengus was ashamed at this injury to his guest and foster father and called for the great physician Dian Cecht to heal him. As soon as he was well, Midir made ready to leave, but Aengus begged him to stay longer, feeling that the spirit of hospitality and kinship also had been injured.

Knowing Aengus's tender understanding, Midir said to him, "I shall stay only if you offer me something that I need."

"Tell me!" begged Aengus, anxious to keep his foster father with him longer.

Midir considered his foster son carefully and asked only what he knew Aengus could afford to give: "A chariot worth seven maidservants and clothing appropriate to my rank."

Aengus kissed his foster father. "Gladly will I give you these, for I know the very chariot for you and the clothes that will suit you best. But, I beg you ask me for a third thing that my giving may be fortunate to me and be a blessing to yourself! For it is in threes that the full power of life's giving is known: for man and woman are made more powerful by the addition of a child, as night and day are strengthened by the between light of dawn and twilight."

Midir looked within his heart, for there was one thing, a secret sorrow that few of the faery folk knew. Many human lifetimes ago, he had taken a wife from human stock, a woman who surpassed all other women for him. Her name was Befind (BAY'vin), Fairest of Women. She was gentle and dear to him. Since the faery women might have looked down upon her as a mere mortal, Midir's gift to her had been the power of healing. He had helped extend her life beyond the mortal span, but, as with all who come from human realms, she had died and her soul departed into the great cauldron of the elements to be mixed again. And if she had come again on earth, he had no knowledge of it, for human souls return in many shapes and not even faery wisdom might look into the night in which souls are reclothed.

Aengus tuned his heart to Midir's silence with wonder, for he saw the image of Befind as if she had been present between them. "Ah! You do not speak your wish, but I can guess it: the fairest woman in Eriu is your desire."

Midir turned a face of such longing and mortal pain to his foster son that Aengus's own soul was full of anguish.

Said Aengus, "I know that the fairest woman in Eriu at this time is none other than Etain Echrade, daughter of Ailill (AL'ill) of Ulster. I will win her for you, if it is your desire."

Midir had no wish to take another wife, unless it might be Befind, but he trusted Aengus's sovereign ability to salve the hurts of the soul. "By your gift I shall be made whole, foster son!"

Aengus set out straightaway for Ulster and was welcomed at King Ailill's house. But when he made his request, that Ailill should give his daughter in marriage to Midir, the Ultonian leader was obdurate. Giving good legal precedents for his decision, the king of Ulster said, "I will not give up Etain, for you and your family are so much greater than mine that if you were to mistreat my daughter, I would have no recourse in law. You are of the faery kindred. Where would I find a judge to rule in such a case?"

Undeterred by this refusal, Aengus asked the king of Ulster to name any price, for he was determined to win Etain for his foster father. Ailill, who had no intentions of giving up Etain, set him a mighty task: "I have twelve tracts of land that are useless to me until they are cleared of trees and scrub: if that is done then I can have assemblies and games, fields for plowing and fortification."

Aengus looked upon the lands in question and grew quiet, but with the help of his blood father, the Dagda, the twelve plains were cleared in one night. He returned to Ailill to ask again for Etain.

Ailill realized that he must ask a more difficult price if he were to keep his daughter. "There are twelve great rivers that cross my land, making it boggy and impassable. Divert their courses to the sea so that the land can be drained and the fruits of the sea become accessible to us."

Aengus looked upon the rivers and his heart sank, but with the help of the mighty Dagda, Father of Knowledge, he diverted those twelve rivers from their courses so that they ran to the sea. Then he returned to demand Etain.

Ailill then set a bride price. "I want her weight in silver and gold." So Etain was brought to the middle of the hall and weighed, which was the first time that she had been aware of a suitor. And such a suitor! Her face burned at the thought of a faery husband.

As the daughter of a king, she knew well that she would likely marry her father's choice, not a man of her own heart's choosing. But she was not displeased to look upon the radiant young go-between who came to beg for her. Aengus spoke glowingly of Midir, praising his virtues, his generosity, his nobility to Etain. "But what does he look like?" she asked the faery matchmaker. Aengus sang, "He is of undying race, like an ash tree in height, his features keen as a hawk, his body slender as a greyhound, his hair dark as the starlit depths of night."

Etain quietly rejoiced. Not for her an ale-sodden reprobate with a violent backhand, no aging glutton with a barrelful of lard for a stomach, but a shimmering, ageless lord with lips of honey.

As King Ailill saw the plentiful heaps of silver and gold, he could have wished his daughter had been a great lump of a girl rather than the fine, long-legged filly that she was. But he was well satisfied that he had got a good bargain.

So Etain was brought to the crystal hostel of the Brugh, which lay crooked within a curving oxbow of the river Boyne. It was a place of awe, avoided by humankind. As Etain's white mare approached the entrance, the pretty beast jibbed and nickered, drawing back her soft pink lips to show her teeth. Aengus steadied the beast's head and asked kindly, "Do you feel it too, Etain—the threshold of the *sidhe?*"

Etain could not explain. "It feels as though I knew this way already—or will know it. . . ." She drew her mantle fast and turned to look upon the fair world of humankind for the last time, and a sudden peace enveloped her. Whatever lay beyond, it could only be fairer than this. With a strange confidence, she took Aengus's hand.

"Welcome to my home!" he said to her. "Within its enclosure you are within the *feth-fiadha,* the magical wall that borders your world and ours. Here you will not grow old; neither will you suffer illness. Come and meet your husband, my foster father, Midir."

Etain found herself within a fair, white place, whose brilliance entranced and dazzled her. Hangings of jewel-like color, devices of strange craftsmanship in white gold and radiant copper, trees of age and majesty, horses and people of different hue.

Birds of bright feathers were calling their unending song over the wellhead of the waters of memory as they gushed from the heart of the earth. Tears pricked her eyes with sharp recollection: she did not know that beauty such as this could exist or that she could ever belong to it; yet, now she was here, it felt wholly right.

Aengus led her with honor to Midir. "Foster father, the chariot and clothes I have given you as promised. But here I present to you Etain Echrade, daughter of Ailill of Ulster, if you will have her for your wife."

Etain looked into the face of the tall, dark man with wonder. His features held a timeless harmony, unmarred by the discontent so often seen in the faces of men. She sensed pride in him and a matchless will, but her blood sang to be mixed with his.

Midir saw a tall young woman whose hands flew continually to her breast as if to shelter a precious flame at her heart. It was the very gesture of Befind when she had been excited! And yet he saw that his new wife had no knowledge of who she had been or of who he was. For Midir, time meant very little, but it would be time that would change and shape this woman and love alone that would rekindle the memory of that which she held in the casket of her soul. The longer she stayed with him, the sooner memory would stir.

In a musical voice of great beauty he said, "Be welcome to my heart, Etain the Horse Rider! Of all women, you are its best companion."

And Etain lay her small hand in his long one and was gathered to his breast. Safe. Forever. . . .

Three nights and days of feasting in the Brugh celebrated the wedding of Midir to Etain. Story, song, splendor, and the long, long afternoons of lovemaking wound Etain into the world of faery. There was little talk between herself and Midir but an unspoken understanding that was intimate and loving.

Tomorrow they were to leave for Midir's home of Brí Léith. But Aengus had prescient knowledge of what would come about, and he warned Midir to take special care of Etain and to beware of a certain woman who was in his household. Midir knew that he spoke of Fuamnach (FOOM'nak), the foster child of Bresal the Wise, she who had no shred of human blood, she who swathed her soul in the magics of the Otherworld.

Fuamnach, the first wife of Midir, married to him when he was but newly come to manhood, aeons ago.

Etain had heard stories of faery cunning and treachery, but having met nothing but kind looks and congratulation, gifts and favors from the People of Peace, she expected nothing other than this when Fuamnach welcomed Midir and his new bride home. But when Midir left them alone together to see to his long-neglected affairs, Fuamnach showed another face to Etain.

Inviting her to her *grianan,* Fuamnach bade her be comfortable. Etain innocently sat in the chair that stood in a pool of sunlight in the middle of the room. With her haughty face twisted with spite, Fuamnach spat, "It is the seat of a better woman you have usurped!" and struck Etain with her wand of scarlet rowan, turning her into a pool of water. There Fuamnach left Etain, returning to her foster father, Bresal's, house, leaving Midir with no wife at all.

Now the heat of the sunlight and the closeness of the air in the *grianan* caused the earth to seethe and boil. The pool of water that was Etain began to evaporate in the heat, and the residue of her human flesh began to corrupt. In the alchemical heat of the sunny room, Etain turned into a worm that could only crawl upon the ground. Enough of Etain's soul remained to make her armless worm body crawl out of the water toward the red-glazed window.

As Etain twisted and turned, testing her new shape, she found that she was transforming again. She looked into the glass reflection and saw that she was a scarlet fly, about the size of a man's thumb. She gave a dolorous cry and found that her voice was sweet and that the beating of her wings was like the accompaniment of musicians. Her huge, multifaceted eyes shone translucent in the growing dark like jewels as she pondered her plight. Even in her distress and confusion, her own cries and movements seemed to soothe her soul.

Attendants searching for their mistress found only the great fly in the *grianan.* They noted, as they tried to catch it, that the color and fragrance of its wings seemed to sate hunger and quench thirst. This wonder needed to be brought to Midir for his judgment.

Taking the fly upon his hand, Midir tuned his soul to its own. The terrible truth was abundantly clear to him: the fly was none other than Etain! What cruel fate had robbed him of his love yet again? He berated himself that he had not listened more closely to his foster son's warning and taken action before Fuamnach could wreak this havoc!

Taking Etain the fly into their private chamber, he spoke to her, soul to soul: "Befind who was, Etain who is my love, do you remember the dear days we had together? I swear to you that they shall be restored, though I wait till the ending of all things when the hills shall cover us, when the seas shall rise up and drown us, when the sky shall fall upon us and the *feth-fiadha* break its sacred protection."

The soul of Etain remained in the body of the scarlet fly, accompanying Midir everywhere and spreading her blessings upon all who came into his presence. She was able to warn him whenever anyone approached who meant him no good. The drops of water that the fly shed from its wings could heal sickness and heaviness of spirits. It was clear to Midir that Fuamnach's magic had not subdued or utterly diminished the essential qualities that were characteristic of Befind and now of Etain.

After many attempts at trying to transform Etain back into her mortal shape, Midir realized that only the one who cast the spell could remove it. But when Fuamnach finally visited Midir, she very carefully brought three of the mighty Tuatha de Danaan as her guarantors of safety, which was as well, for Midir's anger against her was immense and he certainly would have killed her. Fuamnach made no secret of the fact that she considered Etain her enemy and that she would do all she could to bring misfortune upon her.

As Midir demanded Etain's restitution, Fuamnach observed that Etain as a scarlet fly was as close to Midir as she had been as a woman. Nothing had been gained, but now the sorceress resolved to part Midir and Etain forever. Smiling her compliant smile, she said she would consider her position and see what could be done. But once out of Brí Léith, Fuamnach summoned a mighty wind with the aid of the spells and incantations that she had been given by Bresal. It was a wind that blew for seven long years; it blew Etain out of Brí Léith, and there was no place that the scarlet fly might rest save only on the ocean rocks and the waves.

The soul of Etain clung ruggedly to the shape into which she had been transformed, but the buffeting of the sixteen winds brought her no rest. With an instinct that belonged only to her fly's body, she dropped from the sky while the winds were changing their contrafugal dance so that her wings would not be caught by their updraft. She found herself falling to earth into a fold of Aengus's cloak. Scooping the fly into his hands, he saw immediately who it was and welcomed Etain with, "Hail, troubled wanderer! You who have yet to find happiness, welcome here."

And he brought her into the safety of the Brugh and placed her in his crystal *grianan*. Now the *grianan* of Aengus was a wonder: though it could be large, it could also become small, and Aengus traveled with it wherever he went. He filled it with health-giving herbs that the scarlet fly might recover from its long wanderings; he shielded it with a scarlet veil that no magic might dislodge it from its sanctuary. He realized that the soul of Etain was but slenderly attached to her fly's body: exhausted and full of grief, she would need much healing.

Now Fuamnach had not lessened her enmity to Etain over this long time, and she resolved to ruin her happiness. She bade Midir invite his foster son, Aengus, to stay with them, pretending that she wanted to restore friendship among them all. But as Midir's messenger arrived at the Brugh and Aengus went to answer him, bringing the glad news that Etain had been found, Fuamnach took herself *tuathal*, widdershins, about the Brugh and raised the sister of the wind that she had called up before. The scarlet fly that was Etain was blown out of the safety of the crystal *grianan* into the wilderness of the elements.

Seven long years that wind blew; seven long years the scarlet fly was blown through the world, till with weakness and wretchedness it landed on the roof of a house in Ulster where the people sat drinking. Far gone with weariness, Etain the fly fell from the roof—plop—into the cup of strong ale that was in the hand of a woman called Etar. Far gone in carousing, Etar swallowed the fly in her ale, and Etain's soul fell into forgetfulness for a long while.

Back at the Brugh, Aengus had long realized that Fuamnach's friendship was pretended. He found the crystal *grianan* empty, and he followed the trail of Fuamnach to the house of Bresal the Wise, where he attacked her and struck off her head. And though Midir, his foster father, had been avenged, now he had no wife at all.

But so it was that Etain the fly died and was conceived and took new life in the womb of Etar and was born nine months later as her daughter. And it was 1,012 years from Etain's begetting by Ailill until her last conception by Etar, for seven years in faery is a far longer time than it is with men, and the scarlet fly had spun about the heavens for twice that compass.

Etar called her daughter Etain, for it seemed to be the name that best suited her. This girl was reared with fifty chieftains' daughters as her companions, for Etar was nobly born. One day the girls were all bathing in the estuary when a rider came toward them wearing a poet's band about his head, carrying a warrior's shield and spear in his hands, and with a green faery cloak about his shoulders. The girls stopped splashing to gaze upon this beautiful creature, but his eyes were solely upon Etain, and the inspiration of poetic vision brought these words to his lips:

Etain has returned to us at Inbher Cíchmane,
She who healed illnesses,
She who fell into the cup of Etar.
Because of her the king will chase the forbidden birds,
Because of her he will drown his two horses.
Because of her there will be fighting and battle,
Many faery mounds will be destroyed.
It is she who will be on all lips,
It is she whom the king is seeking.
Once she was called Befind—Fairest of Women,
Now again she is called Etain.

Once the faery apparition had passed, the girls shrieked and giggled at these strange, prophetic words, teasing Etain who stood in the rushes, her long fair hair sticking like weed to her white limbs. There was something in the rider's demeanor that reminded her of something deeply forgotten. It was like the contents of a chest whose key had been lost, and try as she might, she could not remember what lay hidden in the casket of her memory.

Now at this time Eochaid Airem (YOK'ee AIR'em) became high king of Ireland. He called together a great assembly of the five provinces to set their taxes, but the kings of Ireland refused to come unless Eochaid took a wife, for they would not attend an assembly that had no queen. So Eochaid made a search for the fairest woman in the land and chose Etain, daughter of Etar—she who had been Etain the wife of Midir in another lifetime.

Now after King Eochaid had married Etain, his brother, Ailill the Valiant, fell desperately and unaccountably in love with her. He knew that it was dishonorable to feel this way toward his sister-in-law, but he couldn't help himself. So lovesick did he become that a doctor was called to attend him.

The doctor's diagnosis was hopeless: "Young man, you have one of the two deadly pangs that no doctor can cure: the pang of love and the pang of jealousy." But, having the confidence of his lovesick patient, the doctor did not tell King Eochaid the true cause of the sickness, merely saying that Ailill suffered from an incurable condition and that all that could be done now was to make his passing a comfortable one.

When it looked as though nothing could be done, King Eochaid went upon his circuit of the provinces, which he could delay no longer, leaving Etain behind to perform the funeral rites for his brother. Now, every day, Etain visited Ailill to talk to him and make him comfortable, and every day he grew suspiciously better and better under her ministrations. The ancient skills of Befind were beginning to resurface in the life of Etain the second.

"Tell me, what has made you ill?" asked Etain, who had reason to doubt the doctor, for Ailill's wasted hands kept straying from under the quilt to touch her in a way that was allowed only to her husband.

Ailill's gusty sigh gave the game away: "Love of you, fair one!"

"You should have told me sooner, and you would have been well sooner," said Etain, who was young enough to know that the appeasing of hungry desires is the quickest cure. She innocently imagined that if she found a woman enough like herself, Ailill would soon forget the king's wife.

"Ah, I can be well if you also desire it," he said meaningfully.

Within a space of three-times-nine days Ailill the Valiant had almost regained his vigor due to the visits of Etain. "There is one thing more will restore me. When will I have it?"

"Tomorrow," she said. "But a king mustn't be shamed in his own house. Meet me on the hill tomorrow at the third hour." Eochaid was good to her, had taken no secondary wife to displace her. She meant no dishonor to him, but perhaps the promise of desire fulfilled would cause his brother, Ailill, to find the strength to walk again, she told herself, though she much doubted his ability to move far after so wasting an illness.

Ailill was so excited at the thought of a tryst with Etain that he was unable to sleep, but, despite this, he did sleep just before dawn. Meanwhile, Etain waited on the hill and met a man who looked and sounded like Ailill. He said nothing but took her in his arms and held her reverently, in an almost brotherly and protective embrace. It roused strong feelings in her, yet she felt that she had done nothing to taint Eochaid's honor. But later, mysteriously, when she returned to the house, she found Ailill lamenting his weakness at having slept through their tryst.

Three times Ailill made an assignation with Etain; three times Ailill fell asleep before the time; three times Etain met the man who resembled Ailill, until she was moved to break the lingering silence that lay between them and say boldly to that man, "You are not the one I should be meeting."

The one who looked like Ailill said to her, "Indeed, it would be better fitting for you to meet me rather than another, for when you were Etain Echrade I was your husband; do you not remember the great bride price given for you by Aengus in land clearing, river diverting, and treasure giving?"

And in the heart of memory, something stirred. "What is your name?" For it seemed that the bluff shape of Ailill fell away to be replaced by someone taller and nobler than he.

"I am Midir of Brí Léith."

At the sound of his name, something stirred, like the shaking of distant stars within her. Etain had heard of such things before: people who were reborn as stars, animals, other people—it made her mind reel to consider such things. "But what parted us?"

"The enchantments of Fuamnach and her foster father. Will you not come away with me?"

Etain was adamant. Shaking the long fair hair out of her eyes, she declaimed, "I will not! Better the noble king I know than one whose race and family I know nothing of!"

"Beloved, it is I who made Ailill fall in love with you, the better to use his shape and meet you." Even for all his ageless patience and searching, Midir felt something akin to human despair in the face of this Etain's blind obedience. It would take great cunning to win her back to him. A faery man can use only what humans give freely or else what he can trick from them. And because of the love that Midir bore to the Befind who had become Etain, he could not so bind her, but he said, "Etain, will you come with me if Eochaid himself bids you go?"

She could not imagine such a thing, so she assented. "Yes, but only then!"

Returning to tend to Ailill, she found him not only cured of his illness but also of his love for her. He yelled at her peevishly from his bed, demanding ale, endearments and sweet-talking completely abandoned.

And when Eochaid returned from his circuit of the land, he was full of praise for Etain's healing skills and loud with rejoicing at the restoration of his brother. But to counter his praise, all that Etain would say was, "Love is its own reward," with a sideways glance at Ailill the Valiant, who had thought little of his brother's honor.

Later that summer, at the end of a successful assembly of the five provinces, King Eochaid climbed the ramparts of Tara to look over the land to consider his kingdom. He noticed with pride the fatness of the cattle that grazed, the activities of the craftsmen, the giving of justice in the courts of the *brehons* where arbitration quelled dispute, the many colored banners and shields of the kings and subkings. Then he frowned and narrowed his eyes, for there, below him, stood a strange gray-eyed warrior with a five-pointed spear in his grasp; he did not remember this man being admitted to the hall of feasts the previous night.

"Who are you?" he challenged.

"Midir of Brí Léith." The name meant nothing to Eochaid—an outlying chiefdom, perhaps?

"Why have you come here?"

"I wish to play *fidhchell* with you."

Eochaid was delighted, for his chief pleasure was the playing of the board game, wood wisdom, in which he was accounted a good player. In *fidhchell,* one player moves the king piece and his retinue, striving to get the king to the edge of the board, proving that the realm is peaceful enough for a king to pass to its very borders and not suffer assault. The other player and his war band, on the other hand, villainously try to prevent this. Eochaid always played king. But then he remembered: "Ach, my friend, we cannot play yet, for the queen is still asleep and the *fidhchell* board is in her chamber. I would not disturb her for all the world." For last night, he had proudly exhibited Etain to the kings of Eriu and sung her praises as a healer. Because of Etain, Eochaid had been able to call together the assembly of Tara.

"No matter," said the stranger. "Here is one I have brought with me."

Now Eochaid had seen some fine *fidhchell* boards in his day, but none compared to this: the board was of silver and the men were of gold, with precious gems set into each corner, all contained within a bag of woven bronze wires. He hurried down the ramparts to greet his new guest and the better to touch the beautiful board with his own hands.

Once within Eochaid's apartments, Midir set up the pieces. "Let us play."

"I never play without a stake," said Eochaid, who loved to gamble at the expense of lesser kings.

"What stake?" Midir's impassive face and blinkless gray eyes discountenanced Eochaid, who wandered whether the stranger was perhaps without great store of goods; his clothes were fine enough, but there was something unchancy about him. Exercising the magnanimity of high kingship, he said stoutly, "Whatever stake you please," leaving the stranger to offer what he could.

"Then," said Midir, "I will give you fifty dark gray horses and their enameled bridles if you win." Eochaid's eyes flew wide open, and he lidded them carefully and played. To bargain such a stake meant the man was a consummate player or else a first-class fool!

They played a lengthy, satisfying game, which Midir lost. "Your horses will be delivered tomorrow," he said and left.

The next dawn, Eochaid rose to look out upon Tara's plain once more, wondering what sureties he should have taken from Midir to hold him to his payment. But he looked down and saw fifty dark gray horses with splendid bridles held by grooms. When he turned around, there was Midir again with his *fidhchell* board.

"Another game, great king?"

"With pleasure, but what stake?" asked Eochaid, rubbing his hands together in the chill dawn.

"I will give you fifty fiery boars with horses' hooves; fifty gold-hilted swords; fifty white, red-eared cows and their calves spanceled with bronze; fifty gray red-headed sheep, each with three heads and three horns; fifty ivory-hilted blades; and fifty bright-speckled cloaks. Each fifty on its own day."

Eochaid was astounded. "Worthy of the high king is your stake!" And he excused himself to go and consult his own foster father, who warned him that Midir must be a man of great and terrible power.

"Test him, my son, with difficult tasks; you should not play against such a man as this, lest he demand a wager that you cannot pay."

Throughout the ensuing game, Eochaid began to sweat: what if *he* should lose and have to obtain such a stake? Where would he find fifty fiery boars with horses' hooves, for goodness' sake? His play began to be ragged and uncertain, but when Midir deftly moved a piece in touch with his king, Eochaid recovered and blocked him smartly. Waiting for Midir to move, Eochaid considered his opponent. The man must be of the *sidhe!* No other could come to Tara so boldly and without being challenged by the guards. Again, Midir lost. Eochaid noted he seemed strangely indifferent to his loss.

The next day, Cruacha (KRUAKH'a), the maid attendant on Etain, came and told her all about the extraordinary stake that Eochaid's opponent had wagered. "And it's true, mistress! There are red-eared cows and three-horned sheep and multitudes of weapons and cloaks. The king has promised a share to you."

Etain rose and hurried to the place where the *fidhchell* board was set in the great hall, the better to accommodate those who wanted a front seat at the next contest. Pressing herself into a dark corner, she watched the tall stranger sit upon the stool, folding his long shanks gracefully under the low table. She could not see his face, for it was shielded by the hood of his cloak. She felt that she should recognize him, if she saw his face, for all his gestures were familiar to her. Even his manner of lifting the pieces reminded her of something beautiful, something strange. She thrust her two hands over her fluttering heart, for it felt as though it might leap out like an ungoverned bird and take wing with the stranger. Neither she nor Cruacha was tall enough to tell what went on, so she sent her servant to find out what the stake was this time.

Cruacha elbowed her way through the close-packed men and back again, with barely stifled complaints, since all were engrossed in the game.

"Eochaid has set him three terrible labors if the stranger loses," she reported. "To clear the whole of Mide of stones, to clear rushes from the barren lands around Tethbae, and to lay a causeway over the bog of Moin Lamhrige."

Etain inhaled sharply. How could he possibly do all that? How was it possible? That it mattered so much to her that he be able to do it, she did not consider. Again, the nature of the stake seemed familiar to her—was it not in some old story that a princess was wooed and won with such a deed? She forgot.

Midir lost the game amid the deafening cheers of the Irishmen. As he rose, they moderated their rejoicings and fell silent as the stranger's keen gray eyes pierced Eochaid's: "Keep your people indoors until sunrise tomorrow, great king. If you do that, the work will be done as you command."

Eochaid sent his steward to the highest point of Tara to look out at what happened, and it seemed to him that all the people of the world were there assembled as the faery folk worked upon these tasks, singing a strange song. When all was done, Eochaid waited to greet Midir, who came with a stern mien. "I have fulfilled these labors; now, shall we play again?"

"What stake?" asked Eochaid with the recklessness of one who wins too often.

Everyone bent forward to catch the stake, only to be surprised.

Midir did not blink: "Whatever stake the winner names."

Eochaid hesitated only a fraction, and then nodded his head. "Of course!"

Etain was on the first bench, nearest to the game, in order to see the stranger for herself. She saw that honest, plain Eochaid was off his game, his fingers hovering uncertainly over the pieces, as one by one the king's retinue was ambushed and taken by the incisive game of Midir.

Midir.

Now that she was close to him again, she felt the fluttering in her heart. It was like a little fly that buzzed and hit itself against the shutter. . . . Only the shutter had been made of glass, that time, she remembered. . . .

By all the beauty of the *sidhe!* Now the casket of memory flew open to reveal that terrible time when Fuamnach . . .

Oh, horror! And her mind snapped suddenly shut again, not to remember the battering of the ceaseless winds, not to recall the enmity of that dreadful woman.

There was an uproar of disquiet, and she came to herself. She looked at the board: the king piece was surrounded on all sides.

Midir had won.

"What will you have?" asked Eochaid, breathing like a winded horse.

Midir's eyes rested at last upon Etain, but to Eochaid he said, "My arms around Etain and a kiss from her."

Eochaid was shocked to silence. It took all his diplomacy as a king to say in a strange, strangled tone, "Return a month from today, and you will have it."

When the company looked again, the *fidhchell* board and Midir were no longer there.

Then Eochaid made preparations. At the close of the month, he assembled rank upon rank of warriors and war bands surrounding Tara, each encircling the other, and shut himself and Etain safely in the central hall. It was a dismal feasting. Eochaid, tight-lipped and apt to snap. His men afraid to drink deeply in case they might have to defend their king and his wife. Etain was held in the vice of memory as one lifetime merged with another. Knowledge of who and what she had been in different lifetimes tumbled over and over in her memory like the ceaseless waves of the ocean. In the merciless undertow of memory's wash, she was incapable of decision.

As she poured the drink that night, they all saw Midir in their midst. He had come through no door but had merely appeared among them. No longer a hooded stranger with a *fidhchell* board under his arm, he now showed all his magnificence and beauty as a faery man. His skin had a translucence and his eyes a sheen that no man there had ever seen. In a deep, commanding voice that carried to the very rafters he said, "I have come for what I was promised."

Etain gazed at him transfixed, as the memory of her lives rose up strongly within her: a terrible knowledge that was hard to think upon.

Eochaid rose to protect her, unprepared for matters to have reached this pass so suddenly.

"Come, Etain, fairest of women! You promised to come with me," said Midir, stretching out his hand to her.

Eochaid stared with unwilling suspicion at his wife. "*When* and *where* did you promise anything to this man?"

Etain ignored him and said to Midir, "I have said that I will go only if Eochaid bids me." But it was clear to all in the hall of Tara with whom she would rather be. To the onlookers, it seemed that the net of her soul rushed toward the tall faery man, even as her body strained to be free of the shackles of a marriage to one she no longer cared about.

"I do not bid you!" replied Eochaid, but not wishing to bring the wrath of the *sidhe* upon his house, he said guardedly, "But he *may* put his arms around you and kiss you, as promised."

It was enough for Midir, who clasped Etain tight to him. The thrill of freedom, of soul's release, washed over her, and she was there again with her beloved. Safe. Forever.

Clutching his weapons in his left hand, Midir bore her upward, right through the skylight of the hall. But when the astounded household of Tara looked upward, all they could see were two swans winging for the *sidhe* of Femuin.

The lifetimes of Etain were as a forgotten memory compared to the joy that now possessed her in the timeless enclosure of the *sidhe*. And for Midir, who had sought her for over a thousand years, the winning of their bliss was as marvelous as the singing of the many-colored birds at the wellhead of memory's beginning: an endless twining of voice and heart that led back to the first day.

CHAPTER SIX

THE STRETCHING OF TIME

I invoke the Silver one, undying and deathless,

may my life be enduring as white bronze!

May my life journey be fulfilled!

May the King of the Universe stretch time for me!

May my seven candles never be extinguished!

—Anon. Irish "Prayer for Long Life,"
trans. Caitlín Matthews

This little-known medieval Irish story, which is nearer to *Romeo and Juliet* than any other Gaelic tale, concerns two lovers parted by rank, location, and parental disapproval. But Fearbhlaidh (FAR'ly) and Cearbhall (KARR'ol) have a clever ally in Duibhghil (DOO'gil), Fearbhlaidh's enchantress nurse. The action moves between Scotland and Ireland, reminding us of the long association between the lands.

EAMAS MAC TURCAILL (SHAM'us MAK TURK'al), the king of Scotland, had but one child: his daughter, Fearbhlaidh. And though many women were said to be beautiful, it was agreed that, beside Fearbhlaidh, such beauties were but pale reflections of perfection.

Because of her beauty and accomplishments, she was sought in marriage by men far and wide. But, for love of her, her father would give her to no man save the one she wished to wed. The high-placed nobles of the king's court began to bicker and argue about Seamas's softness, and many raiders began to attack his lands, thinking to overcome a weak ruler who didn't know how to strengthen his position by arranging a dynastic marriage.

Seamas took his daughter aside, saying, "I have no successor because of you. No allies flock to my side in kinship because of your delay. I would rather marry you to the meanest slave than continue to indulge your fancy. Tell me now, this very day, who is the man whom you find most pleasing, and you shall be wed to him without delay."

Fearbhlaidh's fair cheek turned color: red as summer valerian, dark as coal, white as flaxen sheets. "Truly, Father, I cannot name the man to whom my love is given."

"Where have you seen him?" Seamas beamed, happy to see the end of his troubles.

"I was sleeping in my *grianan* when I beheld the vision of a beardless man with black curly hair. There was a purple cloak about him and a harp set with crystal in his two hands. His voice sat upon the music of those strings like a tuneful bird, and it stole the life of my heart away with it. I shall never be able to join my mind or heart to any man save him, though I see him nevermore."

The king was greatly disquieted. "Fearbhlaidh, I order you to disregard such otherworldly apparitions."

Fearbhlaidh laid one white hand upon her father's arm. "Father, it is not within my power to change what has happened; neither is it right for you to reproach me." She spoke so softly yet so resolutely that he knew that some lover must have stalked her fame and beauty, filling her heart with unappeasable longings.

Seamas tore at his hair and beard in a frenzy of apprehension, babbling, "Now the curse of our race comes upon me! Ah, Fearbhlaidh, it is the nature of Etain (AY'thaw'in), your foremother and ancestress, that comes upon you now! Was she not stolen away into faery by Midir? [See "The Casket of Memory," p. 107.] From her are you descended, and the blood of the bird people is in your veins." And he made a great cry of lamentation at the fate that had fallen upon himself and his daughter.

Fearbhlaidh was astounded at his outcry, unable to make sense of his words. "Father, do not grieve; I shall somehow find out about that man within the year, or, if I fail, you shall marry me to whatever man seems best to you." And she fled back to her *grianan*, determined never to take the latter course. No man whom her father might find could equal the vision that had visited her and laid his head beside her on the pillow.

Now Fearbhlaidh's nurse was Duibhghil, a woman skilled in the magical arts who could shape-shift into any beast, whether it be the insubstantial midge or the mighty seagoing whale. Fearbhlaidh took her nurse into her confidence, staring imploringly into her face for help and advice.

Duibhghil looked kindly upon her charge's desperation. "I have waited a long time for you to tell me of your visitor. Your father is right; you are descended—through fourteen generations of mothers—from that Etain who changed her shape and was found and lost again by her faery lover. It is because of your lineage that I am your nurse, for we both of us have faery blood in our veins. Be cheerful, my dear. If that man exists in Europe, Africa, or Asia, I shall bring news of him before the year dies." And Duibhghil prepared her magical regalia, called upon the spirits whom she served, lay down upon her couch, and fell into an enchanted slumber, wherein her soul rode across the seas upon a magical wind so that she might encompass the lands of Scotland and Ireland within a day. To every secret house and every field of assembly she went, scrutinizing the hearts of all men as time stretched for her.

Finally, she reached Finnyvara on the stony edge of the Burren in Ireland. A sound brought her to the school of the poetic teacher, Donnchadh Mór ó Dálaigh (DONN'ca MOR O DAL'y). Her seeking soul found the man amid all the students at their practice—a curly-haired youth, eyes blue as hyacinths, and a voice sweeter than the honey of bees. "So, you are the one whose soul has sought out and visited my young lady!" She remained long enough to hear the youth rise at the calling of his name. Satisfied that her quest had been successful, she returned to the Fort of Maidens in Scotland and to the *grianan* of

Fearbhlaidh, who was astounded to see her nurse arise so soon from her enchanted slumber.

"I have been through southern Scotland and northern Scotland; I have searched the net of islands, I have traversed the five provinces of Ireland and found the one that you seek."

Fearbhlaidh clapped her hands with delight, but Duibhghil's expression was forbidding. "It would have been better if I'd not found him, for he is hardly your equal in rank or disposition. He is a skilled poet from the west of Ireland, son of Donnchadh Mór ó Dálaigh. He is not of faery kind, but he has gained the magical skills through his study of poetry and seership."

Fearbhlaidh was impatient of the details. "But his name?"

"He is Cearbhall."

And at the saying of his name, Fearbhlaidh breathed exultantly. Night after night, she had dreamed of his dark curly head lying beside her. He had harped and mastered her with his voice, teaching her passions she never knew existed, and now she longed for that which had been promised in his music. She would gladly pay that promise with the gage of her body.

"Take me to him tonight," she demanded.

"Do you promise to come back with me again?" asked Duibhghil, searchingly.

"I do!"

"Then, because of your kinship with the bird people of the *sidhe,* we shall go as birds." And, striking them both with her wand of transformation, Duibhghil changed them both into the shape of doves, and they flew to Finnyvara, landing outside the window of Cearbhall's chamber. The power of his harping caused both the doves to fall into a slumber, for it was far from Scotland to western Ireland. And when they woke in the morning, it was to find that Cearbhall had captured them both and put them into a cage to show them off to his fellow students.

Duibhghil waited until Cearbhall's companions left and spoke in a human voice, "Cearbhall, son of Donnchadh, do you know who we are and why we have come to you?"

Cearbhall's fingers froze upon the harp strings. "Tell me!"

"If I tell you, you must give your word not to harm us and to release us."

Upon his solemn promise, Duibhghil told him the whole tale from beginning to end. Cearbhall then said, "Show me yourselves in your true shapes."

As soon as he laid eye upon Fearbhlaidh, Cearbhall humbly realized that the power of thought and the force of inspiration taught by his father was not just a poetic fantasy but really the truest of the truths. By his own poetic vision he had perceived the beauty of Fearbhlaidh from across the length of the two lands that parted them, and she had received that vision and seen him, so strong was his desire for her.

Duibhghil, seeing how it was with them, discreetly left them together, flying out in the form of a dove to wait till their tryst might be done.

Cearbhall drew Fearbhlaidh to him, almost fearful that she would be a vision woman of no substance, but his hand caressed her slender neck and white shoulder, stroked her long, honey-colored hair, and his mouth closed over her eager lips.

Their lovemaking was insatiable. Three days and three nights saw no end to their twining limbs or to the fever of their desire. No matter how many times their bodies arched in the grip of ecstasy, they sought once more the inexhaustible quenching of their mutual, long-denied yearning.

On the dawn of the fourth day, the iron resolution of Duibhghil brought an end to their tryst. She called through the door, "Although time may not have passed for you, time is hastening away: we can stretch it no longer. Fearbhlaidh, you promised to return home with me, and now we must go."

With great sighs, Fearbhlaidh rose. With many kisses and promises, Cearbhall swore to persuade his father to bring him to Scotland that they might be reunited. Then the two women winged home to the Fort of Maidens, where they were received with great rejoicing, for the king had assumed that his daughter and her nurse must have been lost in the faery mounds, never to return.

Cearbhall began to beg his father to go on a poetic circuit of Scotland, but Donnchadh was slow to persuade. It took him the best part of three months to prepare for the journey, during which time Cearbhall fell sick with frustration. He sent messages to Fearbhlaidh of his illness.

Fearbhlaidh's agitation knew no bounds. "We must make him well again, though I fear he will never be well while we are parted so cruelly." Duibhghil gave a crooked smile. "Hidden gifts often reveal themselves at the edge of necessity. Your foremother, Etain, was a great healer, and that ability flows in your blood. Here!" and the nurse brought from the treasure box a dense black stone, shaped like a beetle, smooth and polished from frequent handling.

"Send this to Cearbhall. It has a quality that heals all diseases and troubles of mind, especially when it bears the loving words and healing intentions of the women of your line."

Fearbhlaidh laid the cold stone reverently between her breasts, willing the healing of her love to be present in the stone. She opened her eyes and asked her nurse, "Is that all?"

Duibhghil smiled, "It is enough!"

When Cearbhall received the stone and the message with it, he too laid it against his heart. The flavor of life and the will to live returned to him once again. He secretly treasured the stone, which shone with a magical light. Were he in the depths of a cave or in a thick forest at the dark moon, it would give out a ray like the sun at midsummer, illumining his way.

Finally the preparations to visit Scotland were all in place, and Donnchadh, Cearbhall, and his fellow students set out. They were received with joyful acclamation at the Fort of Maidens, for the poets of western Ireland were famed for their skill. King Seamas sat Donnchadh in the seat of honor beside him, while Cearbhall was seated between Fearbhlaidh and Duibhghil at the feast.

Now Cearbhall had begged to be given the honor of performing first before the king of Scotland, and Donnchadh, proud of his son's skill, assented gladly. With every ounce of skill at his command, Cearbhall set his fingers to the strings of the harp and played the strains of enchantment first played by the ancient gods of the Irish. He played the sorrow strain, by which all who listened were able to purge their hidden grief with tears; then he played the joy strain, which caused the company to fall into a blessed rejoicing; lastly he played the sleep strain, which plunged the company into a deep sleep—all save himself, Fearbhlaidh, and Duibhghil, whose magical skills could not be overcome by such enchantments.

As the company in the feasting hall lolled in their seats like those frozen into stone in an old story, the lovers poured out their hearts to each other, purging their own grieving anxiety and long parting with tears of their own. Fearbhlaidh cried, "I curse my fate and my lineage, my birth and my conception, that ever I was born to suffer like this!"

"Sweet soul, do not speak so!" Cearbhall stopped her mouth with kisses. "You sent me healing in my darkest hour. Now I come to bring consolation to you, for we shall be together and have joy and pleasure again."

And during the enchanted period of sleep that lay upon the court of the king, the lovers renewed their vows by the union of their bodies.

Later, when everyone woke, continuing with their feasting exactly as before, Fearbhlaidh still sat demurely upon her chair and Cearbhall upon the harping stool, so that no one knew with what passion they had conjoined only a short while before.

The next day, the king invited Cearbhall to a game of *fidhchell*. Fearbhlaidh sat beside her father to watch, her eyes twinkling at Cearbhall as the two men concentrated on the game. Despite the distraction, Cearbhall won several games in a row. They were well into the eighth game when Cearbhall removed his sandal, stretched out his foot, and made to covertly rub Fearbhlaidh's leg beneath the *fidhchell* table. But it was the king's leg that he scratched with his toenails.

Without betraying his anger, King Seamas won the last game and called his counselors to him, telling them what had befallen. "It is clear to me that this Irish youth has ideas above his station. He has set his desires upon my daughter."

The council advised their king to summarily kill Donnchadh, his son, and their retinue for this gross insult. Now poets enjoyed a special immunity, and their persons might not be injured without a high honor-price being paid, but, as Seamas grimly remarked, "Ireland is far from Scotland!"

Now also with the poets was Donnchadh's brother, Macaomh (MAK'eev), who was skilled in discerning the secret intentions of people and their hidden dealings, and he guessed what had happened. Coming innocently to the king's chamber to wish him good-day, he bowed and then, catching sight of the *fidhchell* board on the nearby table, looked up, as if alarmed. "Oh!"

"What is it?" asked Seamas, unable to understand why Macaomh had called upon him.

"I've just had a terrible thought! I do hope that my nephew, Cearbhall, wasn't playing *fidhchell* with Your Highness? It's a way of his, you know, to stretch out his foot while concentrating and to absently scratch the foot of his opponent. No one has ever been able to break him of this disagreeable and potentially insulting habit."

After Macaomh had taken his leave, the king realized how near he had been to committing a terrible atrocity, so that when Donnchadh made to leave later that week, Seamas begged that Cearbhall might be allowed to remain so they might enjoy his skillful company longer.

❦

The year was almost at its end, when Fearbhlaidh would have to reveal the name of the man she loved. She went fearfully to her father, hoping to convince him of her choice, uncertain that he would consent to a little-known Irish poet for his son-in-law.

"The time of revelation is come, Fearbhlaidh," said Seamas, gravely regarding his daughter. "The borders of my land need a strong man to defend them. Come, tell me, on whom has your choice fallen?"

Fearbhlaidh gathered all her courage, lifted her chin, and said sincerely, "Of all the men I have ever looked upon, only one could I marry, and he is Cearbhall."

Seamas went pale, then red. Her words undoubtedly proved his previous suspicions of the youth. He ordered that Cearbhall be cast into a prison of stone and loaded with bonds and fetters that he might not escape.

For many days, Fearbhlaidh recognized no one, so great were her shock and grief. She left off washing or changing her clothes; she neither ate nor drank; sleep never closed her eyes. The light had gone out of her.

Only the urging of Duibhghil brought her back to herself. Throwing a concealing mantle about her, Fearbhlaidh went to the jailer and begged to be allowed to sit with Cearbhall in his narrow cell. The guard refused her twice, and it was only when she returned with gold and silver that he would agree to take the bonds and fetters off his prisoner. Then Fearbhlaidh returned with her most precious jewels and made the jailer let her in.

She said to the guard, "Please stand from the grille and give us privacy! There is no possibility of escape save through this door." And the jailer turned his back, grinning, thinking that the lovers might be allowed some brief kisses and caresses in return for the wealth that the princess had given him.

Meanwhile, without speaking, Fearbhlaidh quickly removed her clothes and put them upon the wasted frame of Cearbhall. Wrapping her thick mantle lovingly around him, she whispered, "Assume my shape and go swiftly into Ireland. As for me, leave me to deal with my father. I will be the grave of his vengeance, and I alone."

Cearbhall shivered then, for his long fasting and solitary confinement had sharpened his poetic powers of seership. "Dear love, never say so! Whatever befalls you shall befall me. I will go, as you bid, but I will return to you as best I may and we shall be together, though the hosts of the world come after us."

And with one last, lingering kiss, Cearbhall walked out of prison, leaving Fearbhlaidh in his place, wrapped in his once-bright mantle. He said to the jailer, "Treat your captive well!"

"I will do that," replied the guard.

Cearbhall made his way to the Irish ferry and returned home to his own country.

Meanwhile, the king decided that he would execute the young poet and ordered Cearbhall to be brought before him. It was not until the prisoner dropped the filthy mantle that the deception was revealed. The sad-faced paleness of his once-beautiful daughter stared defiantly back at the king, who groaned, "Well, daughter, you have been honest to your heart to the very end. I forgive you, and I also thank you for saving the poet's life." Seamas thought chiefly of his reputation now and how he might limit the damage caused by their affair and yet still have a marriageable daughter at the end of everything.

"Release her!" he ordered. "And send word to Ireland that if Cearbhall mac Donnchadh ever sets foot in Scotland, it will be his death." And to ensure that no legal redress could be sought by Donnchadh for the imprisonment of his son, he sent twelve boxes of treasure with the messenger, fully equal to Cearbhall's honor-price under the law for such an insult.

In the west of Ireland, Donnchadh also considered how this messy affair might be effaced without loss of reputation. Since leaving Scotland and after his terrible ordeal in prison, Cearbhall had been like a madman, his hair unkempt, his speech wild, and his manners thoughtless. So Donnchadh consulted druids skilled in healing, who prepared a drink of forgetfulness that would cause Cearbhall to forget Fearbhlaidh and restore his son to his former strength, ability, and good spirits.

Uncaring of what he drank, Cearbhall took the potion and was healed of his dementia. No memory of Fearbhlaidh remained; all that he knew was that he had been ill for a long time, which accounted for the strange blankness of his brain. In every other respect he was restored to strength, and he threw himself back into his craft with enthusiasm. He was even flattered and pleased when his father arranged a marriage for him with the king of Connacht's daughter, Ailbhe.

Meanwhile, back in Scotland, Duibhghil had sad work with Fearbhlaidh. The loss of Cearbhall had eaten holes in her soul. She was like a woman on whom the burden of sorrow fell first and heaviest, like one of the great northern mountain peaks that was always mantled with snow, thought Duibhghil.

When news of Cearbhall's wedding came to Scotland, something of Fearbhlaidh's former energy returned. Seizing Duibhghil, she commanded, "Take me to the wedding chamber of Cearbhall now, this instant!"

"To what end?" asked Duibhghil, cautiously, knowing well that shape-shifting coupled with this intensity of emotion was dangerous to the traveler. Fearbhlaidh's eyes were red, raw, and wild, her heart capable of any violence.

"I go to give him a message, that is all," she grimly replied.

So Duibhghil turned them both into birds, and away they sped to the empty wedding chamber where Cearbhall and his bride would sleep. Only Cearbhall's harp stood in the corner on watch. Fearbhlaidh stalked about, muttering to herself, reining in a rage that would break her in pieces. Taking out a knife, she slashed her arm, pressing up the welling blood into a pool and etching this message in *ogham* letters with the point of the knife, scoring them deeply into the neck of the harp with her own blood:

> *Donnchadh's hall rings with rejoicing,*
> *Hurting my ears with its raucous din.*
> *My friend Cearbhall prefers this uproar*
> *To marriage with my father's daughter.*
> *This is my long curse on the woman*
> *Who believes any man after Cearbhall.*

When Cearbhall came into the room later to fetch his harp, he read these words and remembered everything. Fearbhlaidh filled his mind and heart again like a long-forgotten perfume. Staring upon what was to be his marriage bed, his previous madness came upon him again, and he composed this verse:

> *The side of my harp is red tonight,*
> *Wounded with my beloved's blood.*

Sweet that hand and blessed that blood:
I bleed too for the love that wounds me.

Over and over, past dawn and beyond the time when he should have bedded his bride, Cearbhall played the harp, reciting this verse over and over. His newlywed wife and his companions struggled with him, eventually dragging the harp from his hands, but he would neither speak nor look at them. It was clear that madness had him in its grip and that he could no longer care for himself, so they took him to the retirement of a house in Aughrim.

And there two swans came daily to greet him, for Fearbhlaidh and Duibhghil did not stray far from his side. The women did not dare resume their own shapes, for a watch was being kept for them and they feared capture. Cearbhall took pleasure in the birds' company, singing to them and sharing his sorrows with them, until one day when the herdsman of that place threw a stone and hit one of the swans and broke her wing. Cearbhall fell upon the herdsman with his sword and left him dead upon the shore for hurting the creatures.

Only then did Fearbhlaidh and Duibhghil resume their own shapes, and Cearbhall was aware of them. Duibhghil's left arm was broken, beyond Fearbhlaidh's ability to heal. "Where is the stone I once gave you that healed all ills?" she cried in her extremity to Cearbhall.

And he stood upon the riverside, weeping with self-reproach, for the healing stone had been lost during his madness or when he had drunken the drink of forgetfulness—he didn't even remember. "Have you skill enough to go homeward, Duibhghil?" he asked, knowing that if the two women were captured, they would suffer for being enchantresses.

Duibhghil's voice was choked with pain. "I cannot fly, that is sure. But I can command a spirit ship to take us home, where I may be healed by my kindred." And she called a strangled cry to the winds. The airs and breezes fashioned themselves into a ship for her.

And Fearbhlaidh, torn between anxiety for her nurse and love of Cearbhall, got into the spirit ship, leaving her lover upon the shores of his own land. "We have stretched time, you and I," she called to Cearbhall. "For though the time that we have had together has been shorter than most, the little we have had is more precious to me because of the dangers we have suffered."

In the year that followed, while Duibhghil was healing, she taught as many of her skills to Fearbhlaidh as she could, since she was sure her charge would have need of the magical arts more than many women. And it was soon rumored that Fearbhlaidh visited Cearbhall in many shapes, and none could hinder her subtle movements in the realm of the Otherworld.

King Seamas had almost lost patience with his plan to marry Fearbhlaidh off to some strong successor who would sustain the kingdom. No one would marry an enchantress, which is what she was becoming. One day, looking over his ramparts, he saw two strangers coming toward the Fort of Maidens. He called them to him, asking whence they had come.

"We are newly arrived from Ireland."

"Then I have a task for you for which you will receive a great reward."

"What is your wish?"

"Only that you tell my daughter that Cearbhall mac Donnchadh is dead."

The two Irishmen agreed and went into the main hall and began to tell the news to those who asked them. Looking down from the gallery, the king thought to himself, "Maybe that news will bring my daughter to her senses."

The Irishmen talked of this and that and finally said, as an afterthought, "Oh, yes, and Cearbhall mac Donnchadh has died of a mysterious wasting sickness. The people of Connacht are grieved to lose so fine a poet."

As soon as Fearbhlaidh heard these words, she fell forward upon the *fidhchell* board where she had been sitting, as if in a faint. But when the people went to raise her, there was no life left in her. Her father flung himself toward his daughter, chafing her hands, whispering the endearments of girlhood into her ears, kissing her, cajoling, commanding her to rise, all to no avail.

King Seamas was forced to accept that his beautiful girl was dead, that he might not marry her now to any man but must bury her. Then he proclaimed that he would hang the two renegades who had brought the death-dealing news, but when the Irishmen stood before him, they appealed to his noble justice. "We spoke only what you commanded to tell. To kill us for obeying you is neither just nor fair."

The king sighed heavily. "It is true. I shall spare your wretched lives on one condition: that you go to Cearbhall and tell him of Fearbhlaidh's death without delay. If you do not obey me now, I swear that *any* Irishman who comes within my territory shall die horribly."

So the two messengers of death came to Donnchadh's school, and there they truthfully told the news for all to hear, that Fearbhlaidh was dead. And on hearing that, Cearbhall laid his head upon the neck of the harp and breathed no more.

And when all the people of Connacht heard that Cearbhall and his Fearbhlaidh were dead, they fasted for three days and nights out of respect for the lovers, whom no one could ever divide again.

CHAPTER SEVEN

HOLD ME FAST AND FEAR ME NOT

If my love were an earthly knight,

As he's an elfin gray;

I would not give my own true love

For any lord that you have.

The steed that my true love rides on

Is lighter than the wind;

With silver he is shod before,

With burning gold behind.

—"Ballad of Tam Lin"

In this Scottish tale, derived from the "Ballad of Tam Lin," Janet goes to disenchant her lover from the realms of faery. Fear of the faery people, who are most actively abroad during the major Celtic festival times of Beltane (April 30) and Samhain (October 31), has become focused on Hallowe'en today—a night on which few of our ancestors would have ventured out. The conditions of Tam Lin's release affect Janet's life and that of her unborn child, which are at great risk.

THE LORD OF Lothian was a troubled man. Since before midsummer, disturbing reports from his stewards and foresters told of women who had been raped or despoiled in the region of Carterhaugh. True, the women did not much complain and were apt to be dreamy in their reporting, uncaring of their loss, but the Lord of Lothian could not have such deeds going on within his territories.

His greatest fear he kept unspoken, for Carterhaugh was on the edge of Ettrick Forest, the lands that belonged to his only daughter, Janet. She, being a headstrong, overindulged young woman, might well take it into her head to go riding or hunting there, and then what might befall? Although he had sent bands of men to patrol the region and to make an arrest, irritatingly, not one of these had discovered the hiding place of the man responsible for these deeds. There had been no reports of attempts to rob or assault any men. This villain must be a cowardly kind of cur to attack women in this way.

Accordingly, the king issued a proclamation to be read throughout the region: "It has come to our notice that some unknown, lordless man lies in wait at Carterhaugh, ready to rob and molest females. Until he can be arrested, the Lord of Lothian gives warning that no young woman should go unattended in the vicinity for fear of theft or loss of her virtue."

Janet was incensed: these lands belonged to her, having been part of her mother's dowry. Why should she not go where and when she pleased?

Nevertheless, she lidded the fire of her dark brown eyes and listened carefully to the gossip in the hall.

"They say his name is Tam Lin!"

"The Earl of Roxburgh's son? Never!"

"Aye, he that disappeared when he was out hunting."

"Has he become some thief or outlaw that he behaves so?"

"Nay! They say that he was taken by Herself," and here the serving woman gave a knowing nod and a wink toward the Eildon Hills—the abode of the faeries.

Janet was intrigued. None of the household servants would willingly utter the word *faery* but rather nodded their heads or spoke of the "Good Folk." They all lived in dread of being spirited away for a hundred years or more, only to return after all their kindred were long dead. On Mayday and Hallowe'en, at Midsummer and Midwinter, they would place rowan branches across the window to keep out any faery spells that might harm any within the castle, with muttered charms and prayers to the saints.

Janet had little time for such superstitious stuff. Such fears were born in ignorance, flourishing in the long winter nights when the winds blew chill and drear about the stone walls, whistling and singing like ancestral voices. Janet lived in the daytime world of youth and enjoyment, loving nothing better than to mount her sweet-natured mare and gallop across the hills of her homeland.

Throughout her life, her father had forbidden her nothing. Now that she was a full-grown woman of fifteen years, she was not going to let his proclamation stand in the way of her pleasure. Without a word to a soul, she slid away to the stables and saddled her pretty roan mare. Then, braiding up her long dark hair against the wind, she tucked up her skirts and rode out, one leg on either side her mare, just as she had always ridden when she was a girl, though her old nurse thought this both inelegant and unladylike. Janet despised the sidesaddle, which was both dangerous and uncomfortable to the rider: only old wives riding to market sat like that.

No one heeded her going. The fields of barley were rising golden to harvest, and the bean rows grew green with their winding stems and heavy with pods. The herds and flocks had young to be tended, and many folk were away to the hills in lonely shielings where they slept during the fair summertime, until bad weather forced the herds back down into the valleys to safe barns and sheltered meadows. The hay harvest was being gathered in and stored, and no one noted Janet's passing.

She rode directly toward the Ettrick Forest, which had been her own special place since childhood. The land around Carterhaugh seemed quiet and peaceful, so she dismounted and tied her mare to a bush where she could reach the long, sweet grasses. From nearby, there came the snort of a horse. Her own mare pricked up her ears and gave a questioning nicker back. Although she gave little account to her father's words, Janet had had forethought enough to bring a sharp little knife, which hung from her belt. Now her hand went to her waist and drew it out.

Circling the bush, she found a milk white stallion, accoutred with fine hangings. It was tethered near the spring that rose from the ground at this spot. It certainly didn't look like the mount of an outlaw. She let the beast lick the salt of her outstretched palm, keeping watch for its rider.

As she stood there, Janet was overwhelmed by the scent of the wild roses, which opened their pink faces all around her, catching the warmth of the sun. She turned her head to thrust her nose right into the center of their yellow-stained petals and cut away a double spray of blossoms to thrust into her hair. But as she went to raise the flowers, someone stayed her hand.

A man had come from behind her, seemingly through the bush, and was holding her against him so she could not see him.

"Who gave you leave to pick my roses?" he asked, turning her to face him.

Janet saw a young, neat-limbed man dressed in green-black leathers. His ash blond hair clung to a narrow head; his tawny eyes regarded her insolently under dark brows that made one line across his fine nose. Recovering from the shock, Janet realized that this man was not much taller than herself, which helped her reassert her indignation. "How dare you speak to me like this! These lands to the edge of Ettrick Forest come to me from my mother's kin, so I'll pluck what flowers I will, young man!"

The young man gave her a wry, insolent grin. "It's a pity her ladyship's authority is marred by so much pollen on her nose."

Janet scrubbed furiously at her nose with the back of one hand and glared back, but such a grin was infectious and she gave a short laugh of self-ridicule and said, "Nevertheless, no man has ever stopped me riding where I will. These are my woods."

The man moved one step closer to her. "They may be yours in the world of men, but in the world of faery, they belong to Another," and he nodded his head toward the east. "I am Her woodward and keep Her realms safe."

The matter-of-fact way in which this pleasant young man spoke raised hairs on Janet's neck. With a rush of fear, she knew that she was speaking to one of Them—the faery kind. He, who looked so human, was anything but, and she had fallen into his way! She began to tremble violently, and the roses fell from her hand.

The young man knelt and picked them up, gazing up consideringly at her. "It is perilous to pluck anything in this wood. Those who do so must pay a forfeit to me."

Janet pulled off an armlet from her wrist and thrust it at him. "Here, take this! Give it to your mistress for the trouble I have brought."

But he did not take it. Neither would he accept her fur-trimmed riding mantle. "Two roses you have taken from over the spring," he said gravely, as if the blooms had been human souls. "Two glad lives lost, their petals spilled upon the ground." He advanced upon her now. "Only one form of recompense can be offered in their place!" And his mouth closed over hers: "A life for two lives."

Until that hour, no man had laid finger upon Janet. From his words, she expected violent death at the very least, but here she lay upon the dewy, green grass beside this unknown stranger unscathed. He offered her no violence. He only drew off her garments one by one and laid aside his own. Trembling between assent and denial, she shuddered with longing as he caressed her. She had never known men's bodies could be so white and strange in their workings. That the wandlike member of his body could enter her own was an initiation into a secret knowledge. His mouth upon hers led her into realms unknown, where he and she were as two roses upon one stem, and inside her the glory of the rose blossomed into suns of brightness until she was filled with the ecstasy of summer itself.

It was only when a thin drizzle began to fall, heralding the first of the summer storms, that Janet's eyes snapped open again. She was naked and alone and getting very wet. Shaking, she drew on her clothes, calling out for the young man to show himself. He was nowhere to be seen. With relief, she found her mare still tethered to the bush and rode home, scrutinizing every hill and homestead for familiar sights, lest the tales be true—that those who tangled with the faery fell out of time, returning home to find their kinfolk long dead in the graveyard and strangers inhabiting their houses.

It wasn't until she and her mare stumbled through the gates mired in mud and a servant called out her name and helped her stable the beast that Janet really knew herself in her own time and place.

Summer passed. Harvest was stored in the barn. Nuts were shaken into baskets. Apples sat in their individual twists of hay in the drying loft.

October winds blew drear about the stones of the castle. The women sat together sewing in the pool of light thrown by the branching candlestick. An altar cloth was forming under their busy fingers, to be a Christmas gift for the abbey. The central image of Mary the Virgin was still to be completed, and this was Janet's task. The women muttered and complained about her long absences from the work.

"She's been very out of sorts!"

"Aye, the mouth on her would sour the milk."

"Perhaps she yearns for a husband?"

"Morelike, she's been trying a few out!"

At this suggestion, the women skirled with laughter, for it was clear that Janet's waist was thickening and that this phenomenon was not caused by greed.

The Lord of Lothian was a pragmatic man. He did not wish his daughter to be publicly shamed. He spoke quietly to one of his old companions in arms, Sir Andrew, and bade him go to Janet.

Sir Andrew bowed his gray head courteously to Janet as she sat at the loathed embroidery. She had been sick three times already that morning, and her complexion was green. "Yes?" she inquired, snapping the silken thread with her teeth.

"Janet, listen to me! You bring all men in this castle under suspicion. Speak but the name of the father, and you shall wed him. If not, then, maybe it would be as well for you to marry with me. I am like to die long before you, leaving you and the bairn well set up."

Janet went from green to palest pale at these words. "Hold your tongue, Sir Andrew! You do well to speak of your death, for die you shall before you marry with me! My baby's father is no one hereabouts, but I shall not grace the child with *your* name, you may be certain!"

Thrusting the needle into the Virgin's blue cloak, Janet began miserably to consider her position. Her lover was a man unknown to her, one out of faery: he would not support her and her child, that was sure. Soon her father would force her into marriage with some loathsome man with dirty teeth and a long pedigree. Her heart yearned after the one with whom she had lain on the woodshore near Carterhaugh. He filled her heart and mind to distraction.

She cursed the peril that falls upon women who love without knowing the name or lineage of the ones with whom they lie and, more especially, her own fate for lying with a man out of Faeryland.

The next morning early, she rode there again, with no little hope in her heart. The wild roses on the bush over the spring grew no more; only their red rosehips peered from the hedge, hard as the growing bulk of her belly. There was no faery lord to greet her. Tethering her mare, Janet saw the narrow-leaved pennyroyal that grew at her feet. As she touched it, she remembered it was one of the herbs that women brewed into a potion when they wanted to be rid of the child in their womb. Until this moment, such a thought had never crossed her mind. This child was got in the heat of pleasure, and she would not give it up.

In the emptiness of Carterhaugh, her heart grew heavy and she berated herself. How foolish she had been to yearn after this man! He who lay with the Queen of Faery would have no use for the likes of her or for a human child! Perhaps it would be better to make an end of things after all? Even as she lay hand upon the herb, she heard his voice. "Do not stoop to touch that wicked herb, Janet!"

She looked gladly up, and there he was once more, her own true love. She was soon in his arms, her face wet with tears.

"Oh, Janet, Janet! What? Would you kill the dear babe we got between us?"

The accusation sank into Janet's heart like a knife. "Dear love, not for the world would I harm it. But I was hard driven with fear and doubt. Forgive me! But tell me, truly, as you love my life, are you one of Them, or were you ever a Christian soul?"

The young man gazed eagerly into her imploring face. "Dear love, I was called Thomas at the font, after my grandfather, the Earl of Roxburgh. I lived with him after my father died, but when I went hunting one winter near the Eildon Hills, the girth of my horse split and I tumbled to the ground. It was there, when I lay in faint, that the Queen of Faery caught me and took me into her hill. She called me her Tam Lin and kept me in her pleasant place."

Janet's eyes grew large at this telling. "Is there no hope of you returning to your own kind?"

Tam Lin's eyes glowed. "Every seventh year, the Queen makes an offering of a mortal man. Seven years is as a day to her, but not to mortal men: she is ever young, but I grow older. I am no longer as fair and fresh as once I was. She will be rid of me in a rite so hideous I dare not name it to you. Then she will choose another to take my place."

"Can nothing be done?"

"It can," Tam Lin kissed her, "but it will take uncommon courage for any to attempt it." He turned away his head. "I cannot ask it of you, for you are with child. The danger should you fail . . ."

"Tell me," demanded Janet, now fully restored to her former resolution. "Whatever will free you from her spells, I will do all a woman can."

Tam Lin drew away from her embrace, holding both palms to ward her from him. "Then, gentle love, listen to me! Tomorrow night is Hallowe'en, when the faeries ride out. At midnight we ride toward Milescross; be sure to be there."

"But how will I know you? How shall I be sure among so many strangers?"

"We ride in procession. Because of my renown, I shall be last. Let the black horse pass and the brown, but when you see my milk white stallion—you know him well, love—then pull the rider of that horse down to the ground."

"But won't there be other white horses in that throng?"

"Love, I will give you these tokens for you to be sure: my right hand only will be gloved; my left will be bare. My hat will be turned up and hair finely combed."

"Then what will happen?" Janet asked, frowning.

"They will turn me into many shapes as you hold me in your arms, Janet. Remember, I'm your child's father. Whatever you find in your arms, hold me fast and fear me not."

"Is that all?"

Tam Lin threw back his head and gave a hollow laugh. "All? Hearken to you, woman!" Then he drew her to him solemnly and planted a kiss upon her brow. "Here's a kiss for the bairn, and a kiss for thee," and he kissed her lips slowly and lingeringly. "These are all the remembrances I have to give you, should you fail."

Janet drew up her skirts and mounted her mare. "Never talk of failure, Tam Lin! I'll be there!" And away she rode.

The night of Hallowe'en blew in grimly. The doors of the castle had been locked and the windows barred against faery intrusion. Janet let herself out of the little postern gate and rode through the darkness to

Milescross. There were no others on the road, this night of all nights. Everyone was safely within. What would once have been a short and pleasant ride for her was now a long and weary way. She was heavier, quicker to tire. The movements of the child within her beat their own anxious rhythm, like the pounding of her heart and the thud of the mare's hooves over the dark earth.

A north wind blew tendrils of cloud across the moon's bright face, revealing the lonely stone at Milescross. It was an ancient monolith that had been carved with scenes from the Passion of Christ. The moon's light threw the western side into relief: the vinegar-soaked sponge extended on a spear by an uncaring soldier, the agonized limbs twisted upon the cross, the sad-faced Virgin with upstretched hands. None of these scenes brought Janet any comfort, nor could she sign herself against the onslaught of the faery hosts. The only talisman against evil at this hour was her love for Tam Lin.

She drew back into the shadows and listened for signs of their approach. The night was thick with dark and ancient movements; they invaded her ears like a fog. Then one sound banished that creeping darkness: a spray of harness bells, bright and clear. Janet was as glad to hear it as she would have been to hear the rumble of an honest plowing team going by, for there had been a vigilant menace in that darkness that stalked her very steps.

A large host was coming down the road, hooves faintly reverberating in the cup of the hills. Over Ettrick Water and Yarrow Water there came a shrill piping, as from thin, oaten pipes, and a deeper piping, as from the wide stems of hogweed. There was a gathering of brightness in the air, of dots that shaped together into presences, riding upon the wind. Soon they were upon her.

Bright, tall forms they were, singing and talking merrily, like people met at a feast who speak above the music, but Janet could catch no word of it. The sudden brightness in the darkness confused her, for it exploded the night into cartwheels of noise and movement. She was careful not to look too closely upon the forms that rode past her, but she was aware of a taller, crowned figure, whose brightness had a crystalline hardness raying forth from it.

Already the end of the procession was coming into sight. "The black, the brown, and the white," she kept saying to herself, and, sure enough, here they were! Oh, Christ! How might she launch herself upon this powerful throng and not be noticed? Fear almost paralyzed her limbs. These were They whom she had once thought but foolish imaginings: beings who were but small beer about the fireside at a winter storytelling. Now, their swirling whiteness, their high mirth, their potent music filled and transfixed her to a mere speck of dirt upon the earth.

It was at this moment that the child chose to kick its mother. This reminder of her urgent task brought Janet back to herself again. What was it? The tokens? The ungloved left hand, the upturned hat, the long, combed hair? She leaped forward and grasped the leg of the last rider, upon the milk white stallion, praying that it was Tam Lin.

The rider tumbled down heavily to the earth, with Janet under him. Then, suddenly, it seemed there was no weight upon her body, only a surging and a writhing. She sat up, still clutching hard. A cloud slid from the face of the moon to reveal that she had a serpent in her hands. Of all creatures, this was the one that had frightened her most in youth: the zigzag pattern down its back reminded her of the horror of the day when she had sat upon an adder and received its bite in her thigh. It had only been the quick actions of her father that had saved her then. Now, she struggled with herself, more than with the adder, to hold on.

After a vain thrashing about, the adder began to be still, and Janet stood up. But something else began to happen. The adder melted into a larger shape: coarse brown hair was under her hands. She was wrestling now with a bear, whose small, senseless eyes glared into herself. Dwarfed by the beast's bulky strength and almost quenched by its terrible breath, Janet still held on, unknowing how long it would be before it overcame her.

Then it turned again, this time into a fierce, snapping, spitting wildcat. Its brindled hair stood up, making it five times its normal size. Its teeth were near her throat; its claws straked her breast. She struggled to hold it further from her but still hold on.

Then the struggling ceased, and instead there grew a burning, searing bar of iron in her arms. Surely she would be scarred forever? And Janet shrieked then, nearly dropping the iron, which glowed red in the ever darkening night. But somehow she held on, believing in her love and saying over and over the name of Tam Lin.

Suddenly, the iron bar shrank into a red hot ember, which she tossed from hand to hand to hand as the bright gleed burned each palm. Nearby stood a pool of water, and she tossed it in, weeping with pain and frustration at having to let it go, but out of the water she spied the form of a naked man, and, throwing her mantle over him, she drew him up into the moonlight.

"Janet?"

"Oh, thank God!" And Janet clasped him to her, with cries of relief.

As they clung together, they were aware of a voice from the road. "I thought to offer up the best knight of my company to the Old Ones, but it seems that he's been stolen away."

Behind them, with the moonlight behind her, sat the Queen of Faery upon her steed. Dreadful was her face, with a murderous glint in her eye, but Janet thrust Tam Lin behind her and shouted, "The only theft here has been yours. This man belongs to our realm, not to yours."

But the Queen of Faery ignored Janet, seeking out the cautious gaze of Tam Lin. "Had I known how you would repay my loving bounty, Tam Lin, I would have been more watchful." She leaned down from her horse and grated, "I would have taken your own two eyes and put in eyes of wood. I would have taken out your own heart and put in a heart of stone."

The lovers shrank back, eyes averted from her baleful face. When they looked back, the faery host was gone by and the queen with them.

Tam Lin drew Janet to the eastern side of the monolithic stone of Milescross so that they might wait for the dawn together. As the sun arose, he turned to her. "I, Thomas of Roxburgh, once known as Tam Lin, take thee, Janet, for my wife and declare myself to be the father of your child."

Janet drew in the light of the wintry sun and turned to him. "And I, Janet of Lothian, take thee, Thomas of Roxburgh, for my husband. For I've held you fast and feared you not, and you are my own Tam Lin now."

And they kissed in the light of All Hallows Day, as the rays of the sun sought out the carving upon the other side of Milescross: where the water pots of the Marriage at Cana overflowed with the bountiful wine of love that passes all understanding.

CHAPTER EIGHT

THE SHAKING OF THE CLOAK

I knew a man whose wife once kissed my mouth

With kiss more sweet than any honeycomb,

And now no other kiss can slake my drouth

Until the ending of all time shall come.

—Anon. medieval Irish poem,
    trans. Caitlín Matthews

The Irish story "The Shaking of the Cloak" uncharacteristically shows Cu Chulainn (KOO HULL'in), the greatest hero of Ulster, at his weakest ebb, prey to love's enchantment, forgetful of his love for his wife, Emer (AY'vor). It is an unusual story in that it starkly exposes the nature of infatuation and the cross-grain of jealousy in its fabric, but it is relieved by episodes that were the mainstay of Irish heroic literature, by the high, almost comic-book, deeds of the hero and the quick-wittedness of the lovers' repartee. A potential eternal triangle is finally laid to rest by the skill of Manannan in this story.

T WAS AT the feast of Samhain, on the eaves of the dark wings of winter, that the many-colored flock of birds was seen. Three times sunwise they flew around the roof of the hall in Mag Muirthemne, to the wonder of everyone. The fact that it was Samhain, the night that the otherworldly gates of faery were open, should have been a warning to them all, but the folk of Ulster were all too busy enjoying the six days of feasting that accompanied it.

Looking upon the flock, Queen Ethne (EN'ya), wife of King Conchobor (KON'a-her), breathed her wish: "Would that I had a pair of birds, one to perch on either shoulder!" Then all the women wanted a pair.

But Emer the Beautiful whispered stubbornly to herself, "*I* should be the first to have such a pair." Her conviction came not from pride but out of a sense of what was fitting. For was she not the wife of the champion of Ulster, Cu Chulainn himself? In countless exploits, he had defended his country by his extraordinary feats and courageous deeds, and he was recognized by all as its preeminent hero.

Lebhorcham (LEV'er-kom) the Satirist noted Queen Ethne's words and slipped out to where the great warrior Cu Chulainn stood with his fellows, and he told them the wish of the women.

"Can the women of Ulster not find another to hunt birds for them this day?" Cu Chulainn cried out peevishly, for he was looking forward to the contests and games that were part of the festivities of Samhain.

Lebhorcham remonstrated with him: "If you do not go, then you will cause them to fall into one of their afflictions." This was the name given to the conditions into which the Ulsterwomen fell when they were thwarted in their desires concerning their special favorites. If Conall the Victorious failed to heed them, the women would walk crookedly, imitating his staggering gait; if it were Cuscraid Menn with his attractive stammer, then they would fall to stammering; but if Cu Chulainn thwarted their desires, then they would affect a blindness in one eye, out of regard for the battle frenzy that came upon him in combat. Distorting his still-youthful features in disgust, Cu Chulainn scowled up at the tall satirist, Leborcham. Though the chief champion of Ulster, Cu Chulainn was short and neatly made. He had never given up the characteristic stance that he had adopted as a boy of eight when he had been thrust by his extraordinary deeds into precocious hero-hood: feet wedged firmly apart, a beardless chin defiantly raised, his left arm upon his hip, his right hand firmly gripping his sword to show off his sinewy arm to best effect. And he still wore part of his hair long to his shoulders, while scraping up the front into a top-knot that gave him the height he lacked.

Now, for all this, Cu Chulainn was both the ugliest and the most beautiful of men in Ulster. In repose, his face held a beautiful sadness, but when it was contorted with the frenzy of battle, it would be as though one eye shrank into his head and the other was starting out of it in a rare ugliness that was hideous to look upon.

To suffer a bevy of lovely women going about with these afflictions was more than the heroes could bear, and they were usually quick to comply with the women's wishes. Cu Chulainn sighed heavily and called to his charioteer, "Yoke the chariot, Loeg (LOYG)!" And off they went to catch the birds.

With careful patience, Cu Chulainn brought down the birds one at a time and tied them in pairs. Then they drove back, distributed the living birds, a pair to each delighted woman, and then went homeward. But Cu Chulainn had forgotten to include a pair of birds for his own wife!

The house at Dun Dealgan was charged with the unspent storm of Emer's anger. "A pair to every women except me, your wife! None loves you like I do, yet I have no gift."

The hero stepped back from his wife's wrath. He had been so busy appeasing the women of Ulster, he had neglected his own woman and so dishonored his own household. Breathing levelly, he promised, "Whenever the next birds fly over Mag Muirthemne, you will have the finest pair for your very own." He felt that his words merely glanced off Emer's stormy heart. Truly he had not meant to single her out from all the other women of the royal court by his thoughtless oversight. It was just that they had been so long together, that she was so much a part of him, that he took her loving presence for granted.

Emer tossed her head and stalked out, unable even to look at him. She should have known from the first moment that he did not belong to her alone. All the signs were there, from his miraculous birth to the high-marked deeds of his youth. His destiny was wound with that of Ulster, and the whole of Ulster treated him as their darling, their special totem against disaster. A woman could not be married to a destiny and not fall into his shadow. She had known all along that he would always think first about his position of honor in the country and afterward he would consider her. Lately, it seemed that he cared little for her at all. The passion of their early days together had subsided into a distant formality. This was partially the fault of his many absences on active service but was also due, Emer felt, to her own childlessness. Though he had never reproached her with barrenness, perhaps her husband was already looking for a more fertile woman to share his bed. This was her secret fear.

It was not thus that he had treated her at their courtship. Then, her dark-browed, beardless suitor had come to the walls of her father's house with the riddling wit of poets upon his tongue, and so they had dialogued, using dark and subtle kennings because her father's body-guards had stood nearby. Though the guards could hear all that the lovers said, they could not understand their secret, passionate drift.

Emer unblushingly remembered what account she had then given of herself: "as the Tara of women, as a watcher who is not seen, as a road that could not be traveled." And of how she had laid *geasa* upon him and how he had unconcernedly taken them up out of love for her. Ah! Those days now seemed an age away! Her self-vaunting boasts had inflamed the hero to flights of outrageous heroism on her behalf. The story of her wooing was a well-told tale. Her famous beauty and present status rested upon that heady legend, but it did not assuage the bitter disappointment at this first clear sign of her husband's neglect. Was this to be the way of things now? A once-honored wife to be cast aside and slighted before her peers, to be the mock of every idle tongue?

Now it happened shortly afterward that Cu Chulainn was out with Loeg and their companions near Mag Muirthemne when they came upon a pair of otherworldly birds yoked together with a chain of red gold. The gentle singing of the birds caused all but master and charioteer to fall into a deep slumber.

Still smarting from Emer's jealous anger, Cu Chulainn called, "Pass me my sling, Loeg!"

"Leave these birds! They have some unknown power," the charioteer urged, looking uneasily over his shoulder.

Cu Chulainn aimed and shot, but the stone passed harmlessly through the tip of the wing feathers, and both birds descended into the lake. Loeg had never seen his master so chastened.

"From the day when I took valor as a man" (and Loeg knew that this was when Cu Chulainn had been only eight years of age), "never have I missed a cast!" And the hero staggered like a sleepwalker toward a nearby pillar stone, his soul sick within him, and slumped against it into a deep sleep.

While he slept, he dreamed that the two birds came again from the lake. As they approached, they changed into women, a dark-haired one in a green mantle and a fair-haired one in a purple mantle. The one in green lifted a horsewhip, and, laughing a mocking laugh, she struck him with the whip. Then the one in purple laughed a laugh that thrilled his blood and struck him with another whip. During the whole of his dream, he was beaten till he felt himself all but dead. Then they departed, leaving him aching in body and soul.

Meanwhile, all Cu Chulainn's companions had awoken and were disturbed by what had befallen them but even more so to see the state in which their friend lay there, twitching and turning beneath the stroke of the lashes that were invisible to them.

"Wake him quickly!" urged one.

"Nay," said wise old Fergus, "he should not be moved while he is having a vision, lest his soul be harmed."

Cu Chulainn's eyelids fluttered open. Unable to greet his fellows, he groaned in a weak voice, "Take me to the sickroom at the Speckled House."

"Surely, you would be better nursed by Emer?" said Loeg.

Cu Chulainn gripped his hand with a remnant of his former strength. "To the Speckled House of the Healers take me!" Some instinct made him seek the safe cordon of the healer's house over the uncertain welcome that he might find within his own home. And no one dared argue him. But to Loeg he whispered, "Go to Emer . . . tell her that faery women have destroyed my strength. . . ."

There he lay unspeaking for the best part of a year, until the feast of Samhain was due once more. His friends took turns to sit with him, but ever at his feet sat Emer, her face bleached of beauty, remembering that the last words she had said to him were of anger and reproof. She blamed herself, feeling that her reproaches must lie heavily upon his honor.

Looking upon his stricken, moveless form, she remembered the time when he had abducted her from her father's house, fresh from his adventures in Alba. She would never forget the day when he leaped from his scythed chariot, leaped the salmon leap over the ramparts of Forgall's house, and killed her nine bodyguards in the time that it takes to draw on a pair of gloves. How fine it had been to be carried off on the shoulders of a hero and to be acclaimed as the wife of the chief hero in all of Ulster! That golden day was like the faded song of a tale told too many times upon the tongue of a drunken storyteller. What good was the luster of high deeds in the face of enchantment's sickness? She would have given anything to snatch back the censure of her reproach now, that she might prove the worth of her love.

As the cheerless company sat in vigil over the sick hero, one in the shape of a man entered the sickroom, his form casting no shadow forward upon the floor as he stood in the doorway.

Conall Cearnach challenged him. "Who let you in?" For it had been a deep secret that Cu Chulainn was lodged in the Speckled House, guarded as it was by the magic of the healers.

With an easy smile, the stranger said, "If that man yonder were in good health, he would be the protector of all in Ulster; but in the sickness that is upon now, he is likely to be an even greater protection to you."

Fergus reached for his weapons at these dark words, but the stranger said, "I have no fear of you; I have come only to give this man a greeting."

King Conchobor raised his sad eyes from his sick foster son to the stranger and gestured his men to peacefulness. "Be welcome, then, and speak! Who are you?"

"I am Angus, son of Aedh Abrat." And he sang,

> *"Listen, Cu Chulainn, your illness will be short.*
> *They would heal you, were they here,*
> *Daughters of Aedh Abrat."*

> *So says Liban of Mag Cruach, wife of Labraid.*
> *So says Fann, whom love pierces to the quick,*
> *She who longs to lie by Cu Chulainn:*

> *"When Cu Chulainn comes to my land, led by love,*
> *Silver and gold will be his, wine in plenty,*
> *Could he but love me, come to me.*

> *"This Samhain night, go to Mag Muirthemne.*
> *I will send Liban to you*
> *And your long sickness will be ended."*

As the words were unsheathed from the mouth of the otherworldly messenger, so each one in the room experienced different wounds.

Fergus felt the wound of dishonor that he had succumbed to sleep at the pillar stone; Conall knew the pain of loss that Cu Chulainn had been absent from their friendly combats; Conchobor knew the pain of age, that the time of his own kingly deeds was gone forever; but in Emer's heart, the sear of jealousy began its slow, smoldering burn. She clutched her side with the agony of it. She felt anger that some woman other than herself should heal Cu Chulainn but then reminded herself that that surely should not matter to her, only that he might be healed of his sickness. But who was this Fann who desired her husband? And had she already enjoyed his body in who knows how many secret assignations? Love warred with bitter jealousy within her.

The song lingered in the air, but the stranger was gone. As they stared at the empty doorway, they did not see Cu Chulainn sit up.

Fergus told him sharply, "Tell us what has passed with you, foster son!"

And Cu Chulainn told them of his vision of the two faery women who had beaten him. "What must I do now?"

And the king spoke with the wisdom of his office. "You must rise and return to the pillar stone where this befell you. It is clearly a threshold place between the worlds."

But Emer clenched her teeth together, to bite back the words spurning this bad advice. Truly men were as innocent of guile in such matters as newborn children! Her husband was still clearly enchanted, for he had not uttered one word to her, and now he was bidden by his own king—whom he might not disobey—to go and seek out this enchantress, Fann of the faery world!

She sought out Loeg, her husband's charioteer, who was buffing the bronze mounts upon the harness trappings with a piece of leather to keep them from the tarnish of such long disuse.

He greeted her news of Cu Chulainn's awakening with joyful relief, but she grasped his arm urgently. "Do not be deceived by the messages of the faery folk. They mean harm to my husband, though they flatter the honor of Ulster. I know you to be a man of caution and discretion. Do not allow Cu Chulainn to venture beyond the limits of his strength. His long sickness has weakened his judgment, and the enchantment upon him is not yet over. I see it in his eyes. A faery woman has fallen in love with him. She means to lure him into the Otherworld, to our loss."

Loeg blushed at her praise and the confidence with which she entrusted him. "I will guard Cu Chulainn with all the skill at my disposal. I will endanger myself before I allow him to stain his honor." And though he sincerely meant these words, there was no way that Loeg could predict the wiles of faery women.

Emer was satisfied, but she retired to her *grianan* to implore the help of all Cu Chulainn's protecting guardians to keep his soul unscathed. She besought Lugh and the ancestors of his line, Sualtrim and Dectire, weaving a charmed breastplate of supplication that would guard his soul.

Cu Chulainn returned with Loeg to the pillar stone where they had first seen the two birds. The hero's pallor was accentuated by the thin winter light. As they looked about them expectantly, Loeg clutched his spear tighter. From the shelter of the pillar stone came the dark-haired woman in the green mantle.

Cu Chulainn demanded immediately, "Why did you come here to do me injury last year?"

"We came to seek for your friendship, not your injury." She smiled, smoothly ignoring the beating that she had given him. "I come on behalf of my sister, Fann. Her husband, Manannan mac Lír, has abandoned her, and she has set her heart on you. I am Liban, wife of Labraid (LOW'ree) the Swift. He sends word that he will give Fann to

you in exchange for one day's service to him, fighting against his enemies."

The candor of Liban's speech robbed Cu Chulainn of what little
wit was left to him. Sulkily he said, "I'm in no fit state to contend with
any man today."

"My husband will grant you back your full health if you will but
come with me to Mag Mell, the Plain of Honey. I will be your guide
and ensure no harm comes to you."

Loeg looked at his master uncertainly. These were deep matters,
beyond his skill to reckon. Cu Chulainn seemed to be gripped with
pain, but with the harsh voice of a blade being whetted on a stone, he
said, "Let your husband come to ask me himself. I never went anywhere under the protection of a woman."

The expectations of too many women pressed heavily upon him. If
it had not been for his cowardly appeasement of the Ulsterwomen in
the adventure with the birds, Cu Chulainn would not now be standing, his strength mostly gone, in foolish talk with an otherworldly
woman. "Let Loeg go and see if what you report is true." He was unwilling to commit himself to an otherworldly adventure whose out-
come seemed uncertain.

Loeg looked alarmed. He had no charms upon him to protect him
in faery realms, but, obedient to his master, he followed the dark-
haired Liban through the pillar stone that was the threshold between
his world and hers.

In that world was no sunlight; only the aftershadow or foreglow of
twilight or dawn illumined the sky. The land was charged with menace
and wonder alike. All things familiar to Loeg were in stark relief, showing sides of themselves never visible in the waking world of the sun.
He was ever conscious of Liban at his side, stronger and more confident than he. This, he told himself with rare insight for one so unre-
flective, is what it is like to be a woman in the world of men: always in

the shadow, bending to the needs and directions of men. For so he felt himself in this realm: a man dishonored.

Liban brought Loeg into the presence of her husband, Labraid the Swift.

"I greet you, Loeg, in the name of your master. Be our guest while you are here!" The greeting was perfunctory and somewhat peevish, for Labraid had expected some expert help, not Cu Chulainn's charioteer.

Sensing Labraid's anger, Liban drew Loeg aside. "Labraid is somewhat heavy in spirits today, for a conflict weighs upon him. Come and meet Fann."

She led the charioteer through halls of women lying upon their couches with varying degrees of lassitude or lasciviousness, until they came to the chamber of Fann. With her hand upon the latch, Liban turned to Loeg. "Our father is Aedh Abrat, named for the fire that is in the eye. But my sister is named for the tear that runs from the eye, for her beauty is like the clarity of a tear upon the cheek." She spoke this as a warning before she opened the door, out of which spilled the most melodious music Loeg had ever heard.

When afterward Loeg related his visit to the Otherworld, his voice breathy, his inner eye still full of its strange sights, he sang:

> *If I had not hastened away,*
> *I would have been wounded by that music. . . .*
> *I have seen the beauty of Emer,*
> *But this woman would drive armies to madness.*

Fann, her fair hair framing a face of heart-shaped loveliness, her gray-green eyes under dark-winged brows, gazed into the core of his being, and Loeg was transfixed. He remembered nothing of their conversation—if indeed they had any. All he could recall was the importance of getting Cu Chulainn to Labraid's aid so that his master might win this prize of womanhood, who would surely bejewel his honor a thousandfold more than Emer ever could.

As he listened to Loeg's account, Cu Chulainn felt the stirring of strength within him. Forgetful that his early reputation had been founded on the exploits by which he had made Emer his wife, forgetful of the duty that he owed to Ulster or to his wife, his attention tumbled headlong into the pervasive nets of the faerykind.

When Emer heard that Loeg had been to the Otherworld on Cu Chulainn's behalf, she came, distracted and alarmed at the thought that her husband might have fallen further into the clutches of her rival, demanding to know what had befallen him. Loeg was still bedazzled by the sights and sounds of his visit to faery. He sang lyrically of his experiences:

I went there in the blinking of an eye
To that beauteous country of wonders.
To the house of Labraid the Swift
Lit by gems of precious stones.

At the western door, a herd of grays
Purple maned, fleet of foot.
At the eastern door, a tree of glass
With birds perpetually singing.

Cauldrons of mead, beds of women,
And one woman, finer than all of them:
Fair and gifted one, wounding all hearts
With her dear words of love.

Emer made a rude noise at this. "Loeg, son of Riangabra, do I understand you rightly? You mean to tell me that you've been up and down between our realm and that of the *sidhe* and have brought no healing for my husband?" And she fell into a loud weeping from anger and frustration. Between her sobs, she keened, "If it had been Fergus or Conall or Conchobor who was enchanted, Cu Chulainn would not have rested until they were free! But sleep encases him. Shame to you, Loeg mac Riangabra!"

Loeg slunk off to the stables to avoid her hot, angry eyes. Emer rose and dusted the earth from her skirts, smoothed down her hair, and went to Cu Chulainn's chamber, where he lay contemplating all that Loeg had reported. She spoke his name, but he never answered her. She knew well enough that it was useless to use the words of an injured wife. With a supreme effort of self-control, she summoned up her powers of persuasion and with a triumphant, ringing voice sang out,

> *Arise, hero of Ulster!*
> *Wake in health and happiness.*
> *Regard your great king!*
> *You have slept long enough.*
>
> *Too long a sleep is the weakness*
> *That follows defeat.*
> *Long sleep is like death's counterfeit,*
> *Long sleep is for drunkards.*
>
> *Arise, hero of Ulster!*
> *Wake in health and happiness.*
> *My words are harsh,*
> *But love inspirits them.*

Cu Chulainn stirred from his dozing and passed his hand over his face. The insistence of a voice that sawed like a tree hornet had penetrated his stupor. But behind that noise he heard another sound, more beautiful by far to his enchanted ears, and its words formed into a song:

> *Labraid's house lies over the lake,*
> *Where women daily congregate.*
> *Easy the way and swift the journey,*
> *If you would be allied to Labraid.*

The song went on to sing of high deeds of battle, which stirred his blood. He rose from his bed and staggered across to the door, thrusting Emer aside, unseen, unrecognized. All he was aware of was the other song that was being sung by Liban, who stood in the doorway.

For one brief moment, it seemed to Emer that he had been awakened by her own song, but soon she realized the truth. However much she tried to prevent him, Cu Chulainn passed out of the room into a far distance into which she could not travel, a place where the light of the sun forked sharply away from where she stood, leaving her desolate and uncompanioned.

When the healers returned later to attend to their charge, they found Emer frantically trying to part the curtain of air through which Cu Chulainn had passed into the realms of faery.

Cu Chulainn followed Liban, finding with every step of the journey that he was refreshed and energized. His limbs answered him again, and he longed to wield weapons once more as a man. The enchanted sleep and lassitude had fallen from him.

Labraid and his court stood to welcome the hero of Ulster to their realms. There was much whispering and wondering from the women who thronged the hall, for Cu Chulainn was as beardless as a youth, yet his body rippled with the muscles and scars of a man.

Labraid took Cu Chulainn to one side and spoke of the combat that had been between him and his enemies: "It is prophesied that these cannot be slain by the hand of one such as I but only by the hand of a man. And it is not any man that I have asked to do this deed, but only the most famous warrior of all Ulster."

The praise was heady and the wine rich. Cu Chulainn's eyes roamed speculatively around the many women in the hall. Labraid pressed his proud mouth into a smile. "The one you seek sits yonder," he said, pointing with his golden cup. Cu Chulainn's eyes rested once more upon the fair-haired Fann, in her many-folded mantle of purple. A cap of birds' wings crowned her hair, and her eyes were ever upon him, wide as a lake, consuming as the deepest, most devouring bog. The look of her caused him to scratch his flesh in memory of the beating she had given him.

Labraid whispered promisingly into his ear, "After the combat, the rewards to the victor!"

Together the men rode out to where the opposing army encamped. The host seemed innumerable. With a warrior's eye, Cu Chulainn took in the dispositions and turned to Labraid. "My lord, depart now, and I will see to this. Be ready at twilight tomorrow to cleanse the land of your enemies."

As twilight the next day gathered, Labraid returned with Loeg. The field was clogged with the dead and dying. Labraid yelled across the slaughter to where the small, furious warrior was still laying men low, "Friend in arms, it is time to stop the slaying!"

Loeg bawled at the faery king, "It is no use! Once the battle frenzy is upon him, nothing will stop him. As it builds in fury, it's like a fire. If he continues, he is likely to kill your troops and us as well!"

"How, then, will he be restrained?" Labraid looked with horror upon his secret weapon, who had laid his enemies low single-handedly and now threatened himself.

"I will show you how!" yelled Loeg over the rattle of the chariot, expertly turning the horses' heads toward Labraid's dwelling. Leaping from the chariot, he called to the women: "Fetch three vats of cold water quickly!"

As they scurried to obey, Loeg explained, "He must be plunged into water. The first vat will boil over; the second one will be so hot after he has been in it that none will be able to bear it; the third will be heated only moderately—at least I hope so."

Soon they could see Cu Chulainn charging toward them in full battle frenzy: his whole frame quivered and his sinews stood out, his face contorted with one eye protruding out and one eye sunken in, his lifted hair spiked like a thornbush, his skin ox-liver dark, with a stream of blood showering from the crown of his head making a cloud of death about him.

"Hold steady!" cried Loeg as he leaped nimbly behind his master and threw him into the first vat. Steam poured forth and the waters evaporated abruptly. The next vat bubbled up darkly and overflowed as he was plunged in. The last vat seethed like a cauldron full of boiling stew.

"Great Plain of Peace!" cried Labraid. "We will all be slaughtered!"

"No!" cried Loeg. "Let the women strip off their clothes as quick as may be, and we will all be saved."

Without second bidding, the women threw off their clothing and stood, without a stitch on them, in a circle around the steaming hero. At the sight of their white breasts and supple thighs, Cu Chulainn's battle frenzy waned, and he was restored to himself.

Fann herself stood before him without shame, her garment carelessly thrown over her shoulder, and acclaimed him,

Who outstrips all men in slaughter,
Found only in the heart of battle,
Wielder of weapons most deadly?
No one but Cu Chulainn himself.

Seven lights shine in each eye,
Four dimples redden his two cheeks,
A single weapon he bears aloft,
Proud, lovesome, ripe for combat.

And such was the lascivious manner of her singing that Loeg blushed. But Cu Chulainn allowed himself to be draped in a fine mantle and led away by the naked women to the chamber of Fann, where he entered another kind of combat entirely.

The intoxication of Fann's victory song still echoed in his ears as, afterward, he accepted the truce of their entwined limbs. He knew now why it had been Liban who had been her spokeswoman: if any man heard Fann speak, he would be besotted forever.

In the great bedchamber hung many garments, including one of birds' wings. "I saw you first as a bird," he breathed, feather-stroking her long back.

Fann smiled. "It was the strength of Emer's wishing that summoned the image of you to my mind. She felt the slighting you dealt her so deeply: it showed me what love really was. . . ."

She kissed him again, as if to taste love at his lips.

"And so you came to me as a bird with your sister?"

Fann laughed. "And you would have caught us and caged us, but we beat you!"

Cu Chulainn wrinkled his brow, trying to remember. "It hurt! I'd never been beaten before—no one would ever dare!" And he burst out laughing at the thought of it, he who would once have killed anyone who but grazed his flesh.

Fann lifted one smooth knee, straddling his body, framing his face in her hair and flicking him with it teasingly, "But every blow that I gave, you may redeem from me for a kiss, for a touch, for a . . ."

Cu Chulainn rolled her onto her back. "I will give you back stroke for blow, my honey, never fear!" And they fell once more to the combat.

Cu Chulainn remained a whole month in that land with Fann, and every day Loeg came daily to remind his master of his duties to the king of Ulster, for he saw that they might never return from faery. He felt that after his first poor showing, he might merit Emer's praise for this persistence. Cu Chulainn's remembrance of past deeds and relationships was becoming fragmentary. He agreed to return home with his charioteer only if Fann might meet with him at the yew tree by the strand of Iubar Cinn Trachta.

So Loeg and Cu Chulainn made their way back to the lonely pillar stone where their adventure had begun over a year earlier. They discovered that a month of otherworldly time was not the same in their own world. The trees were already covered with blossom, and the March winds were already tasting the rains of April. They had been gone for a full season of their own time.

"The winter is over!" cried Loeg, joyfully glad to be back upon his home ground once more. Although he had passed the time riding and grooming the purple-maned horses who were a charioteer's delight, he would give them all up for but one handful of Ulster's earth.

"It seems to me that winter is but beginning," said Cu Chulainn, as the heaviness of mortal realms began to press upon him. As soon as he had breathed the air of Ulster, remembrance of his long sickness and its cause came back to him in full measure. And the miserable face of Emer, her reproachful words, and his failure to be a true husband to her began to scratch at his soul like branches against the shutters.

In the long absence of her husband, Emer had not been idle. In order to maintain her hope, she had visited seers, poets, druids, and diviners for help in restoring Cu Chulainn to his rightful place again. Now she heard that he had returned and that he planned to continue his dalliance with Fann, and she drew upon a deeper magic—her innate womanly skills. She took knives to the whetstone till they glinted green as the jealousy in her heart. Calling upon fifty of the women of Ulster as her witnesses and supporters, Emer made her way to Iubar Cinn Trachta.

Cu Chulainn and Loeg sat by the strand of the yew tree playing *fidhchell,* waiting for Fann to dress. They had constructed a bower out of the spring trees to be their trysting place. So engrossed were both the men in their game that they didn't notice the approach of Emer and the women. But Fann, looking out of the bower's branches, saw them and cried out, "Look! the daughter of Forgall comes with whetted knives! Her face is like thunder."

Cu Chulainn leaped up. "Come up into the chariot with me, Fann, and I will protect you. Whatever warfare Emer thinks to bring, she will not prevail against me."

Emer came level with the chariot and saw with disgust how the lovers clung together. She noted a new and boyish petulance about the mouth of Cu Chulainn and saw how the knives she bore in either hand brought pain to the faery woman. Like all the *sidhe* folk, Fann could not abide cold iron, and these knives were wholly of iron, sharp as wolves' teeth to bite and ruin the beauty of the one who had stolen her hero.

Cu Chulainn spoke evenly, "I avoid you, woman, as warriors avoid their friends on the opposing side of a conflict. Those blades in your shaking hands do not worry me. No power of woman can draw my strength."

"Oh, and if that is so, who then has shamed and weakened you before the whole of Ulster?" cried Emer, tartly.

Cu Chulainn had the grace to look ashamed at the truthfulness of her taunt.

Emer let the knives fall to the ground, her anger spent. With imploring eyes, she said, "Dear heart, if you leave me, what do you gain by it?"

Cu Chulainn felt again the dynamic magnetism of Emer as he had first known her, acknowledging that it was she had brought him to full manhood and honor in the eyes of Ulster. She had been the instrument of his formation and therefore was part of himself. Unconsciously, he fell into the deft riddling mode that had marked their courtship. "So, woman, should I not remain with this lady? Pure, bright, and skilled she is, able to ride the ocean's waves. Skilled in crafts and with a mind of crystal."

Emer matched him with an equal levity that she did not wholly feel, but she was now aware of her fifty companions' interest in their dialogue, and she made the best of things: "It is true that the woman you cling to is no worse than myself. All things red are beautiful, all new things shine, all things high are bright, and sour are all familiar things. Men lust after the thing they lack and despise what lies within their arms. By this reckoning, you are wise when it suits you." But the stream of sardonic words stuck in her throat and she wailed, "Oh, Cu Chulainn, once we lay in honor together, and so we would again, if only you favored me now."

Cu Chulainn was moved by Emer's pleading. "Upon my word as a warrior, you do have my favor and shall have it as long as I live!"

Fann drew back, appalled. "You would desert me?"

"No!" cried Emer bitterly. "It is me you should desert. Desertion sits well upon me after all this time!"

"No! No!" wailed Fann, who felt now the double blow of desertion as a certainty. First her husband, Manannan, had left her and now Cu

Chulainn. "It is I who must be given up, since it is my destiny to be forsaken!"

Cu Chulainn relinquished Fann from his protective embrace and looked upon her for the first time under the skies of his own world. Pale she seemed, ethereal as the blossom beneath his chariot wheels, unable to stand the troubles of the way. He looked upon Emer, staring steadfastly into his face as though into the eye of the sun. No amount of troubles would alter that steadfastness, he knew.

Fann approached Emer humbly yet without fear. "It is I who will go away, though I would rather remain, indeed. Emer, this man is yours. Though my arm bears him no more, yet I can wish you well the wearing of him!"

Quick as summer lightning, Emer cried scornfully, "I take no castoff of yours, woman; I but reclaim a jewel I had lost!"

Still speaking to Emer, Fann turned to look her last on Cu Chulainn. "It is an ill thing to give love to one who spurns the gift. It is better to turn away unless you are loved back in equal measure."

It was then that Manannan mac Lír, Fann's husband, found his errant, castoff wife. In the far realms of the western seas, he had heard rumor that she was engaged in an unequal contest with Emer, and he came upon the wings of the wind to fetch her home. But no mortal present saw his coming or heard their talk.

In the privacy of their bower of spring branches, Manannan took in the full misery of Fann's grief and spoke gently: "I have not left you, Fann. I was merely about my work in the deep oceans. You took my occupation for coldness and returned to your sister's house, but my love for you was constant. Will you come home now or remain with Cu Chulainn?" For he fully understood how Fann had used the desire of Emer for a brace of birds as the opportunity to win the bravest hero of Ulster and so help soothe her own hurt.

Fann looked upon her mighty husband, whom she knew to have wives and lovers in every estuary of the sea's expanse. "Either of you would be a good husband to live with. Neither of you is better than the other, since all men—mortal or faery—are alike. Yes, I will go with you, Manannan, since Cu Chulainn has betrayed me."

And from the branches of the bower, Fann called out to Loeg, "Loeg mac Riangabra, I am going hence with my husband, Manannan. He will meet my desires and not disgrace me. Tell them, Loeg, so that no one will say I crept away secretly!"

But Cu Chulainn saw Fann leaving the bower and retreating into the far distance where the sunlight seemed to bend and melt. "What is happening there, Loeg?"

The charioteer dragged the wounding words to the surface. "Since she has displeased you, Fann is going away with her husband, Manannan."

At this news, Cu Chulainn gave a great cry, and the horses of his chariot bolted and galloped across the center of Ireland until the chariot reached Tara Luachra in the southwest. There Cu Chulainn lived for many weeks upon the mountains without meat or ale, sleeping upon the high road that winds through the Luachra mountains, in the grip of madness in which the memory of Fann and of his own loving foolishness ran like a song out of tune, jangled by the full realization of his faithlessness to Emer.

When word came to Emer of what had befallen her husband, she went to Conchobor the King, and he sent out his druids and people of the gifting skills to find the hero and bring him home again. Cu Chulainn fended them off with blows and would have killed them had they not been chanting spells and charms to keep his death-dealing violence at bay. Binding his hands and feet, they brought him back to the Speckled House of the Healers and kept him without water until he begged a drop from their hands.

It was then that they gave him a drink of forgetfulness in the water so that he might have no more memory of Fann. When the healers looked upon Emer, seated at the door of the Speckled House, they prepared a similar potion for her. Wasted by jealousy, her beauty dimmed by the memory of Cu Chulainn's desertion, Emer was unable to sleep, while waking dreams plagued her remembrance like a rash of mosquito bites. Emer drank the bitter brew that they gave her. In the hearts of husband and wife, there came a raw peace over the wounds wrought by love and jealousy.

Over the great oceans, Manannan mac Lír learned of Cu Chulainn's plight. With Fann restored to him once more, the mighty ruler of the Blessed Isles could afford to be generous. The night that the druids gave the ailing couple the potion of forgetfulness, he visited the Speckled House. Taking his bright blue mantle, dyed with every shade of the western seas, he shook his cloak between Cu Chulainn and Fann, that all trace of their affair might pass from memory and so that Fann and Cu Chulainn might never, ever meet again.

And it for this reason that this story is known as "The Shaking of the Cloak."

CHAPTER NINE

THE BLOOD IN THE SNOW

Yes, let us make our claim recorded

Against the powers of earth and sky,

And that cold boon their laws award us—

Just once to live and once to die.

Thou sayest that fate is frosty nothing,

But love the flame of soul that are:

"Two spirits approach, and at their touching,

Behold! An everlasting star!"

—William Larminie,
   "Fand"

"The Blood in the Snow" tells the story of Deirdriu (DEER'dre) and Naoisi (NEE'shee), which is known among Irish storytellers as one of the "three sorrowful tellings." Deirdriu is raised from her mother's womb to be the wife of Conchobor (KON'a-her) of Ulster, yet she chooses the freedom of her desire—a modern woman's decision. It is interesting to note that here, as in many Celtic stories, it is the woman who does the seducing, not the man. (Men are understood to be more sexually retiring than women in popular Celtic culture, where women are historically the predators!) But once Naoisi has chosen to put aside his military and manly service to Conchobor, he abides within his forbidden relationship with Deirdriu with a faithful commitment that is praiseworthy in any era.

INTER EMBRACED THE secret house in the glen where Deirdriu grew secretly to womanhood. Snow lay so deep that Elathan (EL'a-han) thought it small risk to allow his foster child to emerge from her hiding place and stand for a brief time in the outside world. He had sworn to King Conchobor that no man, save himself and the king, would set eyes upon her. But surely, no traveler would be abroad on a day like this?

Long afterward, he would blame Lebhorcham (LEV'a'kom), that trouble-making, sword-tongued old bitch of a satirist. It was Lebhorcham who had urged the harmlessness of letting the girl out of her close confinement. Now, he set himself to the slaughter and flaying of a calf for his foster daughter's supper.

The girl clutched Lebhorcham's arm, awed by the chill immensity of the white-cloaked land. No wider vista had ever been hers in all her fourteen years. "Is the world so white then? I had never thought it!"

Lebhorcham gave a crooked smile and said nothing. She had been sometime visitor and companion to the child, banished here by fearful men who had commanded her death at the moment of her birth. The girl was yet unknowing of the sharp, admonitory prophecies surrounding her. Now, as womanhood blossomed upon her, so waxed the girl's power for good or ill.

Elathan worked in a cloud of breath with ax and flaying knife, stripping and jointing the carcass. From out of the still and cloudless blue, a raven swooped to thrust its beak into the sinewy remnants of the calf. And, seeing the raven feasting upon the blood in the snow, the girl went into a reverie, transfixed by the combination of the whiteness, the redness, the blackness.

Lebhorcham was careful not to break the rapture, for the girl's first exposure to the world brought visions of truth. Eventually, the girl spoke her thought aloud: "If there were ever a man whose hair was as black as that raven, whose cheeks were as red as that blood, whose body was as white as the snow, then my love would be given to him and no other till my doom."

And Lebhorcham, who had the art of prophecy as well as the skill of the well-fitting insult, replied without thinking, the knowledge already upon her tongue: "Fortune favors your wish, for such a man is near: Naoisi, son of Usnach (ISH'nek)."

"Then I will never again enjoy good health until I see him," replied Deirdriu and suffered herself to be led from the world back to her confinement.

King Conchobor rode out with a merry heart to inspect his treasure.

The secret house lay in a fold of the hills, forested thickly with arbutus, hazel, and oak. As Elathan stabled the king's great horse, Conchobor demanded, "How is she, Lebhorcham?"

She led the way up the ladder to the gallery that surrounded the girl's enclosure, skillfully lifting the secret wickerwork shutter through which the king had watched her grow these many years.

The girl was playing with a kitten in the lawned courtyard below, her tawny head bent over her task. A kitten was trying to catch the wool she had plaited, and she suddenly gave over her task and leaped up with the speed of a young doe, shrieking with glee as the kitten pounced after the broken, trailing string. Conchobor held his breath as he gazed down upon her. Her unbound hair brushed the dewy grass, and her short tunic revealed legs of white slenderness.

"Perfection," he permitted himself to breathe. Lebhorcham swiftly shut the flap before the girl could look up and spy them.

With all the reined-in discipline of his lineage, Conchobor tried to keep the youthful eagerness from his voice. "Is she ripe to be my queen?"

"She has seen three moons of bleeding."

"She has never seen a man?"

"Only her foster father and whatever male beasts we have here." The satirist bit back her riposte: what does he think, with an enclosure surrounding the girl that was three spear lengths tall, and a constant watch upon her movements?

"I hope you are not teaching her your insolence?" the king growled, for not even a king was exempt from the satirist's sharp tongue. "Ah, what is this?" he asked, picking up a square of embroidered linen worked with interwoven patterns of red, white, and black.

Lebhorcham said, "It is some of Deirdriu's work."

Unknown to the satirist, Conchobor secretly pressed it to his lips before stowing it in the breast of his shirt. He grasped the old woman's wrist: "I charge you, make her ready for me. I will come with an escort of honor to conduct her to Emain Macha within the month."

Lebhorcham watched him ride away. Mother of all! She would have to work swiftly if Deirdriu was to have any liberty from her fate.

❧

Deirdriu rummaged through her work box with growing agitation. "It's not here, it's not here!"

"What have you missed, my heart?" The nurse continued her spinning, knowing full well.

"My *aisling* (ASH'ling) is gone, my vision token." The blood in the snow that raised such longings in her was her constant vision, her *aisling*. Her heart full of it: amid the ice of winter, the fire of desire. The intertwining threefold red, black, and white pattern of her embroidery was her talisman of that longing, a half-understood, unfigured reaching out toward what she could not say. But yet, Lebhorcham had named a name, had she not? A man called Naoisi.

The satirist carefully did not comfort Deirdriu within her arms as once she would have done. "You are now a woman, and the time for love's toys is past. All my life I have cared for and tended you, and I love you too much to consign you to Conchobor who has kept you here since you issued from your mother's womb into these hands. She died bearing you, and I am all the mother you have ever known. Now I rend the cord that has kept you prisoner in this kingly womb of watchfulness." So saying, she sheared through the thread she had spun with a sharp knife.

Deirdriu gasped, like a child taking its first breath, all anger ebbing from her in surprise. "What is this story you have kept from me? Tell me!"

"It begins in autumn, season of your birth, when the berries clustered on the mountain ash, when Conchobor and his Red Branch

Warriors came to the hall of your father, Fedlimid. Your mother, Dearbhla, was called to pour the mead, though she was full to the brim with you at the time, but honor required it. But as she rose to leave, there came such a shrieking and wailing from her womb that the warriors in that band turned pale as women. She was brought before Cathbad (KA'vad), the king's druidic father, and she appealed to his prophetic vision. "Handsome, powerful druid, I do not have the white words of vision. No woman knows what she bears in her body. Who cries out?" And he, without touching her, uttered this prophecy:

> From your womb's cradle a woman cries out.
> Champions will contest her, kings woo her;
> A harvest of warriors will be reaped
> And laid in her lap.

"And only then he laid his hand, with its seeing fingers, upon her belly, and he said, 'It is indeed a girl; Deirdriu will be her name, for so we call sorrow.'

"And at your birth, he uttered verses of your fame."

"What did he say?" The girl's uplifted face was enthralled in the firelight.

"Oh, that you would be envied by queens for your fame and beauty and that many warriors would come to grief for love of you."

"Then how did I come here?" Again Deirdriu asked the question that Lebhorcham and Elathan had carefully never answered till now.

"When the warriors heard that you might be the cause of their death, they urged the king to kill you, but he, noble and honorable man that he is," she said, and Deirdriu did not notice the bitterness in Lebhorcham's voice, "he set a mighty *geis,* a sacred binding, upon you. He said that he alone would have the trouble of rearing you, since the power of a king would overset all contention, and that he alone would have the trouble of bedding you. You are to be his wife, and for that reason have Elathan and I been your foster parents in this quiet place."

The silence lengthened as the words fell and formed themselves into a pattern she could understand.

"How is it with you, child?"

Deirdriu raised her eyes from the fire. "It is as though I have always known this—here," she struck her breast, "and here," she clutched her womb. "Ah, nurse, I am trembling."

Lebhorcham pulled a cloak about her shoulders, but the girl continued to shake. "Come!" she commanded. "It is time to break the *geis*."

Deirdriu held back in fear, for a *geis* might never be broken without offense or the retribution of the elements.

Her nurse stamped her foot with impatience. "Do you not want your freedom? Freedom to follow your heart's desire?"

And Deirdriu's *aisling* returned to her as strong as the sense that impels the migrating skeins of geese to lands they have never seen. Inarticulate with expectation, she nodded. Lebhorcham opened the outer door, pulling Deirdriu through the labyrinth of screens that obscured the passage between the house and the world outside, until she was truly born to the freedom of the wide world.

Still trembling, her teeth chattering, Deirdriu for the second time stood outside the womblike house that had sheltered her for fourteen years. The night was moonless, yet the stars brightened the sky as goose eggs in grass.

Deirdriu spoke like one in a dream. "Twice have I seen this world. First it was white; now it is black. What color will it be when next I see it?"

And Lebhorcham's mind screamed an answer that she did not voice at this time: "Red, I see it red; the red rain of Ulster will be your tears, and your grave will be in every heart."

Lebhorcham led Deirdriu through the night to Emain Macha. From time to time the girl, who had never know anything but comfort and the immediate answering of desire, would stop and cry, "It is a dark world you have brought me to! I want to go home to the fire."

"Stay close, and you will have your heart's desire, child."

She led on relentlessly, along the highway, until the walls of Emain Macha stood before them and the dawn was upon their right hand. And with the dawning, a quietness fell upon Deirdriu as she looked into the northeast, for a song began.

The singing was the melodious dawn greeting that Naoisi always raised, for it was said that the singing of Usnach's sons would cause each cow that heard it to give two-thirds more milk and that men who heard it would wake content and full of pleasure. It was the voice that brought peace and plenty, thought Lebhorcham.

But for Deirdriu the song and the sunrise were one thing, indivisibly and mystically connected. "Ah! now I see why you have brought me to this place, good guide! This is the third world, red as the blood in the snow in my *aisling*."

As the disk of the sun rose red, the docile cattle rose from their grassy beds in the pasture and began making their processional way toward the milking sheds. Deirdriu ran to urge them on, caught up in the music of the moment.

The singing ceased, and the singer said to her, "What a fine heifer leaping past me!"

Deirdriu halted, turned, and saw the man of her *aisling*. A man with skin so pale and hair so dark that his features might seem like wounds in the whiteness of his face were it not for the healthy color in his cheeks. She suddenly understood from the lifting of the hair upon her body, from the strange and pungent smell of his body, the meaning of maleness—a tangible and overwhelming presence that was not female but wholly different.

As fast as her heel had turned, her tongue responded, "Well might the heifers be fine when there are no bulls running with them."

Naoisi looked upon the tawny hair and the amber eyes of the woman before him and was troubled, for he suddenly guessed who she might be. "Ah, but your bull is the chief of the province, is he not—even the king of Ulster himself?" He spoke softly.

"Then I would choose between you both and take the younger bull for my own—even yourself, Naoisi mac Usnach."

Then Naoisi knew that he was right and that she must be a seer to know his name, when all Ulster knew that she had been incarcerated since her birth and had seen no living man but her foster father and the king in all that time.

"That cannot be so!" he said, courteously repelling her charm. "I fear the prophecy of Cathbad."

Deirdriu's brows joined together. "Are you rejecting me?"

It was Naoisi's turn to look down. "I am indeed!"

Deirdriu's anger swelled then, and with the art of Lebhorcham and an instinct entirely her own, she seized both his ears and cried out her own *geis* upon him. "May these be two ears of shame and mockery unless you take me with you!"

"Get away from me, woman! Would you shame me to my ruin?"

"Too late, for I will never let you go," she cried, desperate that the *aisling* of her heart should not depart.

Then Naoisi raised his voice in a singing that brought no pleasure to the hearer. The Red Branch Warriors within Emain Macha leaped from their beds and began fighting one another, so powerful was the confused urging of his song. Naoisi's brothers woke bewildered and rushed out to restrain their brother. "You have set the Ulstermen by the ears with your terrible song!" they cried.

"No! Here is the one who has set them on!" Naoisi swore. "A more perilous foe has never come against these gates till now!"

When Ainle (ANN'ly) and Ardan mac Usnach grasped who had suborned their brother, they went pale indeed. "Evil will come upon us because of this, and you will be reproached and shamed for it as long as you live," said Ardan, eyeing Deirdriu coldly. But Ainle, the youngest, had a more tender heart. "Let us go with her into another province. There is no king in Ireland who will refuse us welcome, for we are the nephews of Conchobor."

Naoisi looked upon her and groaned. It seemed to him that the girl could not know her power. Was she not a child in a woman's body? And from some secret territory of his heart there arose the scent of strange freedoms that he had never allowed himself. His whole manhood training in arms and in clan responsibility began to melt and buckle like bronze in a crucible.

"I will take her and let no man sunder us," he swore aloud, "though the world turn against us."

Lebhorcham set aside her satirist's weapons and sang praise to the young man: "Courage and swiftness of foot be yours! Then I leave her in your care, for none ever impugned the honor of the Sons of Usnach. May your shield arm shelter her and your sword arm defend her against the world!"

Then she beckoned Deirdriu to her. "You have seen the whiteness of winter, the blackness of night, and the redness of the dawning. Now I send you out into the many-colored world with the man of your desire. In my teaching, I have given you such weapons as women alone can use and none can take them from you. No woman will reproach you for your love."

Deirdriu asked, "But what of the reproach of men?"

Lebhorcham's lips drew tight as a miser's pouch. "Though the white world turns till doomsday, women will never want for that!"

Deirdriu and the Sons of Usnach fled, making camp by Loch Erne. Too tired to talk, Ainle covered the embers of the fire with earth to give no warning of their whereabouts, while Ardan stood guard near the horses.

Naoisi looked to Deirdriu to make up their bed and fetch water but soon saw that she had no more idea of it than a child and directed his hard-ridden brothers to the work, though they grumbled sorely at having to do a woman's work. Deirdriu stared into the fire, forgetting to turn the hastily made bannocks on the flat stones, unaware of the resentment she was causing. She knew it was too late to go back to her house of fosterage and was glad. Today she had precipitated events for the first time in her conscious life, but now she must trust to the skills that Lebhorcham had taught her.

When they had eaten and his brothers and followers had withdrawn to a decent distance from the smoored fire that had been covered with ash, Naoisi turned to her. "You can put shame upon me, but you cannot make me shame my lord and king." And with the deliberation of a condemned man, he tore a blanket in half and laid both parts upon the young bracken, with a careful space between them. He lay down upon the one, hunching his back toward her, and fell into uneasy slumber.

He woke suddenly in the deep night to find her upright, her head turned as though listening, her eyes glittering.

"What is it?" He rose on one elbow to reach for his sword, fearing the expected pursuit.

She gave a laugh full of tears. "That you should have known this freedom all your life, while I have been severed from it!" And the curve of her hand described the wide, wooded hills, the deep and silent lake that reflected the mesh of stars hung above them.

With a wondering exactitude, as though following a preordained ritual, Naoisi held out both hands to frame her face. In the dull fire's glimmer he read the waste of childhood, the lonely, bitter imprisonment of the heart, without friend or foster sister. Resentment and duty dropped from him.

What had *he* been? But one steer in the Bull-Lord of Ulster's run! As near confined by duty as this little one had been by walls. But even as he relinquished his duty to Conchobor, his uncle, he took up new service. His destiny henceforward would be to give back what had been stolen from Deirdriu.

He drew her down and folded his cloak over them both to keep out the reproach of the world.

Their progress through the kingdoms of Ireland was speedily reported to Conchobor as he sat in his hall. "Why did you not counsel me to kill her when she was born?" he asked of his druidic father, Cathbad.

His forehead gleaming with the prescience of his kind, Cathbad was the only one not to flinch from the king's jealous rage. "The fact of Deirdriu's existence was preceded by a cry that is not yet silenced." His grave, level voice brought some measure of calm to Conchobor, who went on resentfully, "Her beauty was mine alone. The Sons of Usnach have robbed me. She shall be restored yet. I will send such weighty messages through the land that no king or chieftain will dare to give them shelter. Is this your counsel?"

It was beneath a druid to shrug, so Cathbad answered, "You are king of the *fidhchell* board and its pieces are yours to command; yet love is a troublesome companion and will not be commanded." After all, the Sons of Usnach were his own grandsons and had a special place in his heart.

Conchobor's bull-like nature was strong upon him: "It is no longer a matter of love, but a matter of property."

"Then Your Highness has judges of legal perspicacity and warriors of swift expedition with which to restrain the ones who rob you. You will be advised by them," replied Cathbad and drew his hood over his face to indicate that, even to the king, he was no longer consultable.

Meanwhile, in the *grianan* at Emain Macha, where the women gathered to weave and gossip, the name of Deirdriu ran like a shuttle of bright thread about the sunny room.

"To think our lord saved her from the death she richly deserved!"

"And now she lies without roof or protection to spread her thighs to that traitor."

"They say she sleeps not only with Naoisi but with his brothers too," shrilled one woman, voicing the suspicions of many.

They did not see the entry of Lebhorcham with her lap harp. "Would you sully the soul of a woman that shines fairer than the sun? As you have spoken, so shall you be judged." And, with dread, the women saw how she threw back her head and closed her eyes, the better to read the prophecy that lies beyond earthly vision, and shuddered: "The black shielded beetle will dissolve your bones to dust and ashes in the wind, and the wise red one will level this *grianan* lower than your foul minds, before Deirdriu's soul rides home along the pathways of the blessed."

And so did Lebhorcham proclaim the doom that awaited Emain Macha.

The next day, a runner came from the corps of warriors Conchobor had set to follow Deirdriu and the Sons of Usnach to tell him that they had fled Ireland for Alba (Scotland).

For a king, the theft of a wife was, after all, a serious matter; it touched the propriety of his kingship, and it was only as king that he might defy the common report that salted the tongues of his people. That they fled toward Alba was both gall and gladness to him: gall that they were beyond his reach and gladness that the cause of his shame should be far from him. He drew off a bronze armlet of curious workmanship to reward the runner. "Let the pursuit cease, but send spies into the land of Alba to discover news of their whereabouts."

Across the sea, in the wilderness of Alba, the Sons of Usnach found a narrow glen in which to hide with Deirdriu. Raised in the pleasant plains of Ireland, they wandered like children among the great clefts of the heather-smothered hillsides, foraging like deer.

It was among the mists of Alba that the love between Deirdriu and Naoisi first drew breath, encompassing them in the same cloak. For there had been no space for them to know each other's heart, harried as they had been in Eriu from shore to shore, never able to lodge freely or engage in the service of any king for fear that Conchobor would suborn any who offered them shelter. It was upon Ardan and Ainle that the chill of exile fell heaviest, for the lovers had discovered the inner country where want, cold, and hardship do not reign.

Into that land of wonder and delight they stepped together, urgent to be always together in one embrace, careless whether they slept when the short nights of summer were crowded with promise of love. They roamed through summer's brightness and autumn's bounty, their love flourishing unchecked. Such was the even temper of Naoisi that Deirdriu often wondered at the harsh words Lebhorcham had winged toward men like so many midges, for his love was equable as June. He was her center, her song, her midsummer's day.

As autumn brought equal day and night, so they found themselves frequently benighted under outcrops of rock to shelter from the rain, heedless of damp, licking each other's faces of raindrops and falling back upon the bracken to rekindle their desire.

But winter laid its thick cloak about them. Game was scarce and the ways hard. Ardan and Ainle had to venture farther afield in search of food. After several days of fruitless quest and empty traps, they returned late one evening with the carcass of a yearling bull calf. They avoided their brother's eye, for, like him, they knew that such sweet meat did not roam unaided into their glen. The days of plenty were over, and the lean, dishonorable days of raiding had begun. Deirdriu and Naoisi hastily skinned the beast and cut it into collops for the cauldron. Deirdriu had become an expert at preparing food in all circumstances and had learned as much about stalking and woodcraft as the Sons of Usnach.

"We ate the raw liver, brother," Ardan said.

Ainle stammered, "We were weak from the cold."

But soon even the last sinews of the animal had been consumed. Then there came a week of thick snows when the men were unable to force a passage through the drifts. They stayed the pangs of hunger by boiling snow with a few precious loganberries in it. At night, the knife-bladed wind cut through their rough shelter, where they lay cold and hungry. The sound of Deirdriu's hungry, sleep-folded moans, she who was so silent and patient with their ineffectual hunting, drove Naoisi to action. He roused his brothers.

"As soon as we can force a way through these drifts, we will seek service with the king of this place. If the snows remain we will be forced to become horse eaters or worse." Ainle gagged at the thought of consuming his patient dun mare that had suffered the voyage from Ireland in an open curragh without fear. "Will the Pictish king take us in?" he asked. Naoisi licked his frost-cracked lips. "He must."

The brothers agreed. "Besides," said Ardan earnestly, "Deirdriu is likely breeding and will need women to attend her soon."

The cloud of Naoisi's breath froze in the still air. "Is it possible?" He stared down at the tumble of bright hair sprawled on the bracken, framing Deirdriu's pinched face, from which all other color had drained.

Ardan grinned at his brother's innocence. "Are you a man? Is she a woman?"

"We should have saved her the liver," rebuked Ainle.

Seven winters passed. The years of her two children's youth passed swiftly for Deirdriu, on the banks of Loch Ness. Naoisi and his brothers were often absent about the affairs of the Pictish king who had taken them into his service, while Deirdriu remained at home. It was the children who filled her days. But it was their laughter and games that were the cause of her sorrow, for it was while she ventured out into the lark-filled air that the Pictish king's steward saw her beauty and rode swiftly back to court. "There has been no woman worthy to be your wife before this time, but now I have found her, the wife of Naoisi the Irishman. She lives on the shores of Loch Ness, and she is very fair."

And from that time, the Pictish king begged Deirdriu to leave Naoisi and come to him, and when his wooing and pleading, his gifts and inducements did not move her, he caused the Sons of Usnach to be placed prominently in every hard combat and every bloody battle. But always they survived.

Naoisi said to Deirdriu, "We must leave this place and settle elsewhere, or the king will find worse ways of binding you to him." And his eye fell upon the playing children so that Deirdriu's heart filled with horror.

And Naoisi, who ever held her needs foremost in his heart, began to feel like a murderer. "My love, though you will hate me, yet the children must be sent to a place of safety."

Deirdriu's hands covered her face to blot out the sight and sound of the knowledge that flooded her heart. Yet Naoisi went on, his own heart breaking, "I have arranged for them to go where they will come to no harm, to my great-grandfather's fosterer, Manannan mac Lír, in Emain Abhlach." For Naoisi was kin to Aengus Og, Lord of the Brugh, one of the undying ones of the faery hills, and Manannan was such as he, Lord of the Seas and a mighty mover in the affairs of the Otherworld.

Like a man on a runaway horse, Naoisi plunged on. "It is better so: Gaiar will become a poet, and our little Aebgreine will marry a faery lord. They will know no sorrow such as we have seen."

Deirdriu raised brimming eyes to him. "No, nor know the laughter and freedom that we have had either!" For, of their short years together, she valued most the freedom to look upon the high hills and then to walk upon them when she would, to wander down to the shores of the loch and enter the double embrace of the land reflected within its depths.

Conchobor sat in his hall, surrounded by his clients and followers, listening to the recitation of his renown among the great of Ulster. The hall was full of people and the fire well banked up. He drew forth from his breast the fine piece of embroidery that Deirdriu had made in her girlhood to mop the fine sweat beading his brow. He had put her from his heart this long while, or so he told himself, but the three interweaving colors on the linen and the place where he kept it told another tale.

Lebhorcham's world reeled. She had not known that he possessed it. She shuddered to herself. "He has the *aisling* of her heart, and now he will find a way to trap her again."

Conchobor rose to his feet, and the steward swung the great musical chain that hung from the ceiling of the hall to bring silence to the company. "Is this not the best of hearths in the whole of Ulster?"

The men roared their good-humored praise, for they had eaten and drunk well. "It is!"

"Is there anything wanting in this household?"

"Nothing!" they bellowed back.

"Well, it is not so with me," announced Conchobor in a voice of tragic gloom, and the virile badinage rippling round the hall swiftly ceased.

"The want that is upon me is for the three best candles that the household ever had, the noble Sons of Usnach."

There was a shocked silence, for it was a brave man who would broach this subject openly in court, and now here it was on the king's own drunken lips!

"They should not be absent from us; their brave deeds should not be denied us . . . because of any—woman." And his voice rose to a drunken mocking bellow that placed women beneath the level of worms in the earth, beneath maggots in the meat, beneath fleas running circuits in a hound's coat.

Lebhorcham pressed her back flat against the wattles of the wall to avoid the foul blast of contempt that emanated from that place. As a poet, she was the only woman in the hall; the servers had retired, and the court women were in their own feasting hall. "Now it comes!" she thought. "Now comes the corroding tide of anger and jealousy; now swells the filth of the Bull King in his little barn!"

Conchobor had them in his hand, for there was no man present who would want to harm the Sons of Usnach; not one was keen to be the instrument of the king's vengeance. They were all glad at heart that he had overset his jealousy to consider them again. "I have sent a messenger to bid the Sons of Usnach home to us, but they have said they will not come unless three men guarantee their safety: Fergus mac Roich, Dubhtach (DU'tak) the Backbiter, and my own son, Cormac."

There was a ripple of wonder round the hall at the three men whom the Sons of Usnach had chosen for their guarantors: for Fergus was stepfather to Conchobor and the most respected commander in the Red Branch Warriors; Cormac was a wise choice, since he was Conchobor's son; but Dubhtach the Backbiter was the most avoided warrior of Ulster, for he was a fierce, grudging, solitary fighter.

Conchobor beckoned the three men to him and sounded them out. "What would you do with me if I should send you to the Sons of Usnach and they were to be slain through me—a thing that I do not intend, of course?"

Fergus answered forthrightly as the elder ambassador: "Your own blood would be safe from my hand, stepson, but no Ulsterman would escape me who harmed the Sons of Usnach."

Dubhtach added fearlessly, "Any that harmed them would get a shortening of his life and know the sorrow of death from me, whoever he was!"

Cormac answered, "Father, I should remain your son and keep faith with you, but know that I must follow Fergus in this matter."

Conchobor nodded, expecting no other answer than this. Dubhtach was but one man, after all, a threat that could be easily averted. "Then, Fergus, I place you under *geis,* as the senior of this expedition, to bring the Sons of Usnach home to me. They are not to eat the food of any other household in Eriu until they have first eaten at mine. See to it!"

A flight of geese passed overhead, honking far up in the cloudless star banks.

"Oh, what is it?" whispered Deirdriu, peering into the darkness. She had slept badly that whole week and had woken everyone only the night before with nightmares about a ghastly hound howling.

Ardan was, as ever, rash in his answering. "Did you never hear of a goose passing over your grave?"

Deirdriu gave a convulsive shudder and closed the door of their shelter. Winter was coming and with it the long battle to survive the cold. All three men longed for the pleasant mildness of an Irish winter. They had not told Deirdriu of the messenger whom Conchobor had sent that summer, but they all longed to return to Ireland that they might rest and put an end to their long flight.

It was not long after dawn that they heard a shout from the harbor, a shout in their own tongue, not in the dark language of the Picts. The three brothers were down at the water's edge as eager as hounds, with no word to Deirdriu.

She followed them at a distance with a heavy heart, for she had long divined that the brothers had held some secret from her. The greeting that the Sons of Usnach gave their three visitors was answer enough—the good humor that was suddenly upon black-browed Ardan, the sudden lightening of Ainle's shoulders, the radiant friendship and gladness that glowed upon Naoisi—and she drew into herself, knowing no like joy, having no kinship or friendship with any save Lebhorcham.

The welcome that they gave the strangers spoke a new truth to her. For the first time she realized that what was freedom for her was imprisonment for the men. For her, Alba was home and Ireland exile. For them, Alba was the exile and Ireland home. There was no reconciling this, and it was worse for her than after the children had gone into fosterage with Manannan, safe in the haven over the water, beyond the druidic mists of the Apple Island.

The strangers checked at sight of her. They saw a tall woman with tawny hair, in a dress so plain that a slave might have spurned it, save that this woman held herself so straight and her hair was so long that she could be no slave. As Fergus looked upon her, old though he was, he felt the dark stir of desire within him, and something like pity for Conchobor rose in his breast and swift comprehension of just why

Naoisi and his brothers had tarried so long in exile. The days of his own passionate youth returned to him as he made a knee to Deirdriu in homage. "Daughter of Fedlimid, I give you greeting! Jewel of the Western World, you are the wonder of all women!" For it seemed to him that her power to instill love was the greater because she bore herself innocent as a girl of the world yet with a woman's beauty.

In Dubhtach's narrow soul, the sight of her was like flame to tinder; here was a woman to die for. To him, Deirdriu had the straightness of a well-forged blade, for he was one for whom the sword alone was companion as long as there was a cause to defend.

His two companions wondered at the fierceness of his bow, like one warrior saluting his enemy before finishing him off, but he flung back his head and said, "Lady, sudden is your attack and certain your quarry!" And he stood as swiftly as he had knelt, but as a man who had been unsworded in combat.

Cormac's bow was more reserved, for he had not yet looked her in the eye, fearful that the spell of her beauty should move him to acts intolerable to the son of a king, but the banal courtly greeting that had hovered on his lips evaporated when he gazed up at her. "Queen of Women, the songs are tuneless that sing of your beauty. Say but the word, and I shall draw down a skein of birds to adorn your neck." And he rose, blushing at his own importunity.

And Deirdriu looked upon all three—the old one, the fierce one, and the young one—and turned her eyes to where the Sons of Usnach stood and said to them, "I never saw men before I looked upon you. Now these men teach me to praise you as you deserve, for you have kept me safely and given me the run of the hills and rivers, for you have hunted for me and sheltered me, for you have brought me comfort and laughter where no laughter was before. And for all this I thank you forever." And she turned suddenly and went from them, never seeing the sudden anger that impressed Naoisi's pleasant features.

He began to say to his guests, "Forgive her lack of welcome," but Ardan clapped his fellow warriors across the shoulders and asked, "What is the news in Eriu? Tell us, for we are empty of deeds!"

When the envoys were abed, Naoisi went to confront Deirdriu. He rebuked her: "Our guests brought us good news and welcome from Eriu where we looked for none. Why could you not have been more courteous?"

"I am not schooled in such things. I was brought up apart from men."

Naoisi moderated his temper. "Come home, Deirdriu?"

"It is not home to me."

"But home is where we are together!" And he drew her into his arms, but she did not kindle to his touch.

"You are mightier here than there and the client of no man. You are all the king I desire!"

Her soft hands upon him suddenly did not signify, for they were embroiled in their first and only quarrel.

"Why will you not return and trust Conchobor's welcome?"

Deirdriu, who knew the grasp of Conchobor's welcome better than any, said, "I had a dream and vision. Three birds came with honey in their beaks to us from Eriu; they left the honey with us but bore back three drops of blood. That honey is the bird lime that will entrap us."

Naoisi snorted and schooled himself again. "But, love, Fergus is our honorable friend, and Dubhtach and Cormac—none of them would harm the honor of the Red Branch war band."

The words spilled from her lips in a torrent of fear: "It is not Fergus I fear or Dubhtach or Cormac, but the one who reaches through them and will not let us live in any quietness but one!"

Naoisi's jaw became hard with the years of exile and the promise of forestalled restoration due to one woman's selfishness. "Oh, so because women dream and dogs howl and geese fly overhead, the Sons of Usnach are not to live in the open sunlight of honor again. Is that the way of it?"

And Deirdriu turned her face to the wall, not to see the mask of hatred torturing that dear face. "I have seen and spoken. You will go and take me with you, and I will not speak of it again."

☙ ❧

As the coast of Alba retreated into the sea mist, Deirdriu alone sat in the stern of the ship, facing the land behind her, which had sheltered their love so kindly. And she sang her farewell to the land, so softly that Naoisi and his brothers might not hear it:

> *Dear to me the land of Alba, land of wonders many;*
> *I would not have left you had Naoisi not brought me away.*

> *Beloved Dún Fídhgha, Dún Fionn, beloved shelter where we lay,*
> *Short was the time we had together, Naoisi and I in Alba.*

> *Glen Massan, tall in wild garlic, deep in hart's tongue,*
> *Broken—but sweetly—was our sleep above your river mouth!*

> *Glen Etibhe, where my first house stood,*
> *A cattlefold of the sun was Glen Etibhe!*

> *Beloved Alba of the firm strand, beloved water over the clean sands,*
> *I should not have left you had it not been for my best beloved.*

And the seal folk brought her song over the gray seas to the land of Alba, a song that was a passionate farewell to its dear land and a deeper farewell to the love that had flourished within its shores.

When the ship landed in Ireland, Fergus was greeted by an old comrade who bade him share a feast with him.

Fergus turned gray, then ruddy, for it was his binding *geis* never to refuse a feast when it was offered; but he was also under *geis* to Conchobor not to let the Sons of Usnach eat at any table save that of the king. Yet worse was the third *geis* that he had sworn: not to allow the Sons of Usnach to suffer any harm while they were under his protection.

While Dubhtach and Cormac fell to arguing how the matter could be arranged, Deirdriu came forward, drawing aside the veil with which she hid her beauty while among men, and very simply kissed and embraced her brothers-in-law. "The journey is finished," she said to Naoisi. "Now the way is but short," and she kissed him also, lingeringly, so that the brothers turned blushing away not to intrude upon their passion. And Naoisi accepted Deirdriu's kiss as one of shared joy at their safe arrival, though her face seemed to him empty of emotion.

The wrangling of the envoys went on, and Fergus came to the brothers saying, "Naoisi, I will not forsake you. Travel on to Emain Macha with Dubhtach and Cormac, and I will send in my place my two sons, Iollan and Buinne, to go with you."

"Wise friend, it is more than we have had this many years, who have been under our own protection till this day!" said Naoisi lightly, sensitive to the warring obligations that had been put upon his erstwhile commander in arms. "We will journey on to Emain Macha."

They made good progress, though the way seemed long, such was the men's desire to be among their fellow warriors once more, but Deirdriu rode more slowly so that they continually had to be waiting for her to catch up. Naoisi rode back for her as they approached Emain

Macha. "Why do you delay? There is nothing to fear, with our friends to stand surety for us!"

Deirdriu raised her head from her breast. "We were always of one mind, you and I. Will you not hear my warning for the last time?"

Naoisi turned his horse's head impatiently. "Speak, then! I have no wish to go against your desire."

"This is the sign by which you will know if Conchobor intends you harm or not: if he invites you into his own house, then there is no treachery in him. But if he invites you into the Hostel of the Red Branch Warriors, then he means to destroy you."

Naoisi kissed her hand. "A portion of your fear upon the high mountains, a portion upon the deep seas, a portion upon the gray stones. With peace we shall be greeted, never fear!"

But when they arrived at Emain Macha, it was to the Hostel of the Red Branch Warriors that they were taken; and when they sat down to eat, it was from Conchobor's own table that the food and drink were brought. But while the men fell upon the food after their long voyage and overland journey, Deirdriu took herself apart, for she could not stomach the bread of treachery.

Now that he was sober, Conchobor had the strength to wrestle with his jealousy. He did not wish to destroy his three nephews, yet . . . It was hard to decide how to act. Since the envoys' departure, he had made a sudden and much-wondered-at peace with his long-term enemy, Eoghan mac Durthacht (YEW'an MAK DER'okt). With Eoghan came a large contingent of mercenary troops from overseas. Thinking to cover his deeds, Conchobor said to himself, "Let it not be said that it was by the hand of an Ulsterman in the service of Conchobor that treachery was done!"

He called Lebhorcham to him. "Go to the Hostel of the Red Branch Warriors, and bring me word: does Deirdriu have the same bloom of beauty upon her that she once had? If she is spoiled and withered, then Naoisi can keep her, but if she retains her former appearance, I will bring her out from there against the Sons of Usnach, whether they are my sister's sons or not."

Lebhorcham's premonitory soul leaped like a salmon in a fish trap at his studied carelessness. As she ran to the hostel, she noted that the whole of Emain Macha swarmed with mercenary troops.

She found Naoisi and Deirdriu playing a desultory game of *fidhchell*. In her sharpest voice, she cut through their distraction: "The time for play is over! Now is it time for deeds of defense, for arming yourselves."

The two looked up, and she saw at once how it was between them, their love frozen by dissension and misunderstanding.

Through hurried kisses and greetings, she sought to arm them with the knowledge of Conchobor's intended treachery. "Keep fast the doors and windows! Defend Deirdriu to your last breath! For the three brightest candles of the Gael are like to be quenched in the wind that follows at my back: a wind from the northeast that shares not the honor of this house. And for this quenching, Emain Macha will be in great darkness."

By the time she had relayed her news, she was glad to see that they were able to repair the damage that had been done to their love. Naoisi's secure complacency was shattered, but at least he now knew the dangers and was readying his weapons. She tried not to see the stark knowledge shining back at her from Deirdriu's dry, opaque eyes.

Lebhorcham returned to Conchobor with a careful, shuttered face. "I have good news and bad, my king. The three bright candles of your court are returned, brave and mighty in soul. But of the woman that you asked about, this is the worst news that ever my lips told: she who was best in form and beauty is sadly without the appearance she used to have," and her voice cracked and trembled with sorrow, though not at the appearance of Deirdriu, who was fairer than ever, but at the lie with which she impugned her poetic oath to uphold the truth before all things.

Conchobor dismissed her, but his suspicion was roused, for this same satirist had been a teacher of Deirdriu. He sent his slave Gelban to verify the satirist's information. But when the man looked through the crack where one of the shutters was unfastened and his eye fell on her, Deirdriu looked up from the *fidhchell* board and blushed fiery red. In one movement, Naoisi cast a *fidhchell* piece into the slave's eye.

Seeing the spy clutching his bloody eye, Conchobor cried out, "You were merry enough in your going, but your coming back is cheerless enough. Speak, what is the appearance of Deirdriu?"

Gelban reported, "If she is changed from what she was I cannot tell: I only know that she is fairer than any woman I have ever seen."

And Conchobor allowed his jealousy to swell up once again, and he gave the order for the mercenaries to attack the Red Branch Hostel but to bring Deirdriu out alive.

As Conchobor gave the order for the mercenaries to attack, Deirdriu seemed to rally from her long quietness. She looked upon the Sons of Usnach with a keen eye as they rested on the long benches, waiting for the assault. "Rise up, Naoisi! Call upon the immortal powers of your grandsire, and take up your sword! While there is life left in your body, sing the song of the Sons of Usnach!"

And the brothers raised their voices once again, the voices that she loved to hear. They sang of joy and companionship, of the long days under the mountains of Alba, of the wonders that they had seen; they sang of fellowship and kinship, of the hearth fire at the day's ending, of the beauty of Deirdriu that was their sun in the dark winters of Alba.

And so, still singing their triumphant song, they forced a way out of the hostel, putting Deirdriu between the three of them behind their shields. Later, they gazed with wonder at the slaughter that they had made: the corpses of the mercenaries smoking in the predawn light while tattered flames of abandoned torches tore across their vision, and white faces upturned to the darkness, all seamed with blood.

Eoghan, who led the attack, bade his men withdraw, for he dared not harm Deirdriu, by whom he meant to win back his full friendship with Conchobor by restoring her to him. He raised his spear and cast it at Naoisi, whom it passed sheer through, breaking his back.

After that it was a short matter to finish off Ardan and Ainle, as the mercenary host swarmed down upon them. Eoghan snatched Deirdriu to his side and held her prisoner while the remaining Sons of Usnach were finished. In that moment, Deirdriu remembered the slaughter of the calf by which her *aisling* vision had come to her: a moment frozen in time, so that she remained transfixed by its memory until they brought the three heads to Eoghan.

Held by the hair in a mercenary's hand, the three heads still resembled the living men: Ardan's features still twitched convulsively in battle frenzy; Ainle's were calm and quiet; Naoisi's eyes looked unblinking into hers, the realization of her warning too late imprinted upon them.

And a terrible keening rose from her that was the echo of the voice she had raised in her mother's womb:

Ochone!
They are gone, the three heroes who rejected homage, the three sons of
the king's sister, three props of Ulster's host.
Let no one think that after Naoisi's death I should live long.
Ochone! Make not their grave too narrow, but leave a place for me!
Three horses, three hounds, three hawks will be without their
huntsmen from this day!
But the reins, the leashes, the jesses of these three wrap my heart round,
binding me to them.

Deirdriu am I: my name is sorrow. The end of my life is near since I have become sorrow!

The totality of her loss and lamentation stilled the hosts of Lochlann and brought terror to their hearts.

And Deirdriu pulled out of Eoghan's grasp and kissed the three mouths before her, licking their blood that they might be yet closer kin to her than marriage had made them.

❦

"Is Deirdriu safe confined?" Conchobor sat with Eoghan after the combat, going over the list of the dead.

"She is. Though she can sing only one song—Naoisi, Ardan, and Ainle—over and over. Grief has demented her."

Conchobor had no feeling left within him. His own son, Fiachna, was dead. His other son, Cormac, with the other guarantors that he had appointed, Fergus and Dubhtach, had returned to Emain Macha to vent their fury upon their own countrymen as they had promised. They were now gone into voluntary exile after leaving Emain Macha awash with blood, indiscriminately shed on both sides.

Eoghan looked at the *ogham* tallies of the slain. "Maine is dead, your noble son, and two of your counselors who sought to stay the combat. Several maidens and women have been raped or slain; their *grianan* was burned to the ground. The ones who stood surety have fled to the service of Maeve the Intoxicator: May they get good of her! Fergus was ever to be found in her voracious bed."

But Conchobor was not listening. He cast down the *ogham* staves upon the ground. The tears stood in his eyes, unshed.

Eoghan roughly tried to rally him. "Your loss is great, but your reward is yet to enjoy! Why do you weep?"

And Cathbad the druid, grieving within the shadow of his hood, for the Sons of Usnach had been his grandsons, said, "The three brightest candles of Emain Macha have been extinguished. May a man not sit and grieve in the darkness for the light that is lost?"

And Eoghan said no more.

They prepared Deirdriu for her wedding. And if she had been pale at her capture, she was bleached as bleak as winter famine now. The women who washed her marveled at the fine-boned frailty of her body, for how had she sustained so many seasons of winter, eating only what the elements provided, and still kept her beauty?

In three short nights, the false report of Lebhorcham had almost become truth. She was no less beautiful, but it was a beauty that becomes a mountain better than a woman—remote and difficult of access.

Deirdriu allowed herself to be dressed in the fine many-colored garments of a queen, which only gave her skin a greenish tinge. One servant whispered to another, "It's like the Queen of the Good Folk among us!"

"Hush your foolish gossip. Can't you see the woman is breeding?"

Only then the shuttered stare of Deirdriu came alive with joy, but it was a joy that had been branded with the sear of sorrow.

They led her to the bulk that was Conchobor. Those many years in waiting for her had been spent more often at table than at feats of arms. Beside her, the king looked nearer to a side of beef than he had ever done. After the feasting, the bedding. His careless grip left bruises on her skin, but they were no deeper than the bruises upon her soul. When he kissed her, her lips were like stone. When he entered her, she lay as responsive as a corpse. She neither laughed nor cried nor spoke.

When she miscarried Naoisi's child the next month, the midwives were quick to point out that she was at least still fertile, but Conchobor had already tired of her. "Let her be given to Eoghan mac Durthacht, that the honor of her fertility might brighten *his* household." And this same Eoghan had been his greatest enemy, just as the Sons of Usnach had been his most faithful kinsmen.

It was on a winter's day that they rode out for Fernmag to convey Deirdriu into Eoghan's keeping. That very morning, the better to savor the coldness of it, Conchobor had asked her, "Whom do you hate most, Deirdriu?"

And for the first time since her capture, she had answered him: "You. And after you, Eoghan mac Durthacht."

"Then you shall have the opportunity to hate him more completely, for I am loaning you to him for a year."

But there was no alteration in her. From her lofty sorrow, she looked down upon him, drear as a day in Imbolc.

Eoghan rode out to greet them, and they rode together, chariot by chariot the last part of the way, boasting about past conquests. Both men ignored the object of their transaction.

Then Conchobor turned and looked for the last time upon Deirdriu and gave a shout of laughter. "You have the look of a heifer between two bulls, Deirdriu!"

But even as he spoke a raven stooped before the chariots. Without a word, Deirdriu sprang onto the side of Conchobor's chariot, stretched out one cusped hand to the raven, and cast herself down between the chariot wheels. The near gray horse of Eoghan's chariot reared up as the raven fell before it and Deirdriu was crushed between the wheels and scattered upon the road.

It was Lebhorcham who lifted her body from where it lay broken and conveyed it to a grave beside the Sons of Usnach. She lay there three nights upon the earth, washing it with her tears and making lament, having set up an inscription in *ogham*, that only those who know the dark tongue of poets might read it:

"The three branches of the tree of Usnach grow straight and strong in the Otherworld. Now is the blossom and fruit come upon them by the further strand. Happy are they who have known Sorrow."

And Cathbad the druid cursed Emain Macha that the lineage of Conchobor might never reign after him, a curse to stand throughout time. And this is the story to bear that curse in memory because of Deirdriu of the Sorrows and the Sons of Usnach.

CHAPTER TEN

WHAT WOMEN MOST DESIRE

I know where I'm going,

I know who's going with me.

I know who I love,

But the dear knows who I'll marry.

—Traditional Scottish folk song

"What Women Most Desire" is based upon a medieval British story that has a long legacy, stretching back into the Celtic king-making legends of Ireland, where the sovereign-to-be encounters the Goddess of the Land in the form of a hideous maiden. The transformation or epiphany of the Goddess always turns upon a test or riddle that only the successful candidate can pass or answer. Here, the testing has a two-level application that goes to the heart of the question in both a general and more particular way, as you will see. Within this story I have reverted to the original Welsh names of the Arthurian characters: Gwalchmai (GWALKH'my) is Gawain; Gwenhwyfar (gwen-HWEE'var) is Guinevere. It is told from the standpoint of a streetwise faery heroine calling herself Ragnell.

OU WHO STRAY within the margins of the dark, silent forest in the depths of winter when the snow lies deep, step carefully! Remember the folk who were here before you and who walked this world in glory before you came to parcel it up and own it. Those who step unwarily into the regions where we still walk will often be surprised by whom they meet there.

Like King Arthur when he came across my brother in the glade. The king had been riding all day under the sun-dappled trees and was under the forest's enchantment, not even realizing how far away were his attendants and companions.

My brother—let's call him Gromer—was a man with a grudge, just as I was a woman with a mission. It hadn't taken much persuasion on my part to manipulate Gromer's outrage to my benefit. You see, Arthur had annexed land belonging to Gromer the summer before.

Not that Arthur had any notion he'd given offense or even been aware of the land having a previous guardian; he had merely taken what seemed to be unoccupied land, without a second thought.

This sort of attitude is typical of most mortals, who have few scruples when it comes to our kind. You ask, what kind?

Well, we are the folk who live on the margins of your world: mortals call us by many names—faeries, boggarts, spirits, demons—but we call ourselves the People of Peace. We live forever, unless we make the decision to become mortal, which a very few of us have done. As you'll imagine, this is a serious, irrevocable step that is seldom taken without considerable heart searching.

Why any of our kind should want to become subject to mortality is a question that has been long debated by wise folk on both sides of the worlds, but I can tell you, with some authority, that the major reason is so that we can experience the bittersweet joys of love.

Don't misunderstand me, we faery folk, as you call us, indulge in bed sport much more frequently than our mortal counterparts. We do not suffer the infirmity of illness or age, we do not die or weep, and we do not often give birth. But then, neither do we experience the tenderness of mortal union. Our kind know little of the human exchange of hearts. Ever since the coming of people to the land, I've longed to know what that means and have been particularly interested in the affairs of mortals—beyond what is usual in faery.

How I achieved my aim you will find out, if you read on. I bent the rules to find a man who loved me above all others and who would be faithful to me forever—at least in mortal terms. I had had my eye upon Gwalchmai for some long time. Tall, golden Gwalchmai! It is true that I could easily have exercised my faery wiles and enchanted him into falling in love with me, by waylaying him in a forest clearing and pretending that my clothes were lost or stolen. It would probably have worked. . . . But I did not desire such an underhand affair. I wanted to know love in full measure.

And Gwalchmai was loveworthy, believe me. Six-foot-three of sheer strength and suppleness of limb, combined with golden wavy hair to his shoulder, a noble but gentle profile, eyes of Maytime green, and deeds of courage.

In addition to this, his heart was tender, his eye true, his courtesy perfect. He had a compassion for women that many men lacked. But the only way I could gain his heart was through his uncle, the king; there was no other way. I knew from my auguries that only under that obedience would Gwalchmai find me and love me.

It was then I went to our queen, the Lady of the Lake, and poured out my need to her: pale, silent Morgen of the healing hand and the gift of shape-shifting. She inquired, with delicate distaste, "Permission to marry a mortal? Do you intend to bring him home? Or do you mean to take the dreaded step and become mortal yourself?"

I shook my head, "Most Royal, I do not seek this man to make him one of us, but rather, I wish to know more about mortal loving while retaining my faery status."

She laughed her clear, cheerless laugh. "There are conditions attached to such a dangerous enterprise."

"Name them, lady!"

They were terrible.

I was not allowed to retain my own shape, I had to make the man I desired answer a riddle most mortals could never hope to answer, and I had to return within the space of two years or else mortality would fall upon me and claim me forever.

"Well?" Morgen inquired, "do you accept these conditions?"

"I do!"

"And tell me, whom do you wish to catch by these means?"

You can't be evasive with the Faery Queen.

"Gwalchmai," I said, but my foolish heart sang: Gwalchmai of the long limbs, courageous Gwalchmai of the quests. . . .

A sickle-thin smile raked the smooth field of Morgen's face—a dreadful sight to behold! Morgen thought the family of Arthur was good sport, in much the same way mortals feel that a running stag makes good venison.

It was then that I decided to enlist the help of my brother, Gromer; no one needs the enmity of Morgen at one's back! A well-placed ally is everything in mortal realms.

I can hear you mortal women thinking: what a nerve, to plan all this in cold blood! Well, you would be right: we do have cold blood—the far stellar light flows in our veins instead of blood, infusing our being with subtle knowledge. But I so wanted to know what it was to be loved in the mortal way!

Like you, faery women have no special abilities to make love happen. It can happen only in its own good time. To provoke lust is the work of a moment, but to invoke love—that is another matter.

Yes, I know we faeries can make ourselves look lovelier than you! But that was not an option in this case, as you'll see. . . .

I stepped through the portal into the forest. On finding that I was on all fours, I trotted through last year's leaf mold to find a pool and looked within it.

This was beyond everything! Morgen had sent me through as a wild sow! Trust her vindictive nature to make me look like this! Well, I did still have some magic at my disposal, and I could at least try to look vaguely human in my shape-shifting.

Calling upon sun and moon and, beyond them, the deep stars that shine in the heights of heaven and also in the depths of the earth, I made my spell and felt myself changing.

You know what happens when you spill milk into a trough of water? You get neither good rich milk nor pure clear water. Well, so it was as Morgen's spell and my spell tussled together.

I peered into the pool to see what had become of me and hurriedly looked away again. I was a monster!

The worst thing was the tusks—thank you so much, Morgen! Or was it the great belly that seemed to start where my breastbone used to be and continued down like a mountain range? Further investigation showed black fuzzy hair like a wild pony's tail, a crooked nose, eyes like coals, enormous knees, and fat ankles. I didn't dare look elsewhere.

This was definitely not part of the bargain!

Behind me, Gromer came through the portal and began roaring with laughter at sight of me. "Stars above! What *do* you look like, sister?"

"Well, I may be no picture, but then, neither are you!" And I beckoned him to the pool to see what he himself had become. He was now a full nine feet tall and sported a grizzled beard down to his knees. Full of bluster, he made the best of it. "Well, I suppose I don't want to look too friendly if I'm going to scare the wits out of Arthur!"

So here we are in the snow-bright silent forest, and here comes Arthur. I dive into a bush, so as not to frighten him any more than he's going to be. He reins in tightly when he sees Gromer blocking the path and looks around for his men, but they're nowhere in sight. Gromer begins his pitch in a deep, booming voice, and Arthur's horse nearly bolts from under him, it sounds so eerie: "Arthur, King of Britain, by what right do you ride in this forest?"

At this point, Arthur is what vulgar mortals call gob-smacked for a minute and then asks, "What is your name?"

"I am Gromer Somer Joure," says my brother in his terrible voice, using a name that the Saxons would know, but not our king of the Britons here. I must say that my brother looked less like a Man of the Summer's Day at that moment than anything I could imagine, but then, he always was vain. "You have done me wrong, Arthur, and now your life hangs by a thread."

"If you have any idea of killing me here, then know that dishonor will follow you all of your days," Arthur replies stoutly. "Only tell me what amends I can make, and I will do the best that I may. Is it gold that you seek?"

Gromer shakes his dreadful beard. "Don't try to cozen me with talk of gold! The only way to save your life is to answer me this riddle: What is it that women most desire? Answer me that, and come here within a year and a day with the right answer."

Arthur puts his head on one side and considers—like all mortals, trying to put another spin on things when in a tight place. "Is it poor women or noblewomen we're speaking of here?"

Gromer leans menacingly over him—having considerable advantage over even a mounted king—and says, "The question applies to any woman—whether of the country or the town, rich, poor, gentle or simple."

"Oh!" says Arthur. "Then I swear by my sword that I will do my best to bring you what you require in a year and a day." Then he blows his hunting horn to tell his men where he is.

Before the trees become thick with his followers, before the smooth, deep snow is stained with footprints, Gromer is away back to Faery. Me, I stay to see what passes.

Men press forward on every side about their king, their angry concern and self-reproach making a wall of protection about him, while he stutters out a feeble excuse about how he came to be lost. He meets the quizzical gaze of his nephew over their heads, and you can see that he knows there's a deeper tale to be told.

Gwalchmai draws the king aside, and they confer in whispers, Arthur telling him everything. My hero says cheerily, "We will go together, you and I, throughout the land, asking everyone we meet what they think women most desire. And we'll write the answers in a book— well, *I* can." He adds to Arthur's doubtful look.

Ah, Gwalchmai! Learned as well as handsome!

I left them to go and seek the answers and made a spell to change my shape again. I needed to see how things went, so the shape of a bird would suit my purposes. With Morgen's meddling, I didn't make a very presentable bird, of course, and I could only go as one by day, for by night I reverted to my loathly shape. But at least I could fly hither and yon and find out how the seekers did.

A fine job they made of it! Arthur insisted that they ask men as well as women, in case a man might know the right answer. (Is there any hope for such a one?) To begin with, Gwalchmai began by writing down every answer; then, after they'd ridden through a few counties, he began to put ticks on a list of standard answers. Most common answers from men were that women liked flattery or pretty clothes. Many of the suggestions were not recordable, being variations on what men would like to do with women in bed. It's extraordinary how unimaginative some of these were, I can tell you!

The women themselves didn't give much better account: having better cows, clothes, husbands (fill in your own blank) than their neighbor; having lots of healthy children; being able to read or ride or travel.

Many mortals of both sexes decided that gold was the answer to all their problems and therefore was itself desirable by women.

Let me tell you, if some of those answers had got back to the realms of Faery, the whole place would have been in stitches for weeks. Faeries have a jaundiced enough view of mortals as it is. Fortunately, I was able to steal the book off Gromer later before he wrought too much havoc in this respect.

The year and a day was drawing to its close, and Arthur was a worried man. To cover more ground, he and Gwalchmai split up, in order to ask more people. Arthur had an excellent memory, as most people without book learning still have, so they agreed to meet at the end of the day and compare answers. This was the moment I'd been waiting for.

Positioning myself and very ably blocking his path, I sat down under a thorn tree and played a bit of music on a *crwth;* after all, there was no reason not to pass the time pleasantly, was there? The one natural asset I still possessed was my voice, and so I sang as delightfully as I could. It beguiled Arthur onto the way.

Once he had an eyeful of me, I greeted him cheerily: "Good day, King Arthur. How pleased I am to meet you here!"

He took in my pendulous breasts, which hung like ripening hams over the gross extension of my mountainous stomach, the slimy tusks poking out of the whey-white blubber of my cheeks, the loathly menagerie of features that just about proclaimed me to be a woman.

"Lady, give me the courtesy of your name, since you know mine," Arthur asked, oh so politely.

I thought quickly: we do not give out our true names to mortals because they have a tendency to make hay with them, bending our powers to their narrow-sighted purposes. (And this is why you won't be reading my true name here or that of my brother, in case you were wondering!) For most of Arthur's people, all foreigners were Lochlanders—meaning the people from Norway—so I gave him a Lochlandish name to call me by: "Ragnell is my name, great king."

I could see he thought it a wholly appropriate name for one so gross in appearance.

"I have advice for you, lord king, and I bid you listen, for I hold your life in my hands."

He didn't seem charmed by the idea! "What do you want with me, good dame?" Ah, they only call you that when they hate your tripes!

"I have good news for you. There is a question to which you seek an answer, is there not?" I'd got his attention now. "Well, I know that unless you have the correct answer soon your life is forfeit. Am I right?"

He nodded miserably.

"If I tell you the right answer, will you grant me my desire?"

"Good dame, tell me what you're talking about. You have true intelligence of my plight, it is true."

But if truth be known and my own shape had been upon me, he'd not have looked at me then as if I were a piece of dung. "Believe me, the true answer is in my possession. But before I tell you, you must hear my desire."

Arthur raised his head and actually looked into my eyes, which was very brave of him. "Speak, woman!"

"I desire a good warrior as my husband, and they say that there are none as bold as those who serve you at the Round Table of Carlisle. I would have Gwalchmai as my husband. Give him me, and I will give you the answer. Only this will save your head."

I don't think *appalled* even comes near his expression! He was Gwalchmai's uncle, after all, and I would be joining the family. "Madam, I cannot make such a promise on behalf of my nephew. All I can promise is to ask him and do all I can to bring your wedding about."

"Ask your nephew yourself, and meet me here at dawn tomorrow."

What else could he do?

I became a bird again and watched their meeting.

Gwalchmai had been waiting for some time and was anxious. He could also see that Arthur's soul was freighted with some extra burden. "Uncle, what has happened? It isn't that damned Gromer again?"

I thought for one dreadful minute that Arthur was going to do the noble thing, for he said, "Nay, nephew. I now accept that my life is drawing to its close."

Gwalchmai was shocked into silence at Arthur's deep depression. "But there's still another day or two.... You *have* met someone, Uncle—who is it?"

Arthur battled unsuccessfully with his better nature and—thank goodness—lost. "The ugliest woman I've ever seen just stopped me and said she had the right answer."

Gwalchmai's face was a sunburst of joy. "But that's wonderful news!"

(Spit it out, Arthur!)

"Listen! It gets worse, I fear. She won't tell it me unless she . . . if only you would . . . oh, confound it! . . . She'll tell me only on condition that you marry her!"

Gwalchmai's face cleared like a shower lifting: it was a miracle to behold his generosity: "Is that all? Of course I'll wed any woman to save your life, uncle! You are my king. My honor is your honor. By saving your life, my honor only increases."

Arthur put the steadying hand of pity on his arm. "I wouldn't be too sure of that, nephew! You haven't seen her yet."

"I don't care what she looks like!" Gwalchmai asserted. (Oh, dear soul! You will. . . .)

❧ ❧

The next morning, Arthur came to the glade, promptly and purposefully, with a new spring in his stride. "Come, good dame, tell me your answer! My nephew, Gwalchmai, consents to your proposal—though I think it ill befits a woman to propose marriage."

Ignoring this jibe—for I could afford to be gracious now—I said, "Well, sir king, I expect you've got a whole lot of answers about women wanting to be beautiful or to have several lusty lovers or to be always young."

He nodded enthusiastically, since these answers were the ones he himself would have endorsed.

I'm afraid I had to deflate his fond illusions. "Well, that's complete rot! What all women want is to have sovereignty over the most manly of men."

Arthur was thunderstruck—as, being a man, he might be. He didn't quite say, "Power over men! Are you *sure?*" but he was certainly thinking it. It was an answer of such totally feminine *lèse majesté,* as French mortals say, that he was utterly taken aback. I seriously don't think it had ever occurred to him before that women might not feel any gratitude for being looked after by men and having all their decisions made for them. It opened up a crack into a sealed room he never knew existed—the treasury of women's hearts.

With a great smile of admiration, as if reluctantly recognizing some particularly praiseworthy quality in an adversary, he said, "Only a true woman could have made such an answer!"

I made a curtesy to him, to acknowledge the compliment—well the best I could manage with knees like mine. "You will keep your promise now?" I asked.

"Assuredly! Meet me at Carlisle at this week's end, and you shall have your desire."

Needless to say, Gromer affected outrage that Arthur had cunningly learned the right answer, but honor had been satisfied. "I don't doubt that it was my wretched sister, Ragnell, who told you! May she be cursed! Well, you have done your part, and I say good-bye to you forever. Farewell!"

And Arthur rode back to Carlisle with, "What a peculiar family!" Until he remembered that Gromer's family was going to be part of his.

That wiped the satisfied smile off his face.

That part had been easy. Now for the difficult bit.

Later that week I duly turned up at the walled city of Carlisle. It looked lovely from a distance but was a lot smellier when you drew near.

To the astonishment of everyone, I was admitted without delay to Arthur's council chamber. "Since you've been successful in answering the riddle, lord king, I come to claim my reward for helping you."

Arthur played for time: "Good dame, if you will be moderate in your demands, you will get what you desire."

I knew immediately that he meant to fob me off with a quiet wedding, to play down the disgrace. "No, lord king! I shall be married with every proper honor to Gwalchmai, in public and before everyone of rank."

Arthur's shoulders sagged. "Very well!" And he sent for his lovely queen, Gwenhwyfar, and her ladies to prepare me for my wedding. They attended me courteously enough, but every now and then, one of them would trail off to fetch a veil or a comb from the closet and sigh, "Poor Gwalchmai!" It seemed that, from Gwenhwyfar on down, all the ladies were a little in love with my intended.

They tried to comb out my fuzzy colt's tail of hair and to drape my tusked jaw becomingly with a concealing veil; they shrouded my misshapen body in a voluminous gown of scarlet sendal and decked my neck with gold and jewels, but when I looked in the polished bronze mirror, the reflection showed me as I was: mutton dressed as lamb— or, to be more strictly honest, wild sow dressed as pork.

The news of the wedding had gone out to the country round about, and the great hall was solidly packed with the curious and the unbelieving alike, all agog to see how bad I could really be. As I stepped into the hall on Arthur's arm, there was a wailing and crying from the women's side and an indignant coughing from among the men. Some little boys made squealing pig noises and were backhanded into courteous silence.

Oh, Morgen! if I could have gone back on my agreement at that moment I would have done so, believe me! Never had I felt so vulnerable. But there was no way out except to carry it through, whatever the consequences.

Oh, mortal women, have you ever been in such a predicament? To be by the side of the one you adore above all other, about to be wed to a man who surpasses even the best-looking men of your country, but to greet him for the first time looking like a monstrous porker? Quell your laughter, if you never stood where I stood!

Arthur released my arm, and at last I stood by Gwalchmai's side and whispered to him over the steady noise of the crowd around us, "I wish, for your sake, that I was beautiful to look upon, but you see me as I am. Will you have me as your wife, Gwalchmai?"

He was surprised and intrigued at my voice, which was at odds with my shape, but he squeezed my twisted hand. "Lady, I gladly take you to be my wife." And I could detect no trace of pity in him for me or for himself. Considering it was the first time he'd set eyes on me, it was a miraculous answer.

He declared his vows to me in a clear voice so that everyone in the hall could hear them. Ill-mannered cries of "shame" came from the gallery where the serving women jostled for a better view, but they were rebuked by the steward.

Then I declared my vows to him, with a sincere heart, opening the true treasury of mortal commitment within my faery soul. I had expected to make some mental reservation about these words or even to whisper some extra clause under my breath, but when it came to the moment, I said them and meant them: "I take noble Gwalchmai to be my husband from this day until the end of time."

It was a promise that would have been binding enough upon the lifetime of a mortal, but for me, this promise was forever—which is a very long time for a faery. If I failed in my quest, I would be bound to him forever, throughout Gwalchmai's every lifetime, until the ending of all things. But as those words were said, so I felt a part of my own heart leave my body and rest upon his heart like a dove.

Too late now, girl!

Arthur and his council acknowledged these vows as truly witnessed, and there was a rush for the benches, everyone wanting to get as drunk as they could to forget the dreadful sight of Gwalchmai's tall, straight body beside my abomination of a shape.

No one really expected Gwalchmai to kiss the bride in public, but he did kiss my hand with consideration and respect and led me to the place of honor.

The feast was sumptuous: oysters, pike, eel, wild fowl, bear hams, beef, heaps of nuts and blaeberries from the northern snows, mead, ale, wine, and fiery *uisce-beatha*. No pork, I noticed—how sensitive of the cook!

We sat together under a canopy, sharing the same dish. It really is impossible to eat daintily when you have tusks: everything just drips down the sides of your mouth when you chew!

Also, when you have nails the length of mine—more like talons than human nails—you make a muck of separating your food. Those nearest to us kept their faces carefully averted while I ate—it was all too disgusting for them. Soon the front of my red sendal gown was blotched with grease and my veil stained with splatters of wine.

If Morgen was watching at that moment, I only hope she enjoyed herself!

The humiliation was of short duration, at least. The feast drew to its close early, no one being in the mood to make merry. Even the musicians seemed distracted from their task and were making a dirgelike music. As the company drifted away from the tables, there was a mounting, shamefaced reluctance to face the fact that we had reached that awkward point of the wedding feast when it is customary to lay the bride and groom in bed together.

My maids of honor, led by Gwenhwyfar, came to fetch me to my chamber. Most of then had tearful eyes only for Gwalchmai and no store of lusty country wisdom to offer me. Gwalchmai's grooms of honor stood around, embarrassed and uncertain; several made such hearty back slappings of encouragement and halfhearted thumps of commiseration that my husband must have been bruised all over.

Neither maids nor grooms of honor felt up to preparing the happy couple but merely led us in funereal procession to the door of our chamber, ushered us within, and pointedly shut the door on us with noticeable relief.

Now for the most difficult part!

I sat on the edge of the bed while Gwalchmai warmed his hands at the fire and poured us out the finest mead into crystal goblets. At last, he was beginning to show the strain, but his courtesy kept him going, bless him!

He handed me the cup, which I grasped in both my hands so as not to break the delicate twisted stem.

"Thank you, husband. Here's to our future happiness!" I pledged him and drank it all down, so as not to see the bewilderment and hurt in his eyes.

"To our happiness?" he echoed, as if to a joke in bad taste.

I put as much enthusiasm into my voice as the wine permitted: "Aye, husband, happiness! Now, since I married you this afternoon, you've not so much as kissed me."

He struggled with himself and bravely entered the fray. "I will do more than kiss you yet, before heaven!" And he took me into his arms—or as much of me as would fit—and laid his lovesome mouth over my tusked and slimy one.

Like a key in a secret door in the deepest recesses of Faeryland, his kiss changed everything, as I had known it would. It was a moment to savor, a guerdon and promise of something more profoundly precious yet to come.

He sprang back as the change happened and I appeared as my true self—no more a tusked monstrosity, but with my own faery skin, my own clear green eyes, my straightness of limb, my shapeliness of form, my own red-gilt hair, my own slender hands and feet.

"Lady, who are you?" He looked about in sad surprise to see where I had gone. Not finding the sowlike wife in the chamber, he took his hands from me instantly. Ah, bless you, Gwalchmai! Even at that moment, you had the goodness to remember your faithful promise to your truly wedded wife and would not lay hand on another woman.

"Gwalchmai, I *am* your wife, your own Ragnell."

He was on his knees before me, as before an apparition of a holy being. "Lady, forgive me for discourtesy! I didn't imagine . . ." but he kept his imaginations to himself. "You are the most beautiful woman I've ever seen . . . yet, even today, you were the most ugly ever seen. What great good fortune has come upon me?"

And without waiting for an answer, he took me lustily in his arms, touching my breast and thigh even as his mouth sought my willing one. Ah! the first throes of passion—was I not even permitted to enjoy these? But no!

Now for the hardest part of all . . .

With great gentleness and all my strength, I pried him away from my bosom and took his face in my hands. "Dear Gwalchmai, beloved beyond all time, listen to me! I know you are pleased by what you see, but I have a question for you. Before you answer, consider well, for much will depend upon your answer. Our entire happiness lies in your hands."

Oh, what it is for a faery to relinquish control over her life. Oh, hardest of tasks! Is this what mortals feel every time life deals ungentle blows to the innocent and the weak? I was empty of power, drained of magic, lost to knowledge of all that I had been in that instant.

"My dearest wife, what troubles you? What question is this?" His urgency pierced through the pain of dread and uncertainty.

"Gwalchmai, noblest of husbands, you must make a difficult choice. I must tell you here and now that the beauty that you see is not fixed and constant but, like the moon, will wax and wane."

He laughed with delighted relief. "Dear one, all mortals suffer age and distress. It will be my pleasure to age along with you and share everything with you, no matter what."

"You mistake my meaning, husband. What I mean is this: you must decide whether you would have me—beautiful as I am now—by day or by night. I cannot be in this shape except by day or by night."

The vise of this terrible decision closed about his understanding, and his dear face became grave. In silence he considered his options: to have me beautiful by day would be to his honor and respect, for everyone would congratulate him on my beauty, but, come the night . . . what horror!

But to have me lovely only by night would mean nights of pleasure followed by days of pitying looks and disrespect, as his peers saw me beside him at every function as a haggish sow.

So much depended on his answer! And for me it was too late, for I had already fallen in love. It was against the rules of the game to help him make the right answer. Only by his own wits could he see beyond the monster he had married to the heart within her and make her true semblance visible.

He leaned forward to settle a log back on the fire and gazed long into the embers, his head an aureole of gold against the red heart of the fire.

Slowly, he turned his head and said, "It seems to me that such a decision is one a loving husband cannot really make. My dear, I put the choice in your hands. Do as you wish. I am bound to you by links of love. My body, my goods, my heart, and all are yours to buy or sell as you will."

I gave thanks to whatever power made this dear world and all within it and knelt beside him in the sweet rushes of our bower. "Oh, Gwalchmai, of all warriors living, you are the most blessed! By your own word, you give me the power to choose what I most want: you shall have me fair by day *and* by night. By giving me sovereignty over your body, your goods, your heart, and all, I am able to be myself in my own true form forevermore."

Whoever would have thought it?—a mortal man able to make such a decision—to let *me* make it! There are few men alive in this time, let alone in those times, who could have so chosen.

Fear and trouble laid aside, we entered that bed together, equals in passion and in love. All that night and the next morning until midday we concelebrated the sacred rites of love.

We might have made a three-night event of it had not Arthur, in the grip of a guilt-induced anxiety so strong that he could not rest until he knew the worst, knocked at the chamber door to see whether Gwalchmai was still on life and not torn to shreds by my tusks and talons.

Grabbing his shirt, Gwalchmai covered the white nakedness of his handsome body and strode to the door, a little smile playing about his mouth. "Who is it?"

I drew the bedclothes up to my nose, trying not to giggle.

"It is your uncle! May I come in?"

"Enter!" Gwalchmai threw back the door so that everyone outside—and there were a suspiciously large number of people attending Arthur that day—was able to look within.

Arthur had eyes only for Gwalchmai. "Ah, nephew! You are all right?"

But he was distracted from the answer by others who had seen. Then he too noticed my long golden hair spilling over the quilt. Gwalchmai ushered all within. "Uncle, gentlemen, ladies—this is my wife, Lady Ragnell."

I could have planted carrots in the number of wide-open mouths before me. They looked and looked, as I sat up in bed, letting my hair cover my breasts—nice and apple shaped now, thank goodness! Looks of pity now became looks of admiration and envy.

Arthur was the first to recover. "I see that there is more to this tale than first appears! Let us leave my nephew and his wife alone now. I hope they will join us for supper later?"

Gwalchmai put his arm about my shoulders and grinned, "Certainly!"

Later, it was Queen Gwenhwyfar who showed most understanding of what had taken place. "So . . . Arthur had to find the answer to what women most desire. But Gwalchmai had to do more than that—he had to enact the answer!" And she shot a look of profound gratitude at my husband for having kept Arthur from certain death and one of very astute understanding at me.

In the wordless way that women have, we exchanged a glance that said, "Yes! That *was* a very good question. Men may rule this mortal realm, but we know the truth of it!"

To save on explanations, I had told everyone that I had been under a spell of enchantment, which was true enough, but I said to Arthur and Gwenhwyfar, "Gwalchmai saved me from degradation and dishonor. And for that courtesy, I shall thank him all the days of my life."

Gwalchmai's dear mouth closed over mine to seal the promise. And I knew a fullness in my heart that told me that his now beat where mine once was.

You want to know how long we were together? Well, long enough for me to bear him a son. When the day dawned and my time was up, I had to consider my bargain with Morgen. Two years only in mortal realms or else become mortal. But to leave Gwalchmai and our little boy was beyond what mortals could bear: it was almost beyond what faeries can bear either.

I made the decision to remain, knowing full well what that would mean. When you have changed hearts with one so beloved as Gwalchmai, I have learned that you need fear neither the encroachments of age nor the pangs of death. The reciprocations of love are finer than the cold unending world of Faery.

Now, you who walk in those lonely forest places, wondering what it is to live with the People of Peace: if you truly wish to become one of them, there is a faery lifetime stretching into forever going spare.

I do not need it anymore, now that I have my love.